HEARTLESS KING

MAYA HUGHES

Editors: Tamara Mayata, Sarah Kremen-Hicks, Sarah Polcher

Cover Designer: Nail Qamber, Qamber Designs

To anyone who has ever lost someone they loved...

1

COLM

"Tonight"—I lifted the corked bottle of champagne high above my head—"we drink my sister's inheritance. Who's with me?" I popped the cork, and bubbles and booze overflowed from the bottle. Below me, people lifted their glasses to catch the stream of champagne. A part of our trust our parents had left in my capable hands when they died eight years ago was being chugged by people packed into the happy hour bar. If Liv didn't want to follow our plan, then she didn't get the money I'd carefully been managing for us.

Responsible Colm was dying tonight in the bottom of *several* bottles.

Setting down the champagne, I ignored the glares from the bartenders and grabbed my bottle of gin. My phone buzzed in my pocket. I grabbed it and checked out the screen.

Declan.

More like *Decline.*

So he'd been nominated to make first contact.

Notifications filled the screen.

Heath. I didn't feel like hearing any of his wisecracks right now.

Emmett. I didn't need him launching into a whole spiel about forgiveness and not being bitter. Maybe I'd take a page out of his book and wait four years to finally figure all this out.

Ford and Liv. Were they together when they'd called?

I tilted my head back, pouring a swig of gin before spraying it out over the crowd of people jumping up and down at my feet. How had I never stood on a bar before? This was king of the world insanity right here. Most my teammates had been living it up for years while I'd been playing Dad, sacrificing my own teen years so my little sister... And for what?

Liv wanted to throw her life away. All the years of hard work, study sessions where we'd sat together going over flashcards at our weekly dinners, practice exams. The hours of science team drills. The free agent position I'd turned down on the west coast to be closer to her. All gone. Poof, up in smoke like that shitty apartment—I'd warned her it was a death trap, but she'd just had to live there.

My brilliant little sister was disproving her top of her class GPA by throwing it all away to be a dance teacher. Out of nowhere. People don't study their asses off the way she did—the way I helped her to—to wake up one day and decide to throw their future away for a hobby. I didn't understand. The only thing that had really changed was Ford swooping in and blowing up her life like the ticking time bomb he was. I wasn't going to help her destroy the future we'd spent years working towards. She could do it without the money our parents had set aside for her and given me control over.

Old responsible Colm was dead. No more reservations.

No more playing by the rules. No more not getting shitfaced because Liv might need me. No more rushing back home or to wherever she was for dance recitals or finals week. No more always being the one who didn't get to have a wild college experience or wade through the mania that it meant to be a pro hockey player. I'd always been that guy everyone could count on.

Fuck that. I was going to live it the hell up. Now it was my turn for a little bad behavior.

The season started in ten weeks, and I'd spend the rest of that time partying like I never had before. Drowning every bit of the old me in overflowing bottles of booze and the company of strangers who didn't give a shit about me or my tragic past.

I took another gulp of my gin. It was a smooth, clean burn. Not whiskey like I usually drank. Ford loved whiskey and I wanted to rip his head off with my bare hands right now; I didn't need to drink his damn booze all night long as a reminder. And I also wasn't going to think about him—shit, too late. Maybe I'd had one too many. Nah, not possible. I signaled to the bartender to set up another round.

He eyed me up and down, shaking his head and grabbing more glasses, and took a step back from the horde ready to take advantage of the free drinks racking up on my lengthening tab.

The way my knee had felt all spring while I'd rehabbed it in California had nothing on the raw ache in my chest. Twelve weeks of intensive physiotherapy to get me to where I was now, standing on the bar. The king of the drunks. I'd take that recovery cakewalk all over again compared to this.

Ford screwed my sister. Went behind my back when I asked him to look after her and moved in on her. For some reason, I'd thought because she was my only family it would be different. That my best friend—already on rocky ground —would protect my family instead of moving in on my baby sister.

And Liv chose him over her only family. After everything she and I had been through. They're both so willing to take this chance on whatever infatuation they have going on and damn the consequences. And what happens when their 'love' blows up? Liv's crushed and I have to hate Ford forever. Ford's totally fine putting Liv's heart on the line after his history. And Liv didn't seem to care one bit about jeopardizing my friendship with him after we'd barely repaired it.

After everything I'd held back from doing and how much I've sacrificed for her since our parents died, she saw nothing wrong with taking my best friend away from me and throwing away the future we'd both worked so hard for.

Losing our parents, keeping our family of two together while I was in college and then turned pro, always sacrificing for her and giving her the best. After all the sacrifices I've made, she turned her back on me like we were strangers on the street, choosing someone she's known for a few short years over me. Because of Ford. It's always Ford. Ford stole my once imagined happily ever after by banging my almost-fiancée, and now he's stealing the future my sister worked so hard and sacrificed so much for —hell that I'd worked and sacrificed for—where Liv becomes a doctor like our parents. Where she's able to do the kind of good they had and save lives every day on the job.

"Hey, are you Colm Frost?" The woman draped herself across the bar, tugging on my pant leg.

"No," I bit out, taking another swig straight from the bottle. "Fucking hate that guy."

"Oh." Her startled response was quickly smoothed over with a wide grin. "Then who are you?" She shoved her arms under her chest, pushing her tits up even higher in her dress. There'd be a nip slip before long, if she wasn't careful.

"Does it matter? You want some of this?" I gestured to the bottle in my hand.

She nodded, opening her mouth.

I tipped the bottle, pouring the clear contents into her open mouth. She caught it like a pro. Like this wasn't her first rodeo with unexpected liquids blasting her in the face.

Servers came out with trays filled with drinks that disappeared before they made it two steps. Everyone lifted their glasses to me, screaming out their progressively inebriated thanks.

Standing up on the bar lost some of its charm after the initial high of blowing through a few thousand dollars.

I jumped down, keeping hold of my bottle, and found myself swarmed by people not wanting the free alcohol gravy train to end. Their fake smiles and faker interest in me made the hollowness inside feel even deeper. Maybe I should've stayed home. But home was empty—filled with no one and nothing but shelves lined with photographs featuring people who didn't give a shit about me.

Everything was too loud now. Was this the seventh drink I'd downed or was it the eighth? Hard to calculate when you're drinking straight from the bottle.

Everyone around me laughed, jockeying for position at my sides. The poor people who'd come in for some bar snacks and a drink to unwind after a hard day's work were being overrun by the bar crowd I'd unleashed with a no-limit credit card and a host of bad ideas for the night.

Noise pulsed through the club like an ever-growing beast. Bottles being put back into their recessed lighting-lined shelves. An overwhelming swarm of voices buzzing around in my head. I needed to be way drunker to get through the night.

When was the last time I'd eaten something? Food was overrated, plus it all turned into sawdust in my mouth. Time was complicated. My girlfriend had left me weeks ago. My sister had turned her back on me less than seventy-two hours ago. My best friend had set our shared history on fire at the same time. Living my best life for sure.

More gin.

Sitting alone in my house had driven me nearly to the point of madness. I'd been staring at four walls the whole time I was in LA, but now my leg wasn't useless. Bailey, the team trainer, had gloated the entire time I was in Philly before they shipped me off to rehab my knee, about being right and calling my injury from the first game she'd watched me play.

No, I hadn't listened to her about changing my workout plans. I'd learned my lesson. Now my knee was stronger than ever, there wouldn't be any more issues, and next season, I'll be a fire breathing dragon out on the ice.

For now, I'd breathe gin fumes in any bar that would have me, surrounded by people who loved a free drink and didn't care where it came from.

I'd destroy anything in my way and I wasn't apologizing for it. This was what I needed to do—now that I was alone. Hockey was what I lived and breathed. What would keep me going.

How could he do that to me?

I'm not supposed to be thinking about it, but fuck! Ford waltzes in and derails my driven little sister from her life's purpose.

But he's all about destroying futures, like when he swooped in and took my fiancée from me. Just like he swooped the fuck in and stole that hottie from my English seminar right from under my nose sophomore year of college. At this point, it was my fault for even still being friends with him. That friendship had sailed, crashed into an iceberg, caught on fire, been attacked by torpedoes and sat as a wreck at the bottom of the ocean.

I tipped my bottle over and a few droplets splattered onto the bar. Holding up another finger, I signaled to the bartender. That's what I needed to be right now. Drunk as hell.

The bartender eyed me again. I pointed to my black card sitting on top of the register. His gaze darted from my card to me. He grimaced and nodded. *That's what I thought.*

So many voices and bodies invaded my space, I could barely keep anything they were saying straight. *Come back to their table. Order bottle service. Let's go dancing. Was there a room we could go back to for some privacy?*

Tonight wasn't the night to bring anyone home. Tonight was the night to put the old me to bed, and not with a woman who only cared about how much I was spending on strangers in the bar. The bartender handed me another bottle of Bombay Sapphire. Tomorrow I'd wake up and know this was a mistake, but tonight—tonight, I didn't give a fuck.

Shoving my hands against the bar, I pushed myself back up on top. "Who's ready for another round?" I yelled. Popping the top off the bottle, I poured out a few more drinks into waiting mouths and glasses.

A gaggle of women from the back of the bar were leaving. It was all purses and limbs, heads thrown back cackling with the laughter of a Girls' Nite as they made their way toward me and the front of the place. They hadn't rushed up for the free drinks being poured non-stop for the past hour.

"Colm?" The word shot through me like a crack of smelling salts. Her voice sliced through the clambering crowd even though she wasn't yelling, but it was her hair that confirmed what I'd already known. It wasn't blonde so much as white, like a glowing beacon. "What are you doing here?" She stared up at me.

Suddenly, being up on the bar didn't mean I was playing the bankrolling big shot. It meant I was a selfish asshole and *she* was seeing it. Fuck, not here when I'm so damn drunk. I blinked, trying to clear the mirage of her away.

Her bright white hair and light blue eyes were just like I'd remembered them. Her eyebrows dipped low, but she stayed back, not trying to push forward to the front of the bar, like she knew I couldn't not look at her.

My body tingled and it wasn't the booze this time. How long had it been since I'd seen her? Six months? How long had it been since that night on the beach? Almost five years. Five years since I'd opened my big mouth and proposed. What the hell was wrong with me?

Blinking at her, I shook my head trying to clear the fog in my brain.

"You guys go ahead," she called out to the women's handbag section of Target.

"Hey, Imogen." I climbed down off the bar, nowhere near as smoothly as I had the two other times. How long had I been slurring my words? "What are you doing here?"

"Where are the guys?" She craned her neck, surveying the bustling bar, checking for anyone else ready to jump up and start making it rain.

"Don't care." They'd taken Ford's side, telling me to calm down and that I was wrong to cut Liv off. They didn't understand. They'd never understand. Their little olive branch of an invite to play with them tomorrow was one I wanted them to shove up their asses, but, whatever, I'd go. I could use the workout after wrecking my body tonight. My penance. At least they'd said Ford wasn't going to be there.

Imo's eyebrows shot way up. She had the most expressive face. I'd thought the same thing that night she looked up at me from the sand on that Jersey Shore beach and the moonlight caught her tropical ocean blue eyes.

"Should I call Liv?" Her gaze darted past me like she was looking for someone to pawn me off onto. Worry and concern radiated off her.

"No," I bit out, barely keeping myself together.

"Colm." She looked at me and cupped her hand to the side of my face. "Come with me."

Her fingers clasped mine and she pulled me through the throngs of people like they weren't even there, around the side of the bar and down the small dimly lit hallway. She didn't hesitate, not even when she pushed through the door with the women's bathroom symbol on it.

I tried to dig my heels in, but, damn, she was strong.

She didn't drop my hand until the door slammed shut. "Where's everyone else?" Her arms were crossed over her chest and she stared into my eyes like she was trying to peel back layers of my soul.

"No idea. They didn't feel like coming out." I shrugged, trying to play at nonchalant, but feeling like I'd been sent to the principal's office.

"So, you decided to come out alone, get up on the bar, and blow through a bunch of money like you guys just won the cup?"

"It's my money to blow. What the hell do you care?" I'd been the careful guy trying to set a good example for my little sister for as long as I could remember. The dutiful son always doing the right thing trying to make sure I lived a life worth—nope, I wasn't going there.

Imogen's head snapped back. The intensity of her stare made my skin tingle as if her fingers were brushing against my skin. Something beyond the clash of emotions in my head was stirring with her touch. Something hungrier.

"Are you okay?" She placed a hand on my shoulder, standing toe to toe with me.

"I'm fine. Why do you ask?" I worked hard to keep the syllables from slurring together into a string of gibberish.

Her thumb brushed along my cheek and she tilted her head, bringing it closer to mine. Her soft lips parted slightly. "You're crying."

I jerked my head back like she'd slapped me for getting so close, and ran my fingers across my face. They came away wet. Fuck! What the hell was wrong with me? I turned to the mirror and saw myself looking like a prom date who'd been stood up, set down the bottle I hadn't even realized I was still holding, and splashed handfuls of water on my face.

I stared back at myself, my eyes ringed with red. Some paper towels were shoved into my line of sight. Without looking at her, I grabbed them and scrubbed at my face like I could wipe away the embarrassment.

"Don't worry about it. You're not the first person to be caught in the middle of an emotional hurricane. I was glad someone was there for mine." Her small smile didn't hold an ounce of pity. Relief coursed through me like it had on the beach when I'd gotten her to smile—a real smile. I could still remember every detail of that night five years ago...

I don't know what was worse: Emmett and Avery turning our summer vacation into World War III or them banging like someone had just announced the end of the world. I needed out of that house. Our slice of Jersey Shore was quiet during the week, even in summer. Most people rented summer houses and drove down on the weekends, but the Kings were here the whole time. Our last summer of freedom—well for Declan and Heath. Ford and I had been playing pro for two years.

Liv had graduated from high school, so it was another reason to celebrate. But damn, did the four-bedroom beach front house feel too small. Probably would've felt less cramped if my girlfriend hadn't broken up with me and I'd been sharing a room with her, instead of bunking with Ford and Liv.

Sexless summer, here I come. Nothing to kill the possibility of picking someone up like knowing I'd be bringing her back to a room with my kid sister in it.

I trudged over the shin-high dune toward the water. Maybe the rolling swell of the surf would block out the sex Olympics going on at the house. Colorful lights from the boardwalk flickered in the distance.

On the wind of the surf, the tinny melody of James Bay whispered in my ear. It was probably some kids making out, but damn, I loved that song. Only it wasn't some kids making out. It was a woman. And she was alone. Knees drawn up and staring out at the surf.

Her white-blonde hair was up in a bun and her yellow shirt stood out in stark relief against the rolling waves and night sky. I froze in my tracks. My feet sank into the warm, grainy sand. I'd eaten at the Surf Shack way more than I needed to this summer because she seemed to have taken at least two shifts a day. The yellow and white uniform she wore hugged her curves and her smile was always warm, even if it didn't always reach her eyes. But even then, she was painfully beautiful. The kind that made me doubt that we were even the same species. Delicate, ethereal, she was like an elf queen from Lord of the Rings.

The song ended and she touched her phone, starting it again.

Staring up at the sky, I took a deep breath. She's just like any other girl. Calm down, Colm.

"I do that too sometimes."

She screamed, jumped, and toppled over, kicking up a spray of sand into my face. Sneaking up on someone—especially a woman—sitting alone on the beach at night hadn't been my brightest idea.

I squeezed my eyes shut, but somehow forgot about my mouth. Turning my head to the side, I spit out the rough grains.

"Colm? I'm sorry." She hopped up, wiping at her face with her arm. Her eyes were ringed with red.

"No, I am. I'm sorry I scared you. Are you okay?"

Her gaze dropped. When her head popped back up, she wore the perfect waitress smile. "I'm good."

Dropping to my haunches, I picked up her phone, dusting the sand off the screen and case. My finger brushed against the home button. The screen flashed on, showing a close up picture of Imogen with Preston's face pressed right up against hers. Her boyfriend. Her dead boyfriend. Fuck, I was an asshole.

I handed the phone back to her. The song was still playing.

She took the phone, and our fingers brushed against each other. The softness of her fingertips nudged against mine. The gentle hum through my body shifted with that small connection.

"Thanks." She slipped her hand away like any polite person would.

I expected her to rub her hands on her pants to wipe away my touch.

"And I do like that song. Have you heard the rest of his album?"

The corners of her eyes crinkled and the corners of her mouth inched up. "I know all his songs by heart."

"I found some old live versions of his first performances

online." I scrolled through my phone and tapped on what I was looking for.

"You did?" She got closer, careful not to touch me while still looking at my screen. The sweet smell of the Surf Shack cinnamon roll pancakes filled my nose, along with sea air and Imo's own light floral scent.

"They're amazing. Do you want me to link it to your speaker?" I gestured to the small cube settled in the sand.

She glanced at it like she'd forgotten it was there. "I'd like that a lot. I never usually have anyone to enjoy his older stuff with."

I connected it and we both sat staring out at the water, our bodies a hair's breadth away from one another. The urge to touch her was almost overwhelming. To run my fingers through her hair. To drag my thumb against her full bottom lip.

"Preston always hated his stuff. He said he was too depressing." The corner of her mouth lifted like muscle memory at saying his name.

And then the exact reason I should do none of those things slammed straight into me. Preston. Her boyfriend. Ex? I don't know what a boyfriend was called after they died. And it was less than six months ago. So there was no way in hell she'd want me doing any of those things I wanted to do.

Our moonlit talk didn't end with one James Bay song or even two. Two albums later, we were still going.

Imo told me the secret sauce recipe for the burgers everyone in our house had been devouring. And I regaled her with my stories of dealing with a little sister like Liv. Imo was an only child. She'd lost her parents eighteen months apart when she was a freshman in college. Her aunt had shown up to Preston's funeral to give her support, but lived in California and had little kids of her own now.

"Sorry to be depressing. Dead parents always bring a party down."

"No, it's not depressing at all. I've been there, remember?" I leaned in conspiratorially. "We're in the club together."

"I guess you're right." She leaned in too. "You're an awesome older brother. Pro hockey player. Lady magnet. You seem pretty close to perfect, Colm."

"Lady magnet?" I lifted an eyebrow.

"Do you think Lady Killer would be more appropriate? You don't think I get requests when you guys come into the restaurant? Requests to be seated next to you. Requests to be seated with you. Requests to be seated on you.

"Just because the waitress shows up at their table doesn't mean people stop talking. Let's just say you're very good for business." She laughed.

I squeezed my hands against my thighs at her sweet gentle chuckle. It warmed me inside. Totally natural and beautiful, just like her.

"Maybe I'll stop by the diner more often to help keep patronage steady."

She nodded. "Maybe you should. We're so far down the end of the boardwalk, sometimes it gets quiet during the week."

"Maybe I'll come in off the beach. Shirtless and still damp."

"Then we'd have to keep you around long term. Lock you in the walk-in fridge to preserve freshness. The perfect way to bring in crowds even after the summer."

"Only if you feed me well."

"I'd make you steak and eggs every freaking day." Her smile reached her eyes tonight. It was full and bright and made her eyes glitter. The long lines and curve of her neck called out to me. Maybe I'd had too many hits out on the ice. Maybe it was that I'd been on a no attachments kick since my last relationship ended. Or maybe it was just that she was so damn hard to resist, but I blurted the words out without even thinking about everything she'd been through and what they might mean.

"If that's on the table then you might as well marry me." It was a joke. Joking words said between two friends sitting on the beach, but I can't say if she'd said yes, I wouldn't have kept her up all night so we could be at the courthouse the second the doors opened in the morning.

Her laugh stalled in her throat like someone had wrapped their fingers around it and choked the sound out of her. And then she did the exact opposite of what you'd want someone to do, fake proposal or not—she bolted. Jumped up like she'd been bitten and mumbled something about needing to get back. To where? I didn't know, but from where was obvious. Away from me.

Sitting alone on the beach after the one woman who'd made me feel something real in a long time nearly leapt out of her skin to get away from my fake proposal hurt in a way I hadn't known it could.

Rain splattered against my skin. I don't know how long I sat out there with my shirt plastered to my chest, trying to figure out why I always ended up alone.

2

IMO

"Thank you for taking my shift last week." Cecily grabbed onto my arm and shook me. Some of my weariness was washed away by her infectious smile. The happy hour crowd had given way to a much bigger one, filled less with suits and button down shirts and more sequins, miniskirts, and guys who wore sunglasses inside—at night.

"Not like I had anything better to do." Sitting home alone was getting old even for me. Netflix had stopped recommending movies after it seemed like I'd watched ALL the things. Maybe I should get out a little more. If I wasn't careful people would stop inviting me, even out of pity.

Cecily rolled her eyes. "That's completely and totally your fault. You get asked out—what? —five times a week by the guys who roll through work."

"I'm not dating a client."

"That's not an official Garfall Rehab Center policy."

"I'm pretty sure that was in the ethics exam we had to take for our last recertification."

A sound halfway between a scoff and a snort shot out of her mouth.

"No exceptions? What about those ripped guys who stopped by last week?"

"Those guys? Old friends both happily married or nearly there." Emmett and Heath had stopped by to invite me to one of their monthly dinners, but it was on a night I needed to head down to the Surf Shack, so I'd asked for a raincheck.

"Shame. But at least we got you to come out tonight. All it took was one year of non-stop asking. We're wearing you down." She laughed and speared the cherry in her drink with her straw.

"I've got a lot going on." The volume in the bar kicked up at least five-fold. There was something going on up front.

"More like a lot of hiding."

A new voice broke in. "If I didn't do this, I'd kick myself for the rest of the month." A guy loomed over our table and crouched down beside me like a server at The Olive Garden.

"And what's that?" Cecily was practically in my lap, leaning over enjoying the view.

"Talking to you." Even with Cecily grinning in his face, he kept his gaze trained on me. "And bringing you this drink?"

He slid the martini glass with clear pink contents much like the one I'd already finished across the table.

Ding. Ding. Ding. Exactly the reason I didn't like going out to bars right here. He was cute, there was no denying that. His suit fit him like he'd taken the time to get it tailored. A happy hour hold over. There wasn't too much product in his hair, but just enough. He had dark eyes framed by long eyelashes most women had to buy in a store.

And he did absolutely nothing for me. Not a flutter, not

a flip, not a flicker of interest. With my best placate-the-guy-in-the-bar smile, I shook my head. "Thank you, but I don't accept free drinks." There was no such thing as a free drink. At a minimum, he'd want conversation and I wasn't up for flirty.

"No strings." He pushed it toward me and then held up his hands, standing and backing away a step.

"We were just leaving, but thank you so much. There's probably another woman in here who'd love to get a drink from you." I craned my neck trying to spot the perfect hook up for him.

"No, it's okay." He shoved his hands into his pockets. "You have a great night." He disappeared into the sea of people now packing the bar like he'd been told to pack up his knives and go from a reality TV cooking show.

"He was so hot!" Cecily shoved at my shoulder.

"He was cute."

"Hot!" She pushed the drink toward me. "At least take the drink."

"I've reached my limit."

"Your limit? You had one. Your limit is one?"

Sweet pink contents splashed over the edge onto the table as I slid it in front of her. "I'm not big on drinking. You have it."

The words barely made it past my lips and she picked it up and downed the whole thing in one gulp.

Furtive looks and not-so-under their breath catcalls swept through my group of friends. I should've guessed something was up. My co-workers from the Garfall Rehab Center had all shed our scrubs for a night on the town and the guy at the front of the bar was the talk of the table.

"He looks like one of the doctors from Grey's Anatomy."

"Which doctor?"

"One of the hot ones."

"Thanks for narrowing that down."

"Is he buying drinks for everyone?"

"Looks like he's pouring them straight out of the bottle."

"Now *that's* bottle service I can get behind."

Short of standing on my chair, I couldn't get a good look at him through the sea of people, but as we left I couldn't help but look.

I should've known it wouldn't be just any guy who whipped my co-workers up into a frenzy. At the center we had local celebrities, run-of-the-mill hotties and pro athletes come in every day, but this wasn't just any pro athlete.

His dark hair was mussed in a cover model kind of way, and I knew the small streak of white was there, even though it was hidden by the swoop of the curl across his forehead. The hanging lights over the bar that he held onto to steady himself lit up his face. Dim lighting from the bar did nothing to hide his body. A machine of muscle and bone built for speed and dominance on the ice. Broad shoulders leading to a muscled chest and powerful legs.

Colm.

Even with all the commotion going on around him, people jumping up and down in front of him like he was a new boy band that had rolled into town, even standing on top of the bar with a cocky smile, there was a sadness in his eyes. It was the kind you kept under wraps by speaking quickly or moving fast, like you're so damn busy you barely have time to breathe. It was the kind I'd found myself on the swampy edges of, stuck in mud so deep I could barely take a step.

My heart lurched. I couldn't stop myself; I never could when someone was hurting.

"Colm?" I called up to him, not even sure he'd notice me in the sea of people, but his gaze locked onto mine.

After I spirited him away from the mob of people surrounding him and got him into the bathroom, I got a close up view of how right I'd been about whatever was going on with him.

He splashed water on his face, the back of his neck and tips of his ears red. His gaze darted away from mine.

I dropped my hand on his broad shoulder. The insanely soft fabric of his tailored blazer caressed my fingers.

"Don't worry about it. You're not the first person to be caught in the middle of an emotional hurricane. I was glad someone was there for mine." My attempt at lightening the mood fell flat.

Our night on the beach. How he'd made me feel like I wasn't alone. How I'd run from the feelings stirred in me when I had no right to feel them so soon after...

"Do you want to talk about it?"

"No." The word was sharp and clipped. His lips were tight, so tight it felt like his face might crack open.

My fingers itched to take out my phone and call the guys, but he didn't exactly seem like he'd welcome their company right now. Or anyone's company.

What the hell had happened? I hadn't hung out with the Kings much lately. A dinner here or there with the girls. A potluck after Christmas. I always felt like they were including me as a pity invite.

Poor Imogen with the dead boyfriend. Poor Imogen, all alone so we should invite her, then shoot sad looks her way all night. Even years later, I couldn't shake the feeling that they only offered because they felt bad. But sometimes I wanted to get out of my apartment. And sometimes I wanted to do the things other people my age did, like hang out with friends. And for a few seconds before I walked in the door I'd think it could be a normal night out, and then I'd be reminded by the looks in their eyes that I'd always be Preston's Imogen. Their voices always dipped lower and they'd get that hint of sadness in every glance, like my presence was a reminder of what we'd all lost. I'd become a walking, talking, breathing memorial to him.

"Then maybe I can just sit here for a while." I hopped up onto the bathroom counter, resting my purse and hands on the cold, smooth surface, staring at him.

"In the women's bathroom?" He stared back at me like I'd suggested roasting one of his testicles over an open fire. "You want to have a conversation in here?"

"It's as good a place as any. Quieter than out there." I smiled, trying to suck some of the tension out of this situation. It wasn't every day I had a big, strong guy break down in front of me, but it happened more often than you'd think when you're trying to get people back on their feet.

I was a get-along kind of person. Agreeable, always trying to help wherever I could, but after my parents and Preston, everyone had always tiptoed around me.

Except Colm. He never looked at me like he was afraid I'd break and needed to be handled with kid gloves. Like that night on the beach. He'd talked to me like a normal person. Flirted even, which was so weird I hadn't even recognized it at first. That's how it went when your eighth grade relationship lasted for eight years—almost eight.

"It's actually pretty nice in here." I picked up the abandoned bottle of gin he'd left beside the sink. "I'll have a drink right here." I kicked my feet against the counter, the backs of my shoes drumming against the hard surface.

"What makes you think I won't walk out of here?" He crossed his arms over his chest.

"You can. The door's right there." I lifted my arm, knowing the clock was ticking on someone walking in and breaking through the cocoon we were in right now.

His jaw twitched, but he didn't move.

I lifted the bottle and took a gulp and winced. "Does that count as a double?" I wheezed out.

"Now you're drinking my booze?"

"I heard you had an open tab for the whole bar. I'm getting my slice of the pie."

He reached for the bottle, but I whipped my arm behind me, crashing my elbow into the mirror. I sucked in a sharp breath between my teeth, glad a cascade of broken glass hadn't showered down around me.

"I'm trying to have a good time."

"By getting blackout drunk?" This was the hard part: getting him to see that whatever the hell was wrong wasn't the end of the world. Life would go on. There might not have been rainbows and unicorns at the end of that tunnel, but it was a hell of a lot better than wallowing until the light was gone.

"You're not my babysitter."

"Nope and that's why I'm drinking this." I tipped the bottle back again, bracing myself for the sharp, crisp hit in the back of my throat. "I hope you didn't have babysitters growing up that would chug booze straight from the bottle."

He plucked the bottle from my grip. "I was the babysitter."

"Lucky girls." I grinned, trying to get him to crack even the slightest hint of a smile.

No dice.

He threw his hands in the air. "What is up with you? Why'd you drag me back here? We barely even know each other. We're not friends."

Ouch. Anyone else feel like they got left out of the school-wide candygram delivery? He was way too drunk to have a serious conversation about whatever was going on. I needed to get him away from the booze and to somewhere quieter that wasn't a women's bathroom.

"Maybe not, but I remember you taking the time to sit down with me once when I was upset and I thought I'd return the favor."

"You don't need to. I'm absolving you of any obligation."

"How magnanimous of you. And from how sloppy those words were, I'm still staying."

He made a noise that sounded a bit like he was trying to snort fire or breathe it. I half expected a curl of smoke to shoot out of one nostril. Fine, if he wanted to be a dick about it, I'd annoy him until he told me what the deal was or got so pissed he forgot about the sadness for a little bit.

"I don't remember you being half this annoying." He tilted his chin to the side, but kept his eyes trained on the door like even he didn't know why he was still in here with me.

"My clients would disagree." The curses people can string together when you're pushing them to get back on their feet—literally—can be quite colorful and creative.

"Clients?" His gaze narrowed.

"I'm a physiotherapist, remember? I went back to school for it."

He harrumphed.

The door flung open, two women stopped short when they spotted Colm, then me. Their eyes widened before one broke free from the other's grip and burst through the stall door assuming the this-is-going-to-be-a-long-night position and yakking in the toilet. Her friend took up post behind her, rubbing her back.

Colm took the distraction to storm out of the bathroom
—fleeing like only a six-two guy who weighed at least
200lbs could. Not that I blamed him.

I bobbed and wove through the crowd to stand
beside him.

His gaze cut sideways. "You're not going to leave me
alone, are you?" The resigned sigh was one I'd heard many
times before.

"Not planning on it." I kept my voice light and my gaze
trained on him. Tension radiated off him, like he might hulk
out of that suit jacket that probably cost more than my rent.
"Why don't we get out of here?"

His head snapped up and he stared at me with narrowed
eyes. I had to rewind a moment before I realized how that
might have sounded.

My cheeks felt like they were glowing under his exacting
gaze, but his pain was palpable. I could taste it in the air,
stinging and deep at the same time. I could never walk away
from that. He needed a friend right now.

"Fine." He waved to the bar manager and said something to him. The guy disappeared before coming back and
shaking Colm's hand.

He lifted an eyebrow like a challenge he didn't know
he'd already lost. "Your place or mine?"

3

IMO

I knew the perfect place. I walked outside, not letting him know I wouldn't be scared off that easily. The noise and heat dropped the second we crossed the threshold.

"Neither." I raised my arm for a taxi as Colm joined me, standing beside me.

"Kinky."

A taxi screeched up to the curb like it had been waiting for him. Perks of being with a hot, well-dressed guy.

He held the door open for me, but not in a way that seemed to be anything other than reflex.

I ducked inside, wondering what exactly this version of Colm had gone through. From what I'd heard he'd gone out to California after an injury and was back ready to play better than ever once the season started. Of all the guys he always had the easiest smile, but not a goofy one like Heath, who epitomized surfer dude chic in the Kings. Ford and Emmett were more sullen and quiet. Declan was more of an every dude, but Colm always had the kind of polish that screamed trips to the Hamptons, private islands, and first class flights.

I gave the driver an address and we pulled into traffic. The taxi ride was pin drop silent aside from the rumble of the tires on the road. A few minutes later, we pulled up to our destination. Big, metal block letters sat above the windows.

"Jones, really?" He lifted an eyebrow.

"Where did you think we were going?" I shrugged. "They have excellent meatloaf." The elevated comfort food always hit the spot after a late night.

Our dinner was what I'd imagine it was like sitting at a table with two parents on the verge of a horrendous divorce, when neither wanted to give way to the other in front of the kids. Colm ordered his food and I couldn't stop myself from getting the crème brûlée brioche French toast for dessert even though it was supposed to be its own meal.

At least Colm wasn't drowning himself in booze. He had ice water and I had an Irish coffee, keeping an eye on him. The rawness of whatever he was going through was there, but he wasn't teetering on the edge of that yawning abyss.

I'd been there. I'd felt that. I was tempted to sneak away and call Declan to find out what the hell was going on.

Maybe Colm's recovery hadn't gone well? "How's your leg?"

He stretched it under the table almost like even he wasn't sure. His foot brushed against mine. That full body tingle from the bar was back.

Not now, Imo.

"Rehab finished two weeks ago. I'll be back on the ice as soon as the pre-season starts."

"I'm glad you've made a solid recovery."

"Once the season starts it'll be like it never happened."

His fingers tightened around his glass, and droplets of condensation dripped onto the table.

"It'll always be something you have to work on, though. I'm sure they gave you exercises you need to be doing in addition to your other training to keep it from happening again."

He grumbled and stabbed at his mashed potatoes.

The rest of the meal was filled with tense silence.

At least my meatloaf was as good as I'd remembered.

I couldn't stop the happy dance in my seat when the French toast came after I'd stuffed myself on comfort food.

"Do you want some?" I nudged the plate toward him.

"No." He drank from his glass.

"You sure? It's so good. It doesn't even need syrup, but if you're going big, might as well go for it, right?"

He tilted his chin and peered over at me.

It took everything in me not to squirm in my seat. The intensity of his gaze made it hard to think straight this close to him. I shouldn't have picked a booth. I should've gone with a table, right up against the window.

He watched me eat the sweet, eggy bread until his attention came to be too much and I was dropping syrup everywhere—well, not just syrup.

I coughed into my napkin and waved over the waiter for the check.

Colm tried to pull the whole I'm-a-man routine, but that was why I'd already given them my card when I dashed off to the bathroom.

He was pissed.

And why did that make me so happy? Teasing him? Making him mad over something so small? It cut through the self-imposed timeout he'd put himself in.

"Why'd you do that?"

"I don't make pro athlete money, but I can spring for a dinner for two."

We walked out of the restaurant. I'd been enjoying needling him way too much, but the way he moved once we hit the late night air killed some of that fun.

His gait was like an animal newly deposited in the zoo. Darting gaze, unable to stand still, body radiating tension and discontent. Apparently, the booze had worn off. What was he trying to drown in a sea of anonymous faces and generous drink pours? "I live not too from here. I'll walk. Let me get you in a taxi." He stepped toward the curb.

I wrapped my fingers around his arm. Beneath the soft fabric, the muscles rippled under my touch. "I'll walk you home." It would take nothing for him to put me in a taxi, go out and do something stupid. If I at least got him home, he'd be less likely to do something that would get him in trouble or that he'd regret in the morning.

His glare was like disgust and annoyance had had a love child. "I already said I didn't need a babysitter."

"Didn't say I was one. I'm walking in that direction anyway."

"You don't even know what direction I'm going."

Looked like he'd sobered up enough to catch me in that lie, but he led the way. It doesn't mean he was happy about it. The grumbling didn't stop. Any lightness in his mood evaporated a little more with every step toward his house. Apparently, 'not too far' meant a twenty-minute walk. He hadn't wanted to get back in a confined space with me.

He pulled his keys out and stopped in front of a modern brownstone nestled in amongst other turn of the century historical homes. "There, I'm home. You've made sure I'm safe and sound. You can go now." He moved to close the door.

"You're really not going to tell me what's going on?"

"What about how tonight has gone so far made you think I'd want to sit down and shoot the shit?" He bristled with anger.

Maybe it's because I've stood my ground in front of clients—usually very physically imposing athletes—when they've gotten in my face with all their bluster and rage at their situations. Or maybe it's because I'd stood in front of Preston when he'd had the same kind of pained outburst that you can only really unleash on the people you feel safe around. Or maybe I'm just a glutton for punishment. Whatever it was, I couldn't let this go.

"Not shoot the shit, no, but you need to get whatever is bothering you out before it poisons you completely. You helped me before. I'm returning the favor before you do something you can't take back."

"You and the beach. It was years ago, forget about it. I have." He ran his fingers through his hair. "Maybe I was being nice to you to get into your pants. Ever think of that?" His silver-tipped tongue was also good with the lashes. But I'd been here before. I'd seen how this could spiral out of control and refused to let that happen to Colm.

"Maybe you were." I approached him with my hand out like I'd stumbled on a wounded animal.

"Would you stop being so nice to me?" He dragged his fingers through his hair again, looking like he was on the verge of breaking down. "Stop it. I can't deal with something real right now." His voice cracked and I had to tighten my muscles to keep my wince at bay. His pain was palpable, hanging in the air like an oppressive fog threatening to swallow him whole.

His red-rimmed gaze clashed against mine.

A step closer and the gap between us evaporated. I

touched my palm to his chest. "Everyone deserves some-thing real."

A look flashed across his face and it felt like someone had plunged a knife into my heart. "Not everyone. It's all my fault." The words were ripped from his throat. This was an old hurt, something deep that had never healed. I'd felt those wounds. Sometimes you had to get good at covering it over because there weren't enough bandages in the world to fix it.

He dropped his hand onto mine. His hold was so fierce and heavy it stole my breath away. There were tears in his eyes, threatening to crest over his lids and fall.

"You need to leave." He slammed his eyes shut.

"You can talk to me. I swear, I won't tell anyone."

"I don't want to talk." His eyes snapped open. Under all the pain, under all the hurt, under the walls he'd put up was something I'd seen before. That night on the beach I'd run from him because the feeling burning in my chest had scared the shit out of me. He'd made me feel alive when it was all I could do to drag myself out of bed every day, but I'd done it for Fern and Charlie, for everyone else who needed me to get through that hard time.

With him, I'd wanted to run out into the surf, laughing and living. To feel his arms wrapped around me. His lips crashing down on mine like the rolling waves of the ocean. Those were things I had no right to feel, a betrayal that shook me to my core. He'd scared me with the glimpse of what could be beyond the loss consuming me.

I was still scared, but there was something else. I'd help him. And maybe, selfishly, help myself quench the longing for connection, the longing to have a second chance at that night and the desire I'd thought had been turned off forever because after that night the door felt closed. Until now.

There was an ache between my thighs that I'd ignored since he'd plucked that drink from my hand and his fingers had brushed against my lips.

"Then don't talk."

My words fell between us like I'd thrown down a glove that challenged him to a duel. His face cycled through too many emotions to name with each excruciating second. My heart beat rabbit fast and I locked my knees so I didn't sway on my feet as doubt crept in. What was I doing? What was I saying?

His lips crashed down on mine, so fast my questions whooshed away in the late spring air.

Our teeth clinked, gnashing as he pulled me up the steps in front of his place. His chest slammed against mine and our bodies collided. The hard press of the circular band of metal that I wore on a chain around my neck dug into my sternum.

He was drowning. I was his oxygen and he was gulping me down. I could say I was doing this to help him, that he needed this to let him deal with whatever was going on, but a part of me had wanted to feel him like this since that night on the beach. It was the night I'd had my heart wrecked all over again.

Who better than another broken person to look through the cracks in the armor he wore?

Who better to make me feel something I hadn't let myself feel in a long time?

Alive.

4

COLM

The question had been running through my head all night: how could I get her to leave? But I didn't want her to go. And now the maple syrup and cinnamon taste of her sent me hurtling close to the edge of my control. Those reserves were running on fumes.

Everyone else had been run off by my anger or blinded by my money, but not Imogen. If anything, she battled me, pushing me like she knew I needed it. She wouldn't let me hide the splintered and cracked pieces of myself that I was barely holding together.

She didn't push me to talk, just slid in past my defenses and got me to say more than I should.

"Do you want me to stop?" I ran my fingers through her hair, tugging on the roots.

Her lips parted in a gasp and I deepened the kiss, needing to taste even more of her. She'd teased me, eating that French toast that smelled like a vanilla and cinnamon factory had exploded when it arrived at our table.

She stared into my eyes, heavy breaths shuddering past her lips. "Hell no."

I'd have laughed if the words hadn't sent me into over-drive. Kicking the front door closed, I dropped my head to her neck and raked my teeth along her thumping pulse point.

She shuddered and shivered in my arms. Her fingers went to the buttons of my jacket, flicking them open like the practiced fingers of a globetrotting playboy. Not to say my fingers weren't doing the same.

There wasn't a preamble.

There weren't soft, gentle words.

There was the ferocious need to get her naked.

I was starving for her. It was like a switch had flipped in my mind and I realized that every meal I'd had over the past four years had been figments of my imagination. Since the first time I'd seen her standing in the hospital hallway after swearing I'd never set foot in one again, I'd wanted this moment. Maybe not consciously; how much of a dick would that have made me? And after Preston was gone, she was so damn sad. The kind of sadness that radiated off someone so thick you could taste it.

She always tried to take care of everyone, make them laugh or make them smile, put them at ease like her feelings didn't matter. But tonight I had her and I'd serve up every blissful feeling on a silver platter, playing out my list of every fantasy I'd had about her in as many hours as it took for her to pass out, only to have her wake up to the second half of that list.

Her jeans hit the wall with a thud. My belt jangled around my thighs on my pants' way to the floor and I kicked them off. They might have landed on top of the TV or fallen into a portal to another dimension for all I cared.

Pushing her against the kitchen's island, I slid my hand down between us and caressed her stomach before dropping my hands lower. I dropped to the floor, not even wincing at the small pinch in my knee. I didn't even care.

She rested her elbows against the granite countertop, her back pressed up against it. Not giving either one of us enough time to think, I flung her legs up over my shoulders. The siren call of her overheated core filled my head—hell both heads—with the need to taste her now.

With the first swipe of my tongue, she dug her heels into my back. I sucked on her clit, running my tongue over it, slipped two of my fingers inside of her.

She moaned and her fingers tightened on the edge of the counter.

This was a heaven I hadn't thought I'd experience with her. That night on the beach, I thought I'd screwed this up beyond belief. An insensitive slip up ruining the chance to be close to her again. But she was into this every bit as much as I was, pouring those feelings out right along with her cries and moans.

I nipped at her inner thighs and she squirmed against my mouth, grinding against my face and working with me to reach her peak. I slipped another finger inside of her and curled them forward.

Her hips shot up off her seat and every muscle went rigid. Her legs squeezed my head like she didn't ever want to move again. I didn't want to move either.

Not wanting to let her come down completely, I laved her clit with my tongue.

She shuddered and moaned, grabbing onto my shoulders and pulling me toward her.

I stood, and for the first time there was no hesitation with my knee. I'm thankful the knee recovered or maybe I couldn't be here tonight with Imogen. I'd been an idiot earlier. I could have fallen off the bar or done something stupid when I was that damn drunk. But I was sober enough now. My leg could've fallen off and nothing would have stopped me from getting inside her when she was clutching at me, pulling me close like this.

Gripping my cock, I ran the head along the seam of her pussy. So damn wet. I gritted my teeth, determined not to come in thirty seconds flat.

"Please, I need this. You need this." She wasn't wrong. Her eyes locked with mine and she dug her heels into my ass and I sank inside her.

"I need you." I couldn't form thoughts. She was so tight and wet my eyes rolled back in my head. Each thrust drew a cry from her lips.

Running the back of my hands along her stomach and up to her breasts, I cupped them and pinched her nipples.

"This is too good." I dropped my hand between us, running my thumb over her clit.

"Colm, I'm—" The word was lost on her cry. Her back arched off the counter and her legs tightened around my waist. The contractions of her walls around me set me off.

"Imo—" It was a choked word, strangled out of me by pleasure. We both hurtled straight over the side of that cliff we'd been balancing on and I collapsed on top of her, bracing my weight with my arms.

My heart pounded like I'd played double overtime out on the ice and sweat rolled down my back. But I couldn't keep the smile off my face. Was I supposed to be playing it cool? How could I when she'd sliced through the storm cloud of my life like a sexy ray of sunshine?

Imo's flutter soft kisses along my neck sent a shiver down my spine. Every part of this felt right: her soft breasts pressed against my chest, our bodies nestled together, my cock inside her.

I'd come already and I was still hard. That was new. Apparently the gin I'd had tonight had the opposite effect of whiskey dick. Like he and I were on the same page about what she deserved. Or maybe it was just her.

I felt her soft touches running up and down my back, and the tingling tickles shot across my skin. Lifting my head, I captured her lips in mine, putting so much more into that kiss than any that had come before. For so long I'd tried to pretend she didn't get under my skin, but I didn't have to pretend anymore. She'd said 'hell no' when I'd asked if I should stop, so there was no doubt in my mind that she wanted to be here with me.

Our journey of sexual exploration took us across every flat surface in the living room and kitchen, as well as some improvised ones. The ottoman. The bookcase. The fireplace. We'd made it as far as the stairs at one point, but ended up heading straight to the floor and then back to the couch. I'd never be able to look at a single surface in my home without remembering how we'd devoured each other on it.

The pillows on the couch pushed her blonde-almost white hair up against one side of her head. She batted my hands away sleepily as I ran the back of my finger along her cheek. If I hadn't been with her for hours and seen her nursing nothing but an Irish coffee—well and the gin she'd stolen from me—I might have been worried. But she'd been there with me the whole time.

I stepped back, separating our bodies, and the ice bucket realization stole over me. No condom. I'd never not worn one. From high school until a few hours ago, it would never have crossed my mind. It was like muscle memory ingrained not only from being a professional athlete, but also coming from a family with resources like mine. I'd always been wary of finding myself ensnared by someone with less than above-board intentions.

Then I looked down at Imogen, and that small knot slipped away like it had never been there. That's not Imo. She's not someone who uses people. She's someone who cares. Look at how she stuck with my surly ass all night.

We could have that talk in the morning and figure it out, whatever it might be. But tonight, I curled up with her in my arms. Sliding them under her, I lifted her from the couch.

Taking a second to make sure my knee was fine, I gazed down at her. She burrowed deeper against my chest, murmuring in her sleep. From the long, fine curve of her eyelashes to the delicate shell of her ears, she was perfect and I could stare at her all night. Goosebumps broke out all over her and I cursed, taking us upstairs to my bedroom before the chill could disturb her.

I tucked her into bed, and smiled as she sighed and rolled closer to me. Then I peeled the blankets back and slipped in beside her. She huddled toward my embrace and I welcomed the weight of her against my chest.

What had I been upset about today? It all seemed like a distant memory. Maybe I should call Ford and Liv in the morning. My shock at thinking Liv had died, coupled with finding out she'd slept with Ford had sent me scrambling to make sense of the world. Intense, crazy emotions had made it hard to think clearly. Throw in my girlfriend leaving me and maybe I'd overreacted a little when it came to Ford and Liv's new whatever-it-was.

I brushed the hair back from Imo's face and the corners of her mouth lifted. One night and I was already thinking crazy stuff. This is what had gotten me in trouble before. Going straight to planning family vacations a year from now.

Asking a woman to move in. Like I was trying to rebuild a family out of thin air.

Slow down.

It's like my game of Life was always jumping thirty spaces down the path, when I needed to stick to spinning ones. Breakfast tomorrow. That would do. I'd take her out to breakfast. Or maybe give her a morning wake-up call that might turn it into brunch, which might slide into a trip back here and lunch in bed.

Wrapping my arms around her, I closed my eyes and smiled as she moved closer, nudging my chin up to rest it on top of her head. I could totally get used to this.

The morning light streamed through the slatted blinds. I closed my eyes and sank into the bed, savoring the feelings lingering on my skin from Imogen's nips, scrapes, and the grip of her supple thighs around my waist.

For once in the past few weeks, I woke up without anger and hurt burning in my gut. A highlight reel from the night before ran through my head. Every word. Every touch. Every taste from her. This had been five years in the making, building up in my head as something that would never happen. But it had, and my imagination hadn't conjured anything remotely as good as the reality.

There was a lot to talk about. What did this mean? What happened now? Did she want to have dinner with me again? The heavy ache in my chest hadn't been as keen when I had fallen asleep last night, and it sure as hell wasn't as sharp this morning.

When I saw her last night, a longing I hadn't let myself indulge in came over me. We hadn't been alone since that night on the beach, but every time I listened to James Bay I thought about her, which meant I'd played those songs more than I should. Anytime the gang all got together, I made a point to find moments alone with her.

Maybe I could deal with this whole thing with Liv and Ford. Take a breather and figure it out. He'd gone behind my back with her and that hurt. The trust we'd been rebuilding was shattered again, but he was my oldest friend. And Liv couldn't just throw away her future to become a dance teacher, but there might be some room for compromise. With Imogen beside me, the uncertainty of the future didn't seem so scary. It didn't feel like, if things didn't go exactly to plan, that they couldn't turn out okay.

Once again, I was flying off into this imaginary life that felt more real than anything I was currently living, but first, I needed to get Imo fed.

Opening my eyes, I rolled over and my hand connected with nothing but blankets. The side of the bed she'd banished herself to after I woke her a second time with the insistent nudge of my erection against her back was cold.

I gave her a few minutes in the bathroom before I shot up, a thread of dread weaving its way through my chest. The bathroom door was open, but the room was empty.

Her scent lingered in the room like a French toast breakfast in a botanical garden. Nothing in my room was out of place, not that we'd been in here for more than sleeping.

Jumping out of bed, I beat back the edges of panic rising in me. Calm down, she's probably downstairs. Maybe getting some food or something to drink.

Out in the living room, my clothes were strewn all over the floor right where she and I had peeled them off my body just like we'd done to hers. But hers weren't there. Only mine, discarded on the floor, like I'd come home by myself and tossed them around, imagining the whole thing.

The clawing rawness in my chest was back. Maybe she'd gone out to get some breakfast. Like in Bridget Jones' Diary. Liv had made me watch that fifty times, probably to see me squirm. In the movie Bridget wakes up and thinks he's gone, but he went out to get her a new diary. Imogen would totally be the person to get up early to sneak out and bring back breakfast, in case I didn't have any food—she wouldn't want me to feel bad about that. Or maybe she was getting that steak and eggs she'd promised me when she sat beside me on the sand.

I turned on the coffee pot. Even if she brought back coffee, I didn't want her to think I was waiting around for her to come back with food. Maybe I could get started cooking something. Maybe French toast. That would be so much better than bagels or whatever the coffee shop a few streets over had.

Had she needed to get up early for work? She hadn't mentioned it last night, not that I'd invited conversation.

I sat at my kitchen island, nursing a long chilled cup of coffee, two plates of French toast with sliced strawberries and a bowl of freshly whipped cream beside me. I kept my eyes trained on the front door, still hoping she'd return from whatever had dragged her from my bed this morning. She hadn't left a note. I didn't even have her number.

Stupid, Colm. What was wrong with me? Here I was, ready to blurt out an out of the blue proposal and thinking about a future, and she'd just been trying to comfort me. Pity sex for the beyond-fucked-up Colm. She was just like everyone else, pretending to care. Pretending they'd be there for me and then disappearing at the first opportunity. I held onto that anger because it was a hell of a lot better than the crushing sadness, the loneliness and rejection that had become the hallmark of my life with everyone other than the Kings. And now we were fractured too.

This was the story of my life. So many women back in college hadn't understood why I needed to bring my little sister along on my vacations. Why I couldn't jet-set like everyone else. But it helped me spot the users a lot quicker when Liv was younger. A de facto single dad with a teenager to take care of wasn't exactly sexy to many twenty-year-olds.

I never cared about anyone who didn't get why my little sister would always come first. It was me and Liv against the world, and anyone who didn't get that could go fuck themselves. Only apparently Liv couldn't wait to break that pact she'd pinky sworn me to out on the jungle gym in our backyard when she was eight.

My phone vibrated on the counter. I shot up like I used to when the ice cream truck drove down our sleepy street when Liv and I were kids. Snatching my cell up off the counter, my heart sped up. Imo?

A punch of disappointment cratered in my chest when I looked at the screen.

Declan: *You're still coming today, right?*

Right, hockey with the guys.

Me: *Yeah, I'll be there.*

Imo wasn't coming back.

Abandoning my sentry post by the door, I got my gear together and headed for the practice rink. The calmness I'd felt earlier this morning had been washed away in less than an hour. I was back to the same burning anger inside, only it was worse now because I'd had a taste of what being with Imogen felt like. But I knew I didn't deserve that happiness —if anything, the Ford and Liv situation had hammered it home.

Out on the ice I was able to bleed off some of my aggression, letting the walls and padded gear on the other guys absorb a shit ton of it, but it all came rushing back the second I spotted Ford in the box ready to get out on the ice.

My day had gone from shit to complete horse shit in a matter of moments. He was here. Staring at me like he wanted to talk, when he was the reason almost everything in my life had disintegrated in front of my eyes.

Ford tensed. "What the fuck is he doing here?"

Fire and blinding rage raced through me. Somehow I was standing in front of him and he was talking to me like I was the bad guy. Like I was the one who'd fucked someone's fiancée. Or I was the one who'd convinced my little sister that medical school, the only dream she'd ever had, wasn't for her. Or I was the one who'd kept the fact that she'd almost died in a fire from me. Like I'm the asshole.

I didn't remember taking the swing, but the thought of splitting his lip and beating the crap out of him was too tempting. Too bad I was on skates and he wasn't. The first time I busted my leg, I'd barely felt it. I tried to get up three times before someone came over and put me down and they hauled me off the ice. It might have been the adrenaline pumping through my veins from the game or that I couldn't hear the crunch over the roar of the crowd. The punch I threw barely connected, but I'd thrown too much weight behind it.

This time, every excruciating pull of muscle, crunch of bone, and twist of sinew was relayed to my brain in crystal clarity. In a split second, all the months of rehab, all the time I'd spent getting my ass back on the ice was wiped away. I stared up at the rafters of the practice rink with my leg on fire like someone had shoved a poker down my thigh.

"Fuck! Don't look." Declan slammed my helmeted head

back to the ground. There was a flurry of activity and shouting and I hoped I'd go numb. I welcomed the numbness because the pain of watching the last thing I had in my life shatter made it hard to see where I could go from here.

And now I was lying in a hospital bed, in the place I'd sworn I wouldn't be again. The doctors had come in. Bailey, the team trainer, had come in with her eyes blazing. Smacking me on my good leg she ground out, "I swear, you're doing this on purpose. What the hell, Frost?"

"You don't think I know already how fucking messed up this is?" I said through gritted teeth, pushing myself up in the bed. I winced as the pain meds took their time ramping back up.

She ran her hand over her face. "I know. I'm sorry."

"Is my place on the squad still okay?"

She grimaced. "If you're up and running before the trade window closes this season, it should be. We'll take a temporary trade to fill out the roster until then. The coaches will be here to give you the official word, so you didn't hear this from me."

I nodded. The angle my leg had been at after I'd thrown that punch at Ford didn't bode well for a speedy recovery. Last time it had been my knee. This time it wasn't just my knee. Part of me just wanted to say fuck it. Wheel myself out of here and never look back. Who'd miss me anyway?

5

IMO

Stretching, I bumped my head against the chin perched on top of my head. Preston smelled different. Crisp and refined like a well-tailored suit. I ran my hands over his chest.

"You're late for practice, P—" The word caught in my throat because this wasn't Preston. He was gone. He'd been gone for almost five years. Gingerly, slipping away from the arms around me, I stared at the muscled and tanned expanse in front of me. Colm.

What if I'd woken him up and he'd heard me? Waking up in Preston's arms was ingrained in my head like muscle memory. I didn't know if I'd ever be able to break the habit.

In the past four years, I'd only let myself spend the night with one other guy. When I'd woken and called him Preston, and then promptly broken down in tears, I'd sworn off trying again. Sleeping over was a no-no. Guilt sat heavy in my chest like a boot pressing down on me. I squeezed my eyes shut and slid to the edge of the bed.

Had I pressed Colm last night because I was lonely? Because I'd wanted him from a time when I had no business thinking about ever kissing anyone else? Because he was even more messed up than me and it felt good not to be the most broken one for a change? He'd been vulnerable and, apparently, I'd thought sex was the best way to help. I slammed my forehead into my hand.

Scrambling out into the living room, I snatched up my clothes. I couldn't even use being drunk as an excuse for doing this. The highlight reel from the night before ran through my head like I'd pulled up to the drive-in with a whole bucket of popcorn.

The abandoned condom sat just under my jeans—still completely in its wrapper. *Fuck!* What had I been thinking? Oh, I know, I was thinking of using my vagina as a new rehab method—well, that and the fact that if I hadn't gotten Colm inside me immediately I'd have jumped out of my skin.

Let yourself get too close and this was what happened. Let your guard down with Colm and now you've banged (without protection) an emotionally unstable hockey player who was eight women deep last night. Perfect.

A shiver shot down my spine at how perfect it had been. There were no kid gloves last night. There was a raw, visceral kind of explosion that had threatened to consume me.

There was a reason I'd kept him at arm's length since that night on the beach. Why I'd avoided sitting beside him when the Kings had dinner or we got together for a game night. It was the way my skin tingled when I remembered those fingertip brushes from when I'd sat beside him in the sand.

He didn't look at me with pity in his eyes that made me want to curl up into a little ball and weep, but with a burning light of desire. I'd longed to feel that heat against my skin.

And that's why I'd run that night. How could I trust myself to get close to someone again after what happened with Preston?

My hand hovered over the door knob. Was I really just going to run out of here? He'd been ready to take home ten women last night. I was sure he'd probably done the same thing before. Lifting my head, I squeezed my eyes shut and took a breath.

Dropping my hand, I tiptoed back to the bedroom. Colm was still asleep, and the slight mussed look he'd rocked last night had turned into bed head. The blankets had dipped down low to his hips, showing off a hint of that V guys only got when they'd dedicated hours to the gym. Even after an injury like his, he'd put in the work. The power of those hips sent another shiver through my body.

I could leave a note. Maybe we could meet up later, somewhere public where I wouldn't want to climb him like a tree and stay in bed all weekend when I was slammed with work. But a note was a good place to start. I was going to message myself with his phone, but it was locked. I looked around the room for something to write on.

Somehow getting caught trying to sneak out seemed a hell of a lot worse than sneaking out. I backed up. Maybe there would be something out in the living room. My foot crossed the threshold and my phone blared in my hand. I nearly chucked it down the hall, before muffling it against my chest and silencing it.

Colm rolled over, dragging the sheets even lower.

I darted out of the room and answered the call in a whisper.

"Imogen! Are you there?" Her tone of motherly concern ratcheted even higher.

"Hi, Fern, I'm here." My whispers sounded like screaming through a megaphone in the quiet of Colm's house.

"Are you okay? Are you on your way?" Her voice had an edge of panic to it.

Shit. The guilt was back with a vengeance, nibbling away at the edges of my memories from last night. "I'm fine, just running a little late." In my Colm-induced, no-alcohol-needed hangover, I'd forgotten. My night of wild and crazy sex with Colm felt tainted. Fern and Charlie were counting on me to help them open the Surf Shack this weekend, and were worried about me, and here I'd been getting my rocks off and sleeping in. Since Preston had died, they were my only tether to that old life I had with him. I'd been taken in by them as my surrogate parents and never wanted to let them down.

"We were worried when you weren't here in time for breakfast."

"I'm so sorry." I tiptoed down the hall. "I'm on my way. Is everything okay?"

"We're having a bit of an emergency down here. Do you know where the warranties are for the walk-in freezer? It's on the fritz. We're scrambling to salvage everything we can after our delivery last night."

"I'll be there in an hour and a half, and I'll call to have a freezer truck arrive until we can figure it out." Rushing out, I closed the door behind me and darted down the street, throwing my arm up for a taxi.

～

Complete and total crisis averted. Charlie, Fern and I managed to save thousands of dollars of meat. My day included hauling giant boxes of it out to the refrigerator truck, stepping in for a waitress who broke her foot on the way to work, and playing hostess and seating people until the dinner shift hostess arrived.

The bright blue, white, and yellow Surf Shack was a Jersey Shore staple. It had survived downturns, hurricanes, and Preston's death, and still kept chugging.

In those first few summers Charlie and Fern needed a lot of help to keep the diner going. Both of them sometimes slipped into a daze of sorts, and it was all any of us could do to get them into the office to close their eyes for a bit. And I'd been back in school, so I'd had summers off.

It was trickier to juggle helping them on the weekends with work during the week now, but I could never abandon them.

I collapsed in the back office with a filled to the brim cup of lemonade, some fish tacos, and a salted caramel chocolate chip cookie. I devoured the food so quickly, I barely tasted it, but the cookie deserved to be savored. As I was lifting it to my mouth, the office door swung open and I froze.

Charlie startled when he spotted me. "Imogen, what are you doing here? I thought you left. You've been here almost twelve hours."

"I'd never go without telling you I was leaving." I cringed a little at the runner I'd pulled on Colm this morning. A busy mind had also helped me push aside the complications that would invite. What had he thought when he woke up and I was gone? I was tempted to call one of the Kings and ask for his number, but that would only invite more questions. What if he had only been looking for a way to blow off steam? If he wanted to follow up as more than fun, he could easily hunt down my number.

"I figured you were probably running off to hang out with your friends or something. We didn't need you to stay all this time. We just needed a little help with the hand we were dealt this morning." He collapsed in the chair in front of the desk.

"Charlie, sit here."

He waved me off. "God knows, half the time in the past few years you've been running this place more than we have." The corners of his eyes crinkled as his cheeks lifted. "Still can't believe it's been almost thirty years." He looked around at the walls. Pictures of famous visitors framed beside those of well-known locals and his family.

"The plan was someday we'd pass that onto the kids." Some of the light in his dark eyes dimmed. "But you know what they say about best laid plans." He chuckled to himself, resting his arms on the chair and clasping his hands across his chest.

"I'll keep coming down on the weekend."

He made a dismissive sound. "That was a good excuse when you were in college, but it's not a good one now. You don't need to spend your weekends down here with us. Even Becca has put in her notice."

"I can't leave you shorthanded."

"You also can't use this place as your hide out." His gaze swung from the walls and met mine.

"I'm not hiding out."

"Sure you are. What twenty-five-year-old wants to spend all her summer weekends cooped up in a restaurant after working a full week?"

"Do most twenty-five-year-olds have access to unlimited salted caramel chocolate cookies like these?" I took a huge bite out of the cookie. The mixture of sweet, salty, chewy, and crunchy staged a deliciously hostile takeover of my mouth.

"We'll mail them to you. Besides, those ones your friend makes from that Bread & Butter aren't anything to sneeze at. They certainly put these to shame."

"You don't want me to come down." That thought turned the cookie stale in my mouth. Had I finally overstayed my welcome? I dropped my hand to the desk.

Charlie shot forward and covered my hand with his, giving it a reassuring squeeze. "Never, Imogen. Never. Of course we want you here. You're welcome anytime, but burning the candle at both ends isn't going to help you move on." He squeezed my hand again and the words came out thick and heavy.

I turned my hand over in his and gave it a squeeze back. "I miss him."

"I know, sweetheart. I know." We sat there, staring up at the pictures. The ones where I'd joined in on the annual family picture. There hadn't been an updated one added since Preston died.

"There you two are." Fern came in and corralled us both out of the office. We finished closing up, and then it was time for me to head back to the city. Even though I usually stayed, I had an interview to prepare for. Charlie's words stayed with me. I hadn't shared the news of the position when it came up. A practice in Philly was opening a new office ten minutes from the Shack. I'd made sure my application was in the second it was posted. How would they feel if I moved closer? Did they want me there?

The drive back to the city was quiet. Not many people left the shore on a Friday night. Stopping to fill up along the way, I grabbed a cup of coffee from the Wawa at the rest stop before getting back on the road. I got back to my apartment and collapsed into my bed. Hour-and-a-half trips down the shore were taking their toll on me. I was so beat it took everything I had not to fall asleep in my shoes and clothes that smelled like—well, a Jersey Shore restaurant.

What would Fern and Charlie think if they knew what had happened last night? I still couldn't wrap my head around it. One second I'm trying to help Colm and cheer him up, and the next it was like he'd tapped into something deep down in me I'd thought was long dead and buried.

I blinked quickly, refusing to let the tears fall. How many had I shed at this point? So many I'd have thought that at some point my tear ducts would have run dry. There were so many emotions all mixed together when it came to Preston. Once the dull ache had receded, there was the keen, slicing pain of loss, the terrifying uncertainty of what would come next, and then the waves of guilt that grew with each passing day.

Every patient I worked with did their best to cope with a debilitating diagnosis and relearn the basics. One client with a knee injury made the transition from pounding the pavement as a marathoner to hitting the pool and building up to 10 kilometer swims instead. It seemed I needed to learn that as well, but how?

Rolling over, I grabbed my phone and texted Emmett, asking for Colm's number. He was the least likely to run around blabbing or give it a second thought, especially if he was anywhere near Avery. When he was near her, nothing else existed. With any luck, he'd forget within minutes that he'd even given it to me.

I typed and retyped the message to Colm. Running out on him this morning had been a dick move, but I'd had a reason. Also, why the hell was his house so clean? There hadn't been a scrap of paper anywhere.

But last night had been...I couldn't stop thinking about it. About him. Everyone at the Garfall Center is always saying I need to put myself out there. And Colm's the only person who made me want to try the whole moving on thing.

I hit send before I could second guess myself.

Me: Sorry about this morning. Something came up. Are you okay?

The phantom buzz caught me at least twenty times over the next hour before I banished my phone to the living room so I'd stop obsessively checking. No response. That was my answer. Colm deserved better than my jumbo jet's worth of baggage. Just leave last night as it was: a perfect night filled with so many emotions that I could ride that high into the next decade.

In a few weeks, I'd be forgotten in the long line of women ready and willing to help him with anything he needed. A small burst of jealousy shot through me. *Get over it, Imogen. You've got no right to be possessive, and things are better as they are right now. You barely have time to get a solid night's sleep; there's no time for a love life right now. Maintain the status quo.*

6

COLM - 3 MONTHS LATER

A pin prick of light broke in through a gap in the curtains, perfectly positioned to blind me through my eyelids. I sat up, and a cold sweat prickled my skin. The dreams of my fall wouldn't stop. A bottle of gin sat beside my bed: a nightcap to beat back the inter-cranial replay and keep it at bay until I plunged into a fitful sleep.

Time had become a more fluid thing over the past few months. My alarm clock had been ejected from the room and my phone had met the same fate after my last talk with Bailey. Every call or message was another hole gouged into the sinking ship that was my life.

Liv wanting to talk.

Ford wanting to talk.

Declan, Heath, or Emmett wanting to talk.

And the one person I'd actually wanted to talk to had gone radio silent. I'd seen her apology text after I'd been released from the hospital, but I could read between the lines: Sorry, you were such a fucking mess that night that I gave you the pity sex you so obviously needed. I hope it cheered you up, but we're not doing that again.

No, I didn't need to have that conversation face to face.

My stomach rumbled. How long had it been since I'd eaten? Days? Rolling over, I groaned. I wasn't exactly the athletic specimen I'd once been.

Swinging my legs over the side of the bed, I paused, staring down at my leg. It had betrayed me more than once. My leg brace sat on the nightstand, taunting me.

Standing, I braced myself for the shooting pain that had been my constant companion right after the injury, but there wasn't any. Only a dull ache from unused muscles.

Clothes littered the floor of my bedroom and the sheets were pulled up from the corner of the bed.

How long had it been since I'd washed them?

Opening the door, a shout and space blaster gun fire echoed up the stairs. My jaw clenched and I headed downstairs. I'd do exactly what I did every other time they came over and tried to coax me out of the house. Ignore them.

"Look at sleeping beauty, finally ready to join us." Heath didn't look away from the TV screen, jamming his fingers into the buttons on the controller.

"And in his good bath robe. Someone's watched The Big Lebowski one too many times." Emmett chuckled.

"With the beard, I can definitely see that. But the smell..." Declan waved his hand in front of his face. "You are ripe, man. When did you shower last?"

I opened the fridge, ducking my head behind the door and sniffing at my pits. Shit, was I nose blind? When had I last showered? Whatever, if they didn't like the smell, they could leave.

The takeout boxes I'd shoved in there were moved to the

bottom shelf to make room for catering trays of pasta, sauce, and meat on the top shelves.

"How much longer until the doc gives you the okay to come back? We haven't been able to play like the Kings yet." Heath jumped up and thumped his fist into the center of his chest.

"Why are you being so secretive about the doc giving you the green light? Did he say it's going to be an even longer recovery?" Declan hung over the back of the couch.

I'd had the all-clear for over a month, but they didn't need to know that. No one did.

"We brought some food since your selection was...lacking." Emmett set his controller on the table. "You need strength for your recovery."

"Avery's got a connection at this Italian place called Tavola. Their food is freaking magic. Grab some of the fettuccini alfredo and the chicken parm, you'd give your left —" Heath stopped with his cup halfway to his mouth. "It's killer. Almost as good as this sixteen-year-old whiskey." He held up his glass, ice clinking against the sides, and drained the last of it.

I gritted my teeth. Whatever, it had been meant as a gift for Ford anyway.

Even though they were all acting like this was a casual conversation, I could feel their eyes on me, boring into me like they were waiting for me to snap so they could cart me off somewhere. I grabbed the carton of milk out of the fridge and banged around the cabinets for a bowl.

Snagging a box of cereal off the top shelf, I dumped half the contents into the bowl and poured out the milk. At least, I tried to pour it. The clumps hit the top of the cereal, mocking me.

I slammed down the carton, sending a few small chunks plopping onto the counter.

"We were going to throw that out for you, but we figured you might want to do that yourself. Or that it was a science experiment." Declan had his tongue clenched between his teeth, slamming his fingers into the controller, trying to take out Heath from his elevated position.

"Remember this combo, Colm? Kicked your ass with this so many times back in our Rittenhouse Prep days." The campaign end flashed up on the screen, and Heath, Emmett and Declan stared at me. A part of me expected Ford to come sauntering down the hallway ready to wipe the floor with everyone in the game. And then it hit me. The lies. The betrayal. The loss. I felt them all over again like it had happened yesterday.

"You just going to glare at that chunky milk until it de-curdles and becomes edible?" Heath got up from the couch and rounded the kitchen island.

"Why the hell are you all here?" My voice came out scratchy like an old door's hinges in an abandoned house, but snapped through their chatter like a shattered glass. When had I last talked to someone? A week ago? Maybe longer. Had it been when Bailey had called to chew me out about flaking on my last physiotherapist appointment? After all, why keep going when no amount of exercises would make it possible for me to get back on the ice?

Heath's eyes widened and his smile dimmed.

Damnit, why couldn't they all just go? I shoved my fingers through my hair.

"We never got to give you a house warming. Plus, Mak's studying for her exams and I think if I bug her one more time about sneaking off with me into her study room, she'll remove my balls and bring them into class for dissection."

Declan rummaged in the fridge, coming back with a whole six pack of beer.

"And Avery's taking on ten new projects at the bakery and not getting home until four every day, so..." Emmett shrugged and picked up another bottle.

"What about you?" I stared at Heath.

"Kara's always happy to see me, I don't know what the hell these clowns are doing." Heath laughed and grabbed a beer. "But I won't turn down a chance to hang out. How much longer before things change and we won't get to?"

"Isn't it a little early for a drink?" The bottle I'd left empty upstairs flashed through my mind, and my hypocrisy wasn't lost on me.

"Dude, it's three pm."

I whipped around and looked at the clock above the stove. They weren't wrong. My stomach protested my thoughts of going back upstairs without eating anything. Cursing under my breath, I dumped out my bowl.

A few minutes later I stood behind the counter, diving into a carb-loaded mountain of pasta. Even cold, the food hit all the right spots.

They pretended they weren't looking at me, but I could feel their gazes tracking my every move. I'd given them all keys when I got the place right before I was injured last season. While I was gone for rehab on my knee, I had wanted them to be able to check in if anything went sideways. Now, I regretted that decision. But I could've changed the locks.

Why hadn't I? Why, when they showed up day after day, didn't I throw the chain across the door so they couldn't get in? Partly because I knew they'd knock down the door if I tried, but also because some part of me wanted them here.

They cared, and they were the closest thing I'd had to an

extended family for as long as I could remember, but that didn't mean I deserved to have them here. They wanted me back on the ice, but that wasn't happening.

Waking up in cold sweats from a dream about setting foot on the ice didn't bode well for my return to the game. The last time I'd walked onto a rink, after the fight, I made it three steps inside before bolting back out the door and puking onto the asphalt. A few weeks later, I'd driven to the stadium at night to see if maybe it had been a fluke, but my hands had been shaking so badly, I couldn't open my car door to even try.

I'd rather they thought I was being a stubborn asshole who'd made a choice to say fuck it than a guy who couldn't bring himself to lace up his skates. The thought was sour, and the food that had gone down so well sat uneasily in my stomach, like I'd eaten the chunky milk.

I don't know what scared me more: that they'd give up on me eventually, or that they wouldn't.

A sharp knock on the door split the tension in the air. No one moved. The guys stared at the TV like they hadn't heard the knock. Was this a test? To see if I'd actually gone full hermit? The season would start soon and they'd be on the road—way too busy to park on my couch, drink my booze and bug me. And that would be when they realized they didn't even need me. The roster was stacked this season, and they'd pull out a win for the cup. It was only a matter of time before the calls became less frequent, the visits nearly non-existent, and then one day I'd walk down here and realize no one had been here in months, and I'd be standing in this kitchen with my chunky milk, completely alone.

Stomping to the door, I flung it open, ready to send whoever it was away.

My eyes narrowed. I didn't even let him say a word before I slammed the door straight in Ford's bearded face. My nostrils flared and it took long silent minutes to unclench my hands at my sides.

"Don't say a fucking word," I bit out, trying to get my breathing under control.

Everyone not standing on my front step stared back at me, Adam's apples bobbing and stealing glances at one another.

"Colm, you want to get in on this game?" Heath held up a controller for me.

A sharp knock on the front door saved me from my long hard stare as a response. Throwing it open, I prepared to launch into my best bellow to get the fuck off my doorstep, but couldn't stop my wince.

"You're alive." Bailey stood on my front step, barely an inch over five-three, but glowering like she was a gladiator sharpening her sword in an arena.

"Rumors of my demise have been grossly exaggerated."

"Not when I get through with you." She shoved the door open and barged into my house.

"Please, come in."

"Cut the shit, Frost."

"So nice to see you too." I closed the door and tipped my imaginary hat to her.

"Are we going to do this here?" With her arms out, she gestured to the guys.

"Fine." My jaw ached. "Follow me."

∼

"Are you out of your fucking mind?"

The office door had barely clicked shut when she

rounded on me. That her teeth weren't snapping for my throat was a surprise.

I leaned against the wall beside the door with my arms at my sides, ready to throw them up to protect my soft tissue at the last minute, if needed. "What do you want from me, Bailey?"

She made a sound halfway between a growl and a grunt of disbelief. "What do I want? How about an explanation for why you haven't gotten off your ass and gotten to work for the season that starts in less than a month?"

"My leg."

"Don't bullshit me. You're seeing a team doctor. Do you think confidentiality with a team doctor is the same as anywhere else? I know he gave you the all clear. I know he's referred you to five physiotherapists." She shoved her hand with her fingers spread wide in my face. "And that you've flaked on every appointment."

The doctor had given me the all clear to start training and get my ass back on the ice, so why hadn't I touched a weight in over a month?

"I've had—"

"A lot going on? Yeah, I can tell, Lebowski." She grabbed the end of her ponytail, yanking on it like she was trying to remove it from her skull.

I shifted from foot to foot. That was the signal that she was three seconds from castrating someone with a pair of dull skates.

With her hands braced behind her head, she turned to me. "My ass is on the line, Colm. You were my first scout. You've got so much talent. Don't throw this away and don't fuck me over." She jammed her finger into my chest.

Damn, for someone so small, she packed a lot of power behind those tiny fingers. "You've got a week to get your shit together or I swear, I've got a set of pliers with your name on them. Get your ass in gear, Frost." Disappointment and anger blazed in her eyes. She dipped her head, shaking it. Looking up at me, all the intensity was gone and the harsh lines weren't painted so deep. She stepped closer and squeezed my shoulder. Without the grimace, I was reminded she wasn't that much older than me. "You can do this."

She stomped out of the room abruptly, as though she'd freaked herself out by not threatening bodily harm. Was she going to rat me out to the guys? A low murmur came from the living room and I stood, holding my breath, waiting for the shouts of outrage at the secret I'd been keeping.

"Bye, Bailey," Declan called out as the front door slammed.

I sagged against the desk, trying to calm myself. It was only a matter of time before they figured it out. I didn't even go back to the living room, heading straight upstairs instead. Staring at my ceiling, my stomach knotted, imagining getting back on the ice. Maybe facing down Bailey and her pliers wouldn't be so bad. At least it would be another excuse for me not being able to skate anymore.

She'd come back. Dodging it had gotten me this far, but showing up at my house? Bailey wasn't going to let this lie forever. Would she tell the guys? Would I lose the only people I had left?

Three months of six clients a day, Monday through Friday, followed by battling shore traffic all summer to work weekends at The Surf Shack meant I could sleep at the drop of a hat. I'd fallen asleep at the gas pump last Sunday on the way back to my apartment. Thankfully, in Jersey it's full serve, so the gas nozzle wasn't pouring unleaded out all over the ground. Instead, I startled awake to the guy knocking on my window like he'd been doing it for way longer than a couple seconds.

My bones ached, but tips were good. Ass smacks from the customers were not, but being with Charlie and Fern and helping them made it worth the winter hibernation I wanted to fall into even though it was only September.

Summer season was ending and I could finally remember what it was like to not pass out in my bed with my shoes on.

I was busy.

I was exhausted.

I was alone.

It was the closest I got to happy nowadays.

Fern had banished me from coming down this weekend. I sat in my apartment half-watching the TV and reading a recent journal article about a new physiotherapy technique for ligament damage after a catastrophic injury. I'd found myself more and more interested in studies and best practices for athletes and their specific types of injuries even though my recertification wouldn't be for another eighteen months.

It wasn't until almost three days after Colm's injury that I heard the news. And it was actual news. I was better at burying my head in the sand than I realized. No one had mentioned it to me and he certainly hadn't. My calls and texts to him went unanswered.

Did he feel like I'd taken advantage of him with whatever was going down? Did the injury have anything to do with that night? Why hadn't I asked more questions instead of jumping his bones? Did he hate me? So many unanswered questions and a few I wasn't sure I wanted the answers to. It changed the memory of that night from something fiery, spontaneous and fun to sadness that I'd let him down.

The descriptions of the injury had been euphemistic in the press. But once you were in the industry for a bit, it got easier to spot what they meant. Like when a realtor said an apartment was "cozy" that was code for you'd better break out your magnifying glass. "Retro charm" meant you'd feel like you've been transported back into the 70s complete with outdated plumbing, appliances and electricity.

Colm's injury meant his next season was in limbo, especially right after his last recovery. If his career wasn't over it would be shortly. Another marble plonked on top of the guilt pile.

If I'd stayed that morning could I have done something

to prevent it? One wrong move and a life could be forever changed. People I cared about could be taken away. My parents. Preston. Did Colm get the newest spot on that list?

The gentle jingle of my phone broke me out of my staring contest with the anatomy breakdown on my computer.

Declan: Hey, Imo. Can you talk?

Tapping on his name, I only had to wait two rings for him to answer.

"Hey, Declan."

"Mak is starting to get offended that you keep dodging our dinner invites." He didn't actually sound the least bit mad, and I did miss them. Summers were always hard with my schedule. I didn't get to see them as much as I did outside of beach season when we were all sort of in the same place anyways. But there wasn't exactly a tactful way to ask if Colm was there and then backtrack out of going if he was going to be there.

"The Shack isn't going to run itself."

"You're working there *and* doing your physio work?"

"Fern and Charlie can use the help, especially with Becca in grad school now."

"They're lucky they've got you to depend on."

"I do what I can."

"You always do. Speaking of doing what you can...we wanted to ask a favor."

"We?"

"Me and the rest of the guys. I don't know if you saw the news or not about Colm, but he's in a bad way right now and he's not doing so well."

"I saw it mentioned in the news." It's bad enough dealing with an injury, but having it plastered all over the national sports news had to be salt in the wound. Preston's decision not to enter the draft had barely been a blip on the campus gossip scene, but Colm was at a different level. "How's he doing?"

"He'd be doing a lot better if he weren't being a total asshat about his recovery. I don't know who they have him going to, but he hasn't even mentioned getting back on the ice. He was ready by now the last time he got hurt." Rustling and his huffs meant he was pacing and dragging his fingers though his light brown curls. Preston had always seen great things in Declan's future, and he was following through on that one hundred percent.

"Sorry to hear that."

"And we wanted to know if you might help. See if there's something his current physio might have missed. You know him. He won't be able to bullshit you the way he can a stranger."

He wanted me to work with Colm. As in be his physiotherapist?

I could barely keep up with my current roster of patients. I was looking forward to falling into a weekend sleep coma after my last weekend at The Surf Shack. And then there was the whole us having sex and him never responding to my message aspect of things. Throwing me into the mix meant stress and possibly drama and that certainly wouldn't help if he was having trouble getting back on his feet. But professional passion made my fingers itch to get ahold of his chart and perhaps make a few recommendations, if what they were doing wasn't working.

I stared down at the phone, unable to form a response for a moment. "There are loads of great people he can work with. People lightyears ahead of me. I can make some recommendations. I don't have the expertise to work with professional athletes. Their needs are a lot different than regular people."

"But—"

"Declan, I know you want the best for him. So do I, and I don't think I'm it for him."

"We'll see." He ended the call there and I tried not to feel like there was an ominous slant to those last words. God help me if they all ganged up on me.

Emmett showed up at lunch. I was surprised his ear drums weren't perforated from how sharp the whisper game was around the lunch room.

No preamble needed, he launched into the pitch. "Colm needs someone who knows him. Someone who won't let him bully them. Our team trainer is about to lose it on him, if he doesn't get his act together."

"Emmett, I'm sure you can find someone else. I can look for referrals."

"He's run off everyone already. Maybe you can talk some sense into him?"

"I highly doubt that—"

"What do you need me to pay you? And don't tell Avery I asked, she'd have my balls in a vise."

"It's not about the money." I threw out my lunch, stomach roiling. The tuna must have gone bad.

"What is it then? Just come and see him. Give him a pep talk. We're shit at that and maybe coming from a professional he'd take it more seriously."

"Let me think about it."

Emmett grinned. "That's all we ask."

Everyone in the lunch room was going to need a few sessions of physio after how quickly their heads whipped around to watch him go. At least I hadn't been with any clients. There would be strained backs and necks all over the room.

I figured I had at least a day or two to come up with an excuse for why I couldn't do it.

I had one hour.

"Hey, Imo."

I jumped and yelped, bracing my arm on the doorway to the locker room. "Heath, what are you doing here?"

"What do you think?" Long wavy hair fell into his eyes and he grinned at me like he was ready to steal the whole damn cookie factory. I'd thought they were going to gang up on me, not bombard me one after the other.

"Don't you all have things to be doing?"

"It's the off season." Heath shrugged and crossed his arms over his chest, leaning against the locker beside mine. I'm sure he struck the same pose day after day in high school and they had to mop the girls up off the floor. "We've got all the time in the world."

I dropped my head back. Just what I needed. Three overbearing hockey players with nothing to do but pester me.

"Excuse me, could you tell me where I could find Imogen Walsh." A deep baritone from the hallway drifted into the room. Heath's grin widened.

Make that four overbearing hockey players. Ford stepped into the locker room, filling the doorframe. I was surprised he didn't have to walk in sideways.

"Oh, Heath, what are you doing here?" Ford's words were as convincing as a dollar store diamond ring.

"Did you all come in the same car? Have you been waiting in the parking lot for your turn to pounce?" I looked between the two of them.

Ford's head snapped up and he looked over my shoulder. The two of them went through an eyebrow and jaw clenching conversation before Ford frowned, gave a growl and picked up his phone, tapping out a message before slipping it into his pocket.

"The locker move didn't work?" Ford crossed his arms and leaned against the wall beside the door.

"It used to be killer." Heath shook his head and looked at himself in the mirror, running his fingers through his long wavy hair. "I'm losing my touch. That always worked back in school."

"You're just not putting out those 'jump into bed' vibes now that you're attached."

"Hello." I waved my arms standing in the space between the two of them. "You two are having a pick-up tactics conversation in an employees-only area of my job like we're hanging out at one of your houses."

"You've been ditching our invites."

Apparently it *hadn't* gone unnoticed. "I've been busy."

"Busy avoiding us." Declan and Emmett strolled up, pointed in our direction by my not-getting-any-B&B-treats-next-time co-workers, who crowded around in the hallway like this was the new touring performance of Hamilton.

"Just get in here." I dragged the two of them all the way into the room and kicked away the door stopper. A distant beep and the distinctive buttery salty smell wafted down the hallway.

"Did someone make popcorn?" I caught the door and stared at my co-workers, who suddenly found the drop ceiling and pristine white walls insanely fascinating.

"Did I miss anything? I've got the—" Cecily darted from the break room, her cheeks glowing like a beacon when she spotted me.

"The absolute worst." I pointed my finger at her. "I'm dealing with them first, then all of you." I glared, slowly moving my finger across the room.

Swinging the door shut, I turned to the overly large men crowded into the locker room.

I opened my mouth and Declan piped up before I could get a word in.

"We know you're busy and have a lot going on, but we're running out of options, Imo."

"Help us, Imogen, you're our only hope." Heath put on his best Princess Leia impersonation.

My glare intensified.

Emmett grabbed Heath, putting him into a friendly headlock with his hand over Heath's mouth.

Declan stepped closer. "Preston talked about how much you helped him that summer when he lost it. When he thought he'd never play again." The words were tight and low.

A lump lodged in his throat. "He told you—"

"Not the specifics, but he told me enough to know that if there's anyone who might be able to get through to Colm it's you. Bailey said his chances are slim, and with everything that went down with Ford and Liv..."

"They're still not talking? What exactly happened?"

"I keep forgetting you haven't been around." Declan gave me the run down. The seeing each other behind Colm's back. The sex tape debacle. The fire at Liv's apartment, and Colm freaking out that something had happened to her. So many heightened emotions running right into the crescendo of him getting re-injured the night after I dragged him into bed. He was in self-destruct mode that night and what had I done? I'd messed with his head and emotions by bolting, because I had more baggage than Paris Fashion Week.

"We're not sure what to do. Right now, we're just trying to be there, even just physically, since he refuses to talk to anyone." Declan had always been Mr. Laid Back, but now his gaze was intent and his words urgent. Preston used to grumble about how much talent he had, if only he'd take things a little bit more seriously. And he'd been right. A championship banner hung in the stadium thanks to Declan's talent and dedication last season. "He's on the edge, Imogen."

"He's not going to be happy to see me." My stomach knotted. Maybe this would at least let me say sorry to his face.

"Welcome to the club," Ford grumbled with his biceps bunching as he crossed his arms tighter across his chest. "If he hasn't actually told you to fuck off, you're doing better than the rest of us."

"What if I make it worse?" Dragging Preston back from that void hadn't been easy, but I'd known how Preston ticked. That inside knowledge had been crucial. Even though Colm and I weren't as close, could I let Colm face the same uncertain future and not even try to help?

Everyone wouldn't be this worried if it wasn't serious.

Ford's jaw clenched. "You're our Hail Mary, Imo. It can't get any worse."

I was the last person who should go near Colm, but I

couldn't come up with a good reason to say no in front of them. My mouth opened and closed. The words wouldn't come. The fact I'd snuck out after having the best sex of my life didn't exactly scream *responsible friend*.

"Let me think about it."

IMO

"You're Imogen?"

A woman who couldn't be over five-one stood from her spot on one of the couches in my apartment building lobby. Despite her size, I was still tempted to run back inside the elevator.

"Yes?" I gripped the strap of my bag tighter.

"Was that a question, or are you Imogen?" Her eyes narrowed and I felt like she was inspecting my skeleton with her x-ray vision.

"I'm Imogen."

Her posture relaxed the tiniest bit. "Good. You're the third blonde I've asked already. Shit was getting awkward." She stalked toward me like she was six feet tall. "But now that I see you, the descriptions make sense."

"And you are?"

"Damn, sorry." She wiped her hand on her jeans and held it out for me. "I'm Bailey. The team trainer. Colm's trainer."

"You're *the* Bailey." My gaze darted to the exit, but I had no doubts she'd tackle me to the ground if I tried to escape.

She eyed me up and down. "In the flesh. I'm sure you expected an ogre from how they talk about me."

"No, you seem about right." Oversized in every way except her stature. She exuded *don't screw with me*, a skill she must have honed over the years working with rough and tumble athletes.

"Oh, nice to meet you." I shook her hand, trying not to wince as her grip threatened to bruise my bones.

"Sorry. I'm used to shaking hands with those oversized jocks. Didn't mean to break out the bone crusher." She raised her hands and backed away a step.

"Did the guys send you?"

"They're not exactly subtle, are they?" She stood with her arms locked across her chest, exuding confidence that I wasn't walking out of here without agreeing to whatever she wanted.

"No, they aren't." As much as I wanted to be mad at them, the way they rallied around one another when someone needed help was admirable. It showed they cared, even if it meant turning my life upside down. "You want me to work with him."

"Yes." Her smile was big and toothy.

"I'm sure there are nine hundred other people out there who'd do better to get him to where he needs to be to get back on the ice."

"But Declan, Emmett, Heath, and Ford keep coming back to you."

"They're so sweet and they think they know what Colm needs, but there are so many other options for him out there." I turned, trying to gauge how quickly I could close the distance to the door. Why did everyone think I was best for him? Why'd they think I could give him something no one else could?

Maybe I could. I shook my head and took another step back.

"And if there aren't?" Bailey stood, bringing herself up to her full height. "Do you honestly think I can't see you trying to get away from me?" Her lips pinched and her eyes narrowed.

My heart skipped and I tightened my grip on my bag. "It wouldn't be a good fit. Like, at all. Trust me, he'd be better off in someone else's hands." I'm ninety percent sure I bolted from the building in only three steps before she could get out another word. Thankfully, she didn't chase me.

The rest of the day went by as it usually did. Cecily had to bust out the duct tape when our water cooler did its shimmy dance across the floor of the break room, and I had to modify my sessions when our bench press bench collapsed. At least no one had been sitting on it at that moment.

"Imogen. Terry wants to see you."

I stashed my folders in my slot behind the desk, trying to close up that pit in my stomach. No one liked being called into their boss's office, even if they hadn't done anything wrong. Had I? I wracked my brain to think of anything I might've screwed up. Now that the summer was finished, my modified schedule was over, but Terry had been cool with that.

Why hadn't she come out to talk to me, if it was no big deal?

I knocked on her door, shifting my bag on my shoulder.

Her 'come in' didn't sound ominous at all. It sounded chipper.

"Hey, Terry, Cecily said you wanted to see me?" I pushed the door all the way open and jerked when I spotted Bailey tossing a baseball from hand to hand beside Terry.

"I can't believe you didn't tell me!" She slapped down the papers in her hand onto her desk.

"Tell you what?" I tore my gaze away from Bailey.

"About the offer! This is going to do so much for the center. Get so much new equipment and make the repairs."

"Imogen hasn't given me her final answer yet." Bailey smirked, tossing the ball up in the air.

"How could she not?" Terry's head whipped from me to Bailey.

"Maybe she wanted to discuss it with you first." The dry smack of the ball hitting her palm punctuated the silence in the room.

"The donation for taking on the case is so generous. Imogen, don't worry if he doesn't make the progress you expected, even that would be enough to tide us over for a while. But if you *are* able to get him back to pro form, that money could change everything for everyone here."

"That's what I told her." *Thwap* against her palm as she snatched the ball out of the air. "But you know how modest she is. Always trying to stay out of the spotlight. She doesn't think she has the skills to get the job done."

Terry made an indignant noise. "Imogen, you're one of the best we have here. Don't ever doubt yourself. And think of the good this money could do for the center." Her eyes shone bright with hope.

I glared at Bailey whose smile widened over Terry's shoulder. Bailey'd played me. She honed in on my weakness and taken me out like a Great White shark attacking a lone swimmer. No wonder the guys were all afraid of her. If this was her playing nice, what did mean Bailey look like?

Twenty minutes later, Terry was laying out all the changes and improvements she'd make to the center, and treating me getting Colm back on the ice like it was a fore-gone conclusion.

"Crap, I have a meeting to get to. Thank you so much for everything, Bailey." Terry clung to Bailey's hand like she might take back everything she'd already agreed to.

"No problem at all. And we're so happy to have Imogen on board."

"Use my office as long as you need." Terry gathered up stacks of paper. "I'll see you later." She brushed past me with flushed cheeks and a Grand Canyon-sized smile, and I was surprised she didn't kiss me full on the lips.

"I can't believe you just did that." I whirled on Bailey.

Her smirk was firmly in place. "You gotta do what you gotta do." She shrugged.

"You don't look desperate."

"I hide it well."

"How am I supposed to get him ready to play this season in such a short amount of time? He's not even cleared to get back on the ice yet."

"Except, he is."

I dropped my bag from my shoulder with the strap in my hand. "What do you mean?"

One quick glance over her shoulder, like we weren't all alone in Terry's office, and she leaned in. "This didn't come from me, but the doctor cleared him for practice four weeks ago. Colm's been ice ready since then, but won't come to the rink. Won't work out with anyone and won't even tell me if he plans on coming back this season."

"And you think I can fix this?" He wouldn't want to see my face let alone work with me.

Her gaze swept over me from top to bottom. "The guys think you're the one who can get his ass back in action, so

I'm trusting them, which means I'm trusting you. I'm willing to try, are you?"

"You don't even know me."

"No shit. I don't, but we're—well, I'm desperate at this point. We have the healthy player bonus and you'd get paid for each session."

"It's not about the money. I just don't think I'm the best person for the job."

"There are no people left. He's blown up every relationship I have with sports physiotherapists in the tri-state area. I'm calling in favors to get other injured guys back on the ice." She dragged her hands over her face. The weight of the situation seemed to be hitting her harder than she let on.

"Look. He was my first recruit. I'm trying to move into scouting more. Colm was my first pick and the four others I've chosen have washed out already. He's kind of my last shot to not be relegated to the team gym for the rest of my career. You'll get paid on top of your regular fee, since you'll need to go to him."

"I'm not doing this for the money."

Her head perked up. "But you'll do it? Will you *please* give it a shot?" She stressed that word and it was probably the closest she got to begging.

I dropped my bag beside the desk. "Can I see his file?"

Rocking back, she reached over her shoulder and picked it up off Terry's desk.

"You came prepared."

"Always."

And that's how I left the center with a new client added to my roster. A client who most likely hated me, but that would have to take a backseat to everything else. He wasn't skating even though the doctor'd cleared him. Preston's reaction after his diagnosis had been hard, probably one of the hardest things outside of losing him, but Colm could get back to his pro career. It was different—less complicated.

I could do this. *Keep it together, Imogen.* How bad could it be?

9

COLM

"Are you going to pretend we're not here?" Liv dropped her purse on the kitchen island.

I knew I should've saved my food run for once the guys had left for the day.

"Anyone else want pizza?" Declan tugged the playing card off his forehead and stood.

Emmett followed right behind. "Lorenzo's?"

"Yeah, let's get the hell out of here before things get even more awkward." Heath raced for the front door with all the subtlety of a fifty-person marching band.

It closed behind them and now it was the three of us.

Ford stood at Liv's side just like he had the morning I'd found out they were sleeping together.

I grabbed a bowl from the cabinet and found a box of cereal.

"This is the game you're playing? The silent treatment? Real fucking mature, Colm." Liv leaned in, splaying her fingers on the countertop.

I dumped the contents into my bowl and took the milk out of the fridge.

"Have you reconsidered the MCATs and med school?" My hand tightened around the cold plastic.

"No. I'm not going to med school. I don't want to be a doctor. I'm going to teach dance."

"Then no, I don't feel the need to talk to you."

"Why won't you hear me out?"

"Because that wasn't the plan, Liv. I didn't sit through summer sessions of biology so I could help you with your homework, or traipse across the country visiting thirty-seven colleges until you decided on the one I'd suggested in the first place, or give up all my vacations to take you to pre-med summer camp in Upstate New York for four summers so you could flip a switch and decide it wasn't for you anymore."

She bit her lip. "And I'm grateful you did all of that. But... It's my life."

"And it was my life too. But did you ever care about what I had to give up? What responsibilities I had to deal with? What *I* wanted to do?"

"It's not all about you."

"And it's not all about you either. You made your choice, so why are you here?"

"I didn't make a choice. You forced a choice on me. I'd never want to choose between you and Ford. You're my brother, you'll always be my brother. But I love Ford. Shouldn't you want that for me?"

"And when that switch is flipped again and you realize you've made a mistake, or he breaks your heart, then what? I already know he can't protect you."

Ford took a step forward.

I bared my teeth at him, clenching my jaw to keep myself from snapping at him like a damn wild animal.

"Come to do a bit more damage to my knee and my career?"

"You took a swing at me."

"After you kept her nearly dying in a fire a secret from me. And after I was forced to watch a damn public sex tape of my sister!" The glass in the cabinets rattled from the force of my yell.

"I'd said it was a mistake. We didn't know anyone was watching." That zapped some of the anger from both of them.

"It shouldn't have happened in the first place."

"We got carried away. No one was supposed to see us. Especially not you."

"But I did. So excuse me if I don't think you're the best person for my sister."

"Shouldn't that be my choice?" Liv stepped closer.

I poured the milk on my cereal and took a bite, not tasting it. "Who's stopping you?" I shrugged.

"That's it? That's all you have to say to me."

"You want to live your own life and do your own thing. Go ahead. I'm not stopping you."

"You're going to shut me out."

"I've cut you off."

"This isn't about the damn money. Not everything is about money, Colm. You think you can use it to control me, but you can't. I'll prove it and then maybe you'll see that I get to decide what happens in my life. Me and only me." She jabbed her finger at the center of her chest, before flinging the front door open.

Ford closed his hand around the strap of her purse. "You were always the one with your head on straighter than the rest of us, but you're dead wrong when it comes to me and Liv. I love her and she loves me. We're not doing this to get back at you or piss you off. We fell in love and I'll do everything in my power to make her happy every day we have together. Life is short, man. You know that. Is this how you want to spend the rest of your days? Old and bitter before your time? She needs a brother, not a dad."

I'd been the only person she could count on for so long and just like that she doesn't need me anymore?

"You don't know what she needs, and you don't know anything about what our lives have been like."

"Like I wasn't there trying to help you along the way. Like I didn't go to those weekly dinners with you half the time. Like I didn't help bake those shitty brownies with you. Or I didn't go buy a new microwave that time you accidentally hit thirty minutes instead of three, trying to make popcorn during one of her sleepovers."

A smile tugged at the corners of my lips, but I forced it away. He'd been there, which made him being with Liv even worse.

"You always tried to cast me as her brother and yourself as her dad. That wasn't how it was. I was a friend. And I stepped back when my feelings for her got complicated, but she's twenty-one now. She'll be graduating from college this spring."

He stuck his hand into her bag and pulled out a white envelope with metallic writing on it. "She came over to give you this." He slid it across the counter. "She's your family, man. Get your head out of your ass."

Without another word, he left, closing the door behind him.

I stared down at the envelope and tugged it open. There was silver writing on the cream card.

You have been cordially invited to the commencement ceremony for

Olivia Frost
On May 13th

Her graduation. In eight months, she'd be a college graduate. Things moved so quickly. Too quickly. This wasn't how things were supposed to be.

I abandoned the cereal bowl on the counter and headed back into my office. Pushing open the closet door, I pulled the box out of the bottom.

Liv had always been big into pictures and reminders of the past. I'd always been less sentimental. From under my letterman jacket, I pulled out the framed pictures. Mom and Dad stared back at me from beneath the dirty glass of the dark wood frame. Seeing my small face wedged between the two of them was like looking in a funhouse mirror: they were my features, but so much smaller.

It was one of the few pictures I had of the three of us. A reminder that there had been a time before Liv was even born and I wasn't a big brother, but just another little kid.

There had been a blizzard. We'd been trapped in the house, but I'd never been happier. Usually, in bad weather they'd stay at the hospital rather than risk not being able to get back to work, but the storm had come out of nowhere, blown in overnight, and they hadn't had the warning.

Two days before Christmas, we had a movie day. They were pulled away for phone calls here and there, but it was a full twenty-four hours I had them all to myself. A rare treat. Then the hospital sent a snow plow for the both of them and they were gone. That was the downside of having renowned parents. People deferred to them and always needed their help, and our parents had never been ones to shy away from that responsibility.

But it meant I'd had to step up too. Once I turned twelve, I told them we didn't need a babysitter anymore. I could handle Liv. I'd wanted them to be proud of how I held down the fort while they were away. And they were always away.

Sometimes I wondered why they'd even had us. They'd missed every parent-teacher conference—I'd gone to Liv's in their place and made sure I never flagged in my schoolwork, so they'd never have to go to mine. They missed every field trip. Every one of Liv's ballet recitals or short-lived volleyball season. They missed every one of my games. All but one.

"We're traveling for a conference that weekend."

"It's my last game of the season. As in no more hockey games at my school. Ever."

"You'll be playing in college."

"Like you'll go to those games. Do you even know what position I play?"

Dad tugged down his glasses and lifted his pen from his tablet. "Center. You're the team captain. You've scored thirteen goals this season."

"You had one of your residents compile a factsheet, didn't you?"

He set his glasses down. "You asked a question. I answered."

"Colm, we want to be there, but we can't. This conference will have over two hundred surgeons from around the world there."

"And you said yes, knowing my last game was happening."

"There will be other games."

I slammed my fists down on the desk. Papers fluttered and a pen rolled off the side. "Not this game. Not this season. Not with this team."

"The same could be said for our work at our conference."

"What does it say about the two of you as parents that me telling you something is important to me doesn't matter to you? That your son, asking that you attend one fucking game in his entire high school career doesn't rank in your world?"

"Language," my mom chided.

"I've packed the lunches. I've gotten up at 4am to drive to the rink with Liv. I've sat down and helped her with her homework. I've been the babysitter every night you're both called into surgery. I've done all that and you can't do this for me? Why the hell did you even have us?"

I stormed out of their office straight to the front door. Flinging it open, I ran into Ford, ripping the doorknob out of his hand.

"You need to get out of here?" He stepped back a step.

"Yeah, let's go."

"Where's Liv?" He looked past me at the closing door.

"She's at a sleepover tonight."

We drove to Ford's house. His place always felt more like a home than mine.

Lifting the garage door, we ducked under and he dropped it down behind me.

I walked over to the door to the house and flicked on the light, not needing to see my way there after traveling this path hundreds of times.

When I turned, a pair of heavy gloves hit me in the chest.

"Put them on."

Ford grabbed the punching bag from the shelf and lifted the chain at the top, attaching it to the hook in the center of the room.

"Looked like you could use a few rounds."

I nodded, shoving my hands into the gloves.

"They're not coming to your game, are they?" He held onto the bag as I drove my fists into the black and red leather panels.

"Nope."

Ford shook his head and stepped back, now that I'd found my rhythm with my punches. The steady cadence of my hits filled the garage. The weights clanked as Ford added fifty pounds to the bench press bar.

"Any reason this time?"

"A big conference they can't miss."

"Sorry."

"It's not your fault."

"Still sucks."

"Just know you're not the only member of the shitty parent club."

"Your mom's a saint."

"True. But dear old dad won't be winning any awards anytime soon."

"One out of two isn't bad."

He grunted, pushing the bar up off the braces and dropping it to his chest.

My arms protested when I threw the next punch. Grabbing onto the bag, I panted and rested my head against the now-warm leather. Sweat poured down my face, soaking my shirt and dripping off the tip of my nose. I yanked off my gloves, leaving the cotton wraps still wound around my hands.

Ford lifted the bar one more time, the left listing a bit to the side. Ripping the gloves off with my teeth, I kept my eyes on him. It clanked against the bracket, metal slamming into metal. Ford faltered. I dove for the bar, catching it less than an inch above his chin.

With the last of my strength, I kept it from cracking him in the head.

"Shit, thanks. I thought I had another one in me."

"Always trying to push yourself too far. You never want to say you need help."

"Eh, I'd have made it out okay."

"With a cracked jaw, you asshat." I laughed and sat beside him on the bench.

"Feel any better?" He leaned back and rummaged around in his mini fridge. He handed me a cold beer.

I cracked it open and gulped down half. *"Damn, these are good."*

"We can thank Heath. You owe him two, though."

"Two? I didn't even ask for this one."

He smirked at me, clinking his bottle to mine. "You needed it."

I had. And my parents had been gone that next week. Killed on the way to my game, racing to make it after presenting at their conference. If I hadn't freaked out at them, would they have tried to make it? No one blamed me, but that didn't mean I didn't blame myself. I'd done all I could to replace some of what Liv lost. But it felt like everything that had gone wrong in my life since then was punishment for my selfishness.

This was what I deserved, and no amount of talking was going to change things.

10

IMO

How bad could it be? Ha!

So freaking bad. My stomach had been a wreck since leaving Terry's office with the file Bailey gave me after signing a thick stack of non-disclosure agreements and other contracts. I'd choked down some toast this morning, but it had almost come back up in minutes.

My hands were clammy and my stomach was flip-flopping like I'd downed a liter of coke and a whole package of Mentos.

Townhouses with flowery window boxes and navy blue shutters lined the street like the whole thing had been coordinated by a designer. Given the price tags on these houses, they probably had been. Perfectly spaced trees lined the streets, their leaves already changing although the fall chill hadn't settled into the air yet.

Looking up at the red brick townhouse nestled in amongst the others with the shiny 37 beside the mailbox, I swallowed against the lump in my throat. The house looked different in the daylight. More imposing and ominous, like there was an old church organ on the corner playing me to my doom. I hadn't exactly looked around that night when we'd fallen through his doorway, taking turns ripping each other's clothes off.

Standing on the doorstep, I figured I'd knock and Colm wouldn't answer or he'd open the door, take one look at me, and slam it in my face. Instead, Emmett held it open and pulled me into his arms in a giant hug.

"You showed." He set me down inside the house and closed the door behind him.

I froze, waiting for the 'get out' from Colm, but one didn't come. My racing pulse slowed.

"I told Bailey I would."

"Not like we didn't do some serious arm twisting to make it happen."

I glanced around the room—no Colm. "Thanks so much for all your hard work in getting me here today." They didn't seem to care about my deadpanned response.

"Did Colm have to go somewhere? We can totally reschedule." Hope sprung from my voice like a leaky bucket.

"Nope, he's upstairs."

Upstairs. The stairs he'd pressed my back against while palming my breasts, teasing my nipples until I threaded my fingers through his hair, dragging his mouth up to mine. "Should I wait for him to come down?" I pressed my fist against my lips like the blistering kisses still lingered against my flesh.

They all exchanged glances, looking at one another like they'd found their sacrifice to a rumbling volcano. Not suspicious at all...

"It's probably best that you go up." Declan held onto my arms and guided me toward the stairs.

"His room is the last door at the end of the hallway," Heath offered.

I caught the 'I know' on the tip of my tongue that threatened to blow my whole, 'I haven't banged Colm six ways to Sunday in this very house' cover. Nodding, I walked to the bottom of the staircase. *You've got this, Imogen. It'll be fine. He'll take one look at you, tell you to get out and then you tell the guys you gave it your best shot. And you kill Terry's dreams of overhauling the center and stop hundreds of people from the quality of care they deserve.*

Looking over my shoulder, I gave them a half-smile and they shot back a thumbs up. The three of them were lined up like my own cheerleading squad minus the pompoms.

I climbed the steps, my heart pounding in my chest like a drum. I ran my fingers along the railing. The same one I'd held onto while Colm pushed himself inside me, sending sparks of pleasure ricocheting through my body.

My shoes sunk into the carpet that had been soft and plush against my bare feet as Colm bracketed me against the wall. The matte paint had rubbed against my skin with each shuddering breath against his shoulder.

The door at the end of the hall was cracked like he was expecting me.

My breakfast was charging for the gates with each step closer to the dim light peeking out through the barely opened door.

Rapping my knuckles on the solid wood, I pushed it open. Three things hit me the second I crossed the threshold:

The musk. It was a cross between a locker room and a bar. Under all that was the hint of the cologne Colm wore, but it smelled nothing like the last time I'd been here.

The mess. Clothes were all over the floor. Discarded

bowls and take out boxes littered most surfaces. The sheets were half off the bed, leaving the mattress exposed.

The man. Colm walked out of the bathroom and froze, locking eyes with me. His scruffy beard wasn't enough to hide his chiseled features, but it hinted at the turn his life had taken.

His face morphed between ten different emotions before settling on one. Anger—no, make that blind fury. "What the hell are you doing here?"

Not the reception I'd hoped for, but not unexpected. He wasn't looking at me like he had that night: hungrily, raw, filled with an all-consuming passion. Now he looked at me like he'd rather I disappeared before his eyes.

I squared my shoulders. "The guys said you could use a little help."

His glare shot through the open door behind me like he could roast them from one floor up. "I don't need their help, and I certainly don't need yours. You can go."

Did he just try to dismiss me?

My eyes adjusted and I got a better look at what he'd been doing with himself since he was injured. His shaggy hair and beard made him almost unrecognizable, other than his bright blue eyes, piercing, sawing through me like he could see straight to my soul. Then his words registered.

I looked around at his room and all the signs of what was going on hit me like the wall of funk. He was in it. He was in the place people went to when they gave up any hope of getting back the life they'd built. I'd been down this road before and the destructiveness could have far reaching implications that didn't need to happen, if the person accepted the help they needed.

"I was invited."

"Sure as hell wasn't by me."

"Colm—"

"Leaving would be best. It's what you're good at." His jaw was clenched and even under the beard, I could tell the muscles were flexing.

"Did you get my messages?" It was a subject I'd hoped we wouldn't have to broach, as though he might have chalked that night up to a fever dream and forgotten all about it. No such luck.

"Messages I didn't need. We had a meal. We f—had sex. You left."

"It was—"

"If you're here for some bullshit apology, you can save it. I don't need it. I don't need you."

Like that night in the bar, he was good at the performance, but not good enough. The cracks were showing. He'd keep pushing until there wasn't anyone left, if we let him.

"The Howard Hughes levels of crap in this room are definitely communicating all types of fine to me. Are the jars of toenail clippings under your bed or in the closet?"

"They're in the nightstand right beside the bottles of piss."

"Must be handy when you've drunk yourself into a stupor." At some point he seemed to have abandoned glasses for drinking straight out of the bottle.

He crossed his arms over his chest. "I haven't—" He moved his foot and it hit a half-empty bottle, knocking it into a completely empty bottle beside his bed.

I lifted an eyebrow and he glared at the bottles like he could turn them back into sand with a look.

"So I'll see you on Sunday at 7am for our first session." I'd have to brute force this, not only for how helping him helped others, but because he needed it. He needed someone who'd get him to see what possibilities his life could have. Keeping my distance would be hard when the pull to him was so strong, but I could do it for him.

"We're not working together."

"You need it."

"But I don't need *you*." That kind of hurt. Okay it really hurt. He was half fire breathing dragon, half lion with a thorn in his paw.

"Unfortunately, you've run off everyone else who could help, so I'm who you're stuck with." I clapped my hands together. "I'll be here bright and early Sunday morning and we'll get you back on the ice in no time."

"Does no one hear me? Is this thing on?" He tapped an imaginary mic. "I don't want, need, or accept your help."

"Glad to see you're in the fighting spirit. You'll need that on Sunday." I turned to hightail it back down the steps.

"Don't come back, Imogen." Was that a curl of smoke coming out of his nostril? The door slam rattled the railing as I hit the first step.

The beard, the gruff attitude—he was lashing out at everyone near him and pushing them away, even though that was the exact opposite of what he needed.

The guys all stood at the bottom of the stairs just like I'd left them, but the thumbs up were replaced by grim faces.

"At least you tried." Declan's shoulders slumped.

"And succeeded."

"Didn't he just say not to come back?" Emmett's eyebrows dipped.

"He did."

"And..."

"I'm sure he's said the same to you guys, right? But you're still here."

"If he's going to be an asshat, you don't have to put up with it."

"How do you think I got Preston through the worst of it? Sometimes you've got to push someone to take those first steps and then after that *they* need to make the decision. But I'm not ready to give up yet, are you?"

They were all hugs and wanted to hang around for a bit longer to make sure Colm was okay and probably finish the paused video game they had going. Even their presence would help Colm. Just knowing he wasn't all alone was a start.

The afternoon sun painted the sky with pinks and oranges that contrasted with the storm brewing inside the stately brownstone I stepped out of.

The summer air was giving way to fall, taking the heat and humidity off the city streets as the sun set. Instead of getting on the bus, I hung a left and walked to my new destination. Home could wait for another hour. I wanted to soak up the green and sun before I was cooped up inside my house and then the rehab center for another night and day.

Even when I went down the shore, even if I wasn't dead on my feet, I didn't get to enjoy the sun. Every time I heard the rolling waves of the beach at night, my thoughts drifted to Colm. Not Preston, even though we'd spent years on the sand hiding out from work at the Surf Shack.

11

COLM

W hy did she have to show up here?

My dick, which had taken a months' long siesta, decided to wake the fuck up within seconds of her walking into the room. It was like my mind jumped back to that night and wanted to pick up right where it left off. Only it wasn't that night and I wasn't that same guy.

So I welcomed the anger. I let it wash over me to strangle back that erection and keep me focused on the task at hand: getting her the hell out of my bedroom.

The way her nose wrinkled when she looked around the room before spotting me was embarrassing. I was an embarrassment, and she needed to stay the fuck away. I'd run her off like I'd done with everyone else in my life, but that didn't keep me from throwing myself into the shower and taking my cock in my hand, pumping my sudsy hold up and down my length remembering how good she'd felt that night.

Her arms wrapped around my neck with her panting breaths brushing against my skin and her thighs locked around my waist working against each of my thrusts to make every slam into her more explosive than the last.

I bit back my groan and came, slamming my hand against the wet tile. Resting my forehead against the wall with my arm braced, I winced at the throb shooting down my leg. Fucking hell. I couldn't even come without a reminder of how screwed up I was.

Drying myself off, I stared at myself in the mirror. Wasn't I supposed to be the one with my shit together? I was the one who looked out for everyone. I was the one who'd given up my teens and twenties to take care of my sister. Resentment threatened to boil over, swiftly followed by guilt.

Of course I took care of Liv. She was my sister. My little sister, and I'd slipped into the parent role long before our parents died. Did it piss me off sometimes when I couldn't go out and party because she'd needed me? When I'd missed out on spring break trips because I hadn't wanted to leave her at boarding school all alone during her break? When I'd stayed sober and played designated driver because I had to serve as a chaperone on her school trip, or help her study? Yeah, but we were a team. At least I'd thought we were a team.

Just like the team I'd been a part of for almost my entire life. And my turn as an irresponsible fuck up had lasted all of three days. My turn to finally be a selfish asshole had been cut short with one botched punch and here I was with a fucked up leg, not even able to do the only thing I was apparently good at, since surrogate parenting certainly wasn't one of them. The wallowing had turned into drowning in a vat of self-pity and it was even starting to piss *me* off.

Fuck, I was screwed up, but how did I fix it? Wasn't it better for everyone to think I was just a stubborn asshole rather than a complete waste who couldn't even get out of the car at the practice rink? I'd been through way worse, so why was this fucking with me so hard?

I'd tried a couple days ago after Bailey's visit. I'd gotten in my car at 4am and driven to the practice rink. There were always cars in the lot. Figure skaters, high school hockey players, anyone who couldn't afford prized rink time had to work around the early edges of the morning.

My fingers had frozen on the door handle. The cold sweat prickled across my forehead and dripped down the back of my neck. I stayed there for what felt like hours as more cars pulled into the lot, each driver stealing a glance at the weird guy sitting in his car. But I couldn't make myself pull the handle and open the door. The sun was already on the horizon by the time I admitted defeat and drove home.

And then Imogen appeared in my house. In my bedroom like she'd never left. Bailey and the guys had to be behind this. Desperate times called for desperate measures and that's the only way they'd subject her to me.

Everyone treated her like she was spun glass. All the voices dropped a little lower when she walked into the room, like if the volume were too high she might shatter. Anytime someone mentioned someone dying, even offhandedly, all eyes would shoot to her.

She always brushed them off like it was no big deal. But they'd never tiptoed around that stuff with me or Liv. Why treat Imo differently? She wasn't really a part of our group, just an extension of a guy who would have been a part of our group, if he'd lived. And it pissed me off.

What happened if she came back? I'd told her to leave, but if Bailey had gotten to her that meant she wouldn't give up so easily. And if she came back could I tell her to leave again?

The sugary sweet smells enveloped me a block away from Bread & Butter, carried on the last of the summer air before the blustery cold moved in.

"Hey, I didn't expect to see you." Avery rounded the corner and pulled me in for a big hug. She smelled like donuts and chocolate. It was one hell of a perfume; no wonder Emmett barely wanted to let her out of the house.

"Emmett told me about the PT session with Colm today, how'd it go?" She held onto my shoulders and smiled at me.

I tilted my head and stared back at her.

"That good, huh? I've got what you need. Grab a seat." She didn't stop at one of the display cases at the front of the shop, instead pushing through the swinging doors back into the kitchen.

There weren't many customers inside, with the morning and lunch rushes well over. I grabbed a table by the big front window and stared up at the trees, where orange or yellow leaves dotted amongst the lush green.

"Try these." She slid a plate in front of me with a cupcake and cookie combo that made my mouth water.

"These don't look like your usual." I took a bite of the huge cookie with salt sprinkled on top.

"They're not," she continued, and although I was interested in what she was saying, I wasn't willing to take the cookie out of my mouth to respond. "You know that web series thing I talked about? I found someone who could help. She made these."

"Not worried about the competition? Is that caramel in here?" I covered my stuffed mouth with my hand.

"Her name's Jules. She's in college and really talented. Who knows if she even wants to do this professionally, but she's adorable and Max refuses to go on camera with me, so I've brought her on."

"You'll bake things together on camera?"

"Posting it on social media. It's not exactly Martha Stewart level, but it's something we're going to try."

"Sounds like it could be fun."

"I hope so. Now you can stop dodging the conversation. How was Colm? We're all a bit worried about him. Emmett said Colm's doing everything he can to make sure he's all alone."

"I can certainly tell. So what do you have planned for this web project?"

Avery scrubbed her hands over her face. "How long do you have? Let's say things are going to be turned upside down for a while."

She launched into the details and I was tired just listening to her. "And I need everything finished by March."

I wiped my mouth with a napkin. "Why March?"

"Excuse me." A guy stood beside our table, looking down at the two of us before focusing on me. He was tall, probably at least a foot taller than me if I were standing. The sleeves of his button down were rolled up to his elbows, showing off a tattoo on his forearm. A professional with a rebellious streak.

"I'd kick myself if I didn't come over here." He had a warm, sweet smile only helped by the bakery boxes in his arms, tied up with pink and white string.

Avery crossed her arms over her chest and sat back in her chair.

"Kick yourself for what?" she piped up.

My foot shot out under the table, but she was too fast and moved her leg out of the way.

The stranger smiled at me. "I've seen you in here a few times before and I decided if I saw you again, I'd ask you if you'd like to get coffee."

"That's very nice of you."

"I'm sensing a but coming my way."

"But I'm not up for dates, even coffee dates right now. Thank you so much for asking. I know it couldn't have been an easy thing to do."

He smiled. "It's better than a lingering *what if*."

"You're right."

Avery jumped up and grabbed a display of fudge brownies off the counter. "And for the ballsy move of the day, you get a brownie on the house."

His smile brightened. "This definitely takes the sting out of it." He took his bundled sweets and left the store.

When the door closed behind him, Avery turned her playful glared on me. "Stop working these guys up or I'll have to give away half my shop to keep them from bursting into tears when you shoot them down."

"I'm just sitting here."

"Giving off that, *I'm sweet, understanding, but will also blow your mind in bed* vibe."

"What the hell?! I do not."

She laughed, raising an eyebrow, crossing her arms over her chest and rocking her chair back onto two legs. "That's what you think."

I had another bite of my cookie and a glass of cold milk.

She sent me on my way with another dozen cupcakes, donuts, and brownies.

Everyone at the center would love getting these tomorrow, but my appetite was gone. My stomach was only able to handle one of her cookies before threatening to revolt. I'd nursed my coffee for the rest of our time together. It wasn't even winter yet and I was already coming down with something. Just what I needed...

With the sugar high wearing off, I couldn't keep my thoughts from Colm anymore.

Did I want to go down this path again? With Preston, it had nearly shattered us both, but when we came out the other side, we were stronger than ever. He was happy. We were happy. A new start that had been ripped away when he died.

Preston had been my first love, so comfortable, and we fit together so easily. Even after his diagnosis, we were ready to head into the future with the new hand we'd been dealt. A previously undetected heart condition had been discovered after he'd passed out the summer before our senior year. It was rare and we were so lucky there hadn't been any complications from it before.

But the health gauntlet he'd have needed to go through to get drafted would've meant no team would touch him. It was over for him. One second he was sitting in the doctor's office thinking they'd tell him to lay off the salt or he was allergic to something he'd eaten and the next, his whole life had been ripped away from him.

Things with Colm were much more complicated. He

was a wild card with no regard for anyone around him. The pain radiated off him in waves and sometimes it felt like no one else could see it or feel it as keenly. All they saw was him acting like an asshole, but he hadn't always been like this, and I saw the neon glowing arrow pointed right at his pain and fear. He felt cornered and the pushing it would take to get him past it might be more than I could manage.

A grimace twisted my lips. There was no fucking reason for Colm to give up like this. Anger replaced the pity. Screw him for putting his friends and family through this unnecessarily! He wasn't dying. He wasn't dead. They needed him and wanted him to be whole again and he could be. Unlike Preston's heart had been, Colm's leg was fine. There were no damn excuses.

Maybe it was the loss we'd both dealt with, but I wasn't going to let him shut himself up in his house and become the weird urban legend that kids on the street talked about.

He could do this. I could do this. We'd slept together, but that didn't mean anything. We'd banged. We'd had hot, crazy intense sex, but people did that all over the city. People were probably doing that right now, and they'd tip their hat to the lady or gentleman on the way out and it wasn't a big deal. He'd slept with tons of women. My roster of men was less sizeable, but I could keep things professional. And if he was pissed at me, there would be one more thing to keep his mind off wallowing in self–pity. That quicksand was hard to pull yourself out of on your own.

He was just like every other client. It was a lie I'd have to keep repeating or we were headed for disaster.

13

COLM

S taring at my phone on the nightstand, I picked it up. It hadn't been off Do Not Disturb mode in months. Probably why Bailey had come to my house. My dodging technique wouldn't work forever.

I held the cold metal in my hands. The screen was pitch black. Holding down the button on top, there was a flicker and the screen lit up.

As it fully powered up and connected, the messages and notifications rolled in, wave after wave. When I thought it was all caught up another onslaught started. My agent. Bailey. Declan. Heath. Emmett. Ford. And Liv.

Her messages were the ones that had made me turn it off right after I left the hospital.

I was a freaking wreck. I was supposed to be the strong older brother. If I couldn't be that, why did she even need me around? I'd failed in every way imaginable. She wasn't going to med school. I hadn't gotten her to move out of her apartment and she'd nearly died. Ford, who was going to break her heart, had swept her off her feet, and I couldn't stop it even though I knew he would hurt her. And now I didn't even have hockey. The whole situation tapped into an anger and resentment I'd kept bottled up for so long I couldn't remember not keeping it tightly bundled and shoved to the back of my mind.

My dreams had been filled with Imogen since she'd left my bedroom. My body had prickled with awareness of our night together the second she'd stepped across the threshold. On my couch. In my room. In this bed. I ran my hands over the blankets.

At least this time I'd been awake to see her go. But the gnawing was back. The hungry gnawing that had been replaced by a dull black and white existence since I'd found out my leg would recover and everyone expected me to get back on the ice and skate into the season like nothing had happened.

Only *everything* had happened. My sister had blown up her future and ruined my relationship with my best friend —or he'd ruined my relationship with her, I wasn't sure which yet. I'd injured myself twice almost back to back. And the one woman my thoughts kept coming back to year after year had given me a night of fireworks that made everyone else feel like backyard sparklers, and then run like an angry mob had been chasing after her. She'd only sent me a message because I was a pathetic mess who'd nearly ruined his career again.

I wasn't going to be the pity guy. So her showing up like we could forget about all that? No, it wasn't happening. It had made me even more restless and I'd gone down to the gym I had installed in my basement to lift some weights when the thoughts had become too much.

She was the muse of a life I didn't live anymore. Maybe she'd sensed my bad fortune coming. Maybe the universe had told her to cut and run before this loser blew up his life.

My comeuppance. No hockey. Here, all alone in my big house with a bum knee. If only the rest of the Kings would stop coming around, I could complete my journey to neighborhood weirdo shut-in.

I scrolled to my favorites: there were only five names. Liv's was at the top of the list. I stared at the picture beside her name. It was from her first day of boarding school in Boston. She'd been miserable and worried about making new friends. We'd started our Sunday dinner tradition and I promised I'd take her to any dance classes she wanted. That had come back to bite me in the ass. She'd been so young then, so small, and she'd needed me so much. Now what did she need me for? The broken brother who didn't know what the hell he was doing.

My finger hovered over her name. Instead of tapping it, I turned the phone off and shoved it back into the drawer in my night stand. Flopping back in bed, I slammed a pillow over my head like the room wasn't dark enough already.

The front door opened and closed. Didn't the guys ever want to hang at home? Maybe sleep in?

"Colm, I'm here. Are you ready to go?" Imogen's voice trailed up the stairs like I'd conjured her from my dreams.

My hands on her hips pulling her closer.

Her hands in my hair tugging at the roots.

My body pressed against hers, breathing in her scent.

Her moans.

My need for her.

I shifted in the bed and my knee ached. All those feelings were washed away and replaced with the reality of my current situation. There would be no scooping her up and throwing her on my bed and sinking inside her.

I groaned remembering how good she'd felt under me. No, she wasn't here for another round of the best sex I'd ever had in my life. She was here to play nursemaid. To give me encouraging words while I walked on a treadmill or did some leg presses. To tell me that I would play hockey again.

I stayed in my bed. My t-shirt and sweats were rank. The books I'd grabbed off the shelves in my office to keep the boredom at bay sat beside the TV remote. There was only so much reading and TV watching I could handle before I wanted to go running down the street like a madman.

There was rustling and banging downstairs. Fine, she could hang out and play video games like the guys, but I wasn't doing any of her hoop jumping today.

Her jogging footsteps up the stairs followed a few minutes later. "Good morning." She burst into my room like rainbows shone out her ass. "Did you hear me? Let's go. We've got a lot to get done today."

Her hair was up in a ponytail that swung behind her. She was in scrubs. Just like a nurse. The black strap of her bra poked out the side of the v neckline. Was it the same bra she'd worn that night? The smooth feel of it had been seared into my memory. *Stop it, Colm.* This isn't a recreational visit, and she wasn't looking for a repeat.

"I'm sleeping. You can do whatever the hell you want." I grabbed my blankets and wrapped them around myself. At least the sheets were clean. After she'd left, I'd given them a smell test and damn they were rank. With her so close my morning wood was turning into something else and I didn't need to embarrass myself even more.

"You're hilarious. Let's go." The bed dipped and she patted my back through the blankets like this was some game we were playing.

"If anyone asks I'll tell them you gave it your all, now leave me alone. How in the hell did you get in here in the first place?"

The jingle of metal on metal. "Declan gave me his keys. Said he had at least twenty sets made up."

Traitors. I'd have to find my phone so I could call a locksmith and get them changed.

"There's loads for us to do, so let's get a move on it."

"What part of 'not happening' don't you understand?"

"Okay, but you can't say I didn't try." The mattress sprung back and her footsteps retreated.

And I must've fallen asleep. All I know is I didn't even hear the attack coming.

Icy needles splashed over my face and rivulets of freezing water streamed up my nose. I shot up from my bed.

Imogen stood over me, holding a bucket I didn't even know I owned, wearing a smile fit for an adorable anarchist.

I spewed water out of my mouth and shook ice off my body. It thudded to the floor and the water splashed all over everything. "What the fuck, Imo?"

"You wouldn't do things the easy way, so I had to improvise." She shrugged like she'd had no choice in the matter. An invisible force had propelled her helplessly through her attempted drowning.

"By waterboarding me?"

"Hardly, I didn't even get out the burlap sack. Let's go." She nodded with a smile like we were on a prank show and I was missing the party downstairs. "Why won't everyone leave me alone?" Gruff hadn't worked. Time for a change of tactics. I'd go full-on dick. That got people to steer clear for at least a few days.

"Because you don't want to be left alone."

"Did you think the flashing welcome sign above my door had burned out? What part of any of this"—I gestured to my dark cave of a room, blackout curtains drawn—"makes you think visitors are welcome?" It was slightly cleaner than the last time she had been here, but I hadn't exactly set out fresh scones and a pot of tea.

She held onto the bucket and stalked toward me. "Why haven't you changed the locks?"

"The locks." Hmm, what was this new word? Never heard of it. Apparently, since I hadn't gotten off my ass to get it done.

"I told you the guys had keys. Declan had enough made for the whole team. They've been showing up for weeks, if not months. If you truly wanted everyone to leave you alone, one phone call would've taken care of that. Hell, you could call the cops on them for trespassing, if you really wanted."

I crossed my arms and glared back at her.

She set the bucket down, water droplets tracing down the side of the plastic, and took a step closer.

"I'm not here to make your life harder."

I glanced down at my drenched clothes and back up to her. My face was set to 'are you fucking serious?'

"Desperate times call for desperate measures. The guys are worried about you. They want to know you're okay."

"I'm fine. They're here almost every day. Everyone can see for themselves. I'm fine. I've told them I don't need their help. I'm fine."

"That was two more 'I'm fines' than anyone who actually has their life together would say." She opened her arms wide and showcased the room. "Does this look like the room of a man who's fine? Does downstairs look like the house of a man who's fine? There was something on the counter down there and I didn't know whether I should run away from it or try to communicate with it."

"They could've taken my word for it." I turned my head to look at the water soaking into the floor.

She shifted and stepped closer. "Do you know the best

way to get them off your back?" Her hand lifted, fingers flexing inches from my arm before she made contact.

That electric charge traveled straight up my skin, tingling and zapping through me.

"Give this a try." She ducked to catch my eye. "For real, put in some work and show them you will at least entertain this."

"My knee—"

"Bailey told me."

I sucked in a sharp breath. "Told you what?"

"Are we going to play this game, Colm? She told me the truth. Something I take it you're keeping from the guys, based on how they've been talking."

I ducked my head, my shoulders inched up.

Her fingers grasped my dripping forearm.

Meeting her gaze, I looked into her eyes and I was lost. Everything else faded away. The stiffness in my knee. The loneliness and anger. The past.

Everything was centered on the two of us in this room. Screw the rest of the world. She'd always been able to make it past my defenses, even the ones that were so ingrained I barely realized I wore them like a shield around me every second of the day.

"Will you do that?"

I shook my head, clearing away the fog of her touch and dislodging her hand from my arm. *Don't get too close, Colm. Remember what happened last time? How deep that burn went?*

"And what's your big plan? How do I get everyone to leave me alone?"

"We work together."

"If you say treadmill and weights, I'll lose my shit." And no matter how much I worked out, I couldn't get on the ice. What was the point, if I didn't skate again? Couldn't skate again? Every trainer was focused on getting me playing again. Probably for the big fat bounty team physios got for player rehabs. They'd have shoved me onto the rink shaking and puking, if it meant they got paid. But this was Imo. Some of the sharp jagged edges of my fear were worn away. Maybe she wouldn't be like everyone else.

Her laugh came out as a huff. "Sick of the standard PT? You're not the first client to feel that way. We can improvise, but you'll have to do some work on your own."

Client. That's how she saw me. I was a broken client she was working to get back on his feet and send on his way. Probably getting paid by the team or the guys.

"For how long?"

14

IMO

I licked my lips, expecting I'd need to pull the bucket treatment at least a few more times before he caved. I'd had to use the ice water bath three times with Preston.

The weight of expectations rested on my shoulders, a heavy burden I couldn't shake. The whole time I'd walked over, I kept trying to talk myself out of it. Give myself all the reasons to tell Terry I was sorry, tell Bailey why it wouldn't work, and tell the Kings that I wasn't the miracle worker they thought I was.

Colm didn't want to see me. He'd made that clear. And the fire in his eyes had been a different kind of ignition than what I'd seen that night months ago. But there had been loss in his eyes, too. How could I walk away from that? How could I walk away from this new and different Colm who was waiting for someone to wrap the lifeline around his waist and drag him from the churning waters and into the comfort of a safe boat?

I was exhausted. I didn't want to be here, but I couldn't walk away. The balance I'd maintained in my life was shaky, and he could topple it. My perch on the chasm of loss and life had seemed safe before he burned a trail across my body with his lips.

Now he stood in front of me, soaking wet with an expectant look on his face. Oh shit, the pitch. My big plan on how to make it all better. Get Colm back on the ice, save Bailey's fledgling recruiting career, get Terry the donation to the center she needed, and keep my life as close to normal as possible. Maybe a nap.

"We meet three times a week, until the trade window opens. Thirty sessions." Meeting that often and building his confidence in his recovery could see us cutting things short and only needing a month.

He crossed his arms over his chest. The t-shirt clung to his wet skin. Even after being laid up for months, his muscles bulged under the soggy fabric. Pecs and biceps for days—well, it seemed months in his case—but he was leaner than he'd been before. "Five, and we meet every other week."

From the boredom on his face, I expected him to start inspecting his nails and yawning.

"Be realistic. Twice a week for twenty sessions." There were people who'd kill for what he had. The healed muscles and bones. The support. The money.

"Every other week. Five." His jaw ticked, muscles tight like a rubber band stretched to capacity.

The gauntlet had been thrown, but I wasn't backing off. Other than Preston, I'd never worked with someone I knew, so I pushed harder than I might with my other clients, rather than respecting Colm's boundaries and slowly easing him into things. If the bucket of ice water hadn't clued him in, I wasn't going to play fair. Stepping forward, I steeled myself and got in his face.

"From what the guys have said, you haven't been working out. We need to recover your lost capacity. Consistent work and form will help your muscle strength, flexibility, and reflexes improve much quicker."

"And the average recovery period for someone with my kind of injury is less than three months. I know."

"Then why aren't you sweating your ass off to be back with your team?"

"Why should I?" He glared at me with defiance teetering on the edge of contempt. The lost guy from our night together had been swallowed up by this angry shell. Based on his charts, he was physiologically primed for gradually building back up to his old regimen. But his head was in the way. Fear had a way of paralyzing people. It could freeze them solid even as a truck bore down on them and their body screamed to move.

As much as he didn't want to admit it, he'd opened the door. He'd given the Kings keys to his house and hadn't change the locks. He could've called the cops when I showed up for my impromptu dunking, or at least grabbed me and tossed me outside. Even that would've been some welcome exercise as long as he kept a solid form while doing it. Hell, he could've had someone pack up his life and gotten on a plane, never to be heard from again.

But he hadn't. He'd rejected every chance he'd had to truly shut everyone out. Colm wanted this. He wanted to recover.

That didn't mean he wasn't going to be an asshole about it. Hope was a cruel mistress and sometimes we fought against the things we wanted most because pretending we didn't want them was a hell of a lot easier than going after them full tilt and falling short.

"Are you going to fight me the whole way?"

"Of course." He shrugged like he had all day—and he did. He had the rest of his life to be a stubborn ass, but once he saw that a full recovery was possible and got over whatever lies he was telling himself, he'd stop fighting. Getting over the hump, though, showing him he could trust his body again...it would be a doozy. "But you've signed yourself up for an assignment when no one asked you to."

"Except for your family, friends, and trainer."

His jaw clenched.

"Fifteen sessions. Twice a week every other week and once in between." I felt like I was haggling at a Saturday Farmers' Market.

"Seven."

"Ten. Less than once a week and you're going to lose out on any progress we make. Give me at least that. And you have to do the program I give you for the rest of the week in between our sessions."

"Eight."

"Colm, don't be an asshole. The people who care about you want you strong and healthy. Don't deny them or yourself that just because you want to be stubborn. Ten." I held out my hand.

His rough calluses slid against my palm, sending a zing down my spine. This was the first time we'd touched since that night.

"Deal, but I'm not getting on the ice."

My jaw and hand dropped. Now it was my turn to stand there like someone had thrown a bucket of ice water at me. "You're..." The plan had been a few sessions to see if he'd kept up with the plan his doctors and previous physio had set out for him, and then see how he'd been on the ice. The guys had said he hadn't skated with them since the injury, but no ice at all? "But how can—"

"Figure it out, Miss 'Let's get you back on your feet.'" He sliced his hands in front of him. "I'm not getting on the ice. If you can't agree to my terms then I can't agree to yours."

How was he going to get back to playing if he refused to even set foot on the ice? Was self-destructing his plan all along? Wait out the season until they had no choice but to cut him?

"Do we have a deal?" He held out his hand with a smirk that told me he was enjoying this.

"Things might get a little unconventional if you're holding firm to that no ice thing."

"Do your worst, Imogen. No ice, but I can handle anything you serve up."

I pumped his hand up and down. "I can work with that, but remember this conversation later. This is me saying I told you so."

15

COLM

I mo shoved the metal handle into my hand before walking over to the pantry.

"What the hell is this for?" I was tempted to let it fall.

"For today's session." She filled the bucket with water at the sink and hauled it off the counter. Rummaging around under the sink, she grabbed a bottle and unscrewed the top. A pungent lemon scent filled the room. "Perfect, I love a citrus smell. It's invigorating."

I could hear the smile in her voice, even with her back to me, and her shoulders shook, like there had never been anything more exciting than a lemon scented cleaning solution.

"Gets the blood pumping, right?" With a glance over her shoulder and a grin out of a 90s sitcom, she screwed the cap back on.

"You're batshit crazy, aren't you?" Maybe I'd missed it, staring into her eyes for too long. I'd missed the crazy whirling around them that could have her standing over me with a bucket of ice water and suggesting that cleaning my house would be our first session together.

"Nope, high on lemon cleaning products." She lugged the bucket over to me, setting it at my feet. Water sloshed over the edge, spilling onto my toes and the floor.

"Whoops, someone should probably clean that up." She tapped her chin and looked up at me, eyes widening at the mop in my hand like it had appeared out of nowhere and she hadn't shoved it at me less than three minutes ago.

Had Imo always been this...mischievous? "This is how you're going to help me? Your plan is to have me mop floors?"

"No."

Some of the tension left my shoulders.

"You're also going to vacuum as soon as I find it, clean out the fridge, and do some laundry. Things are piling up." A quick pat to my shoulder and she turned.

"I'll do the dishes." She grabbed the sponge beside the sink and turned on the faucet.

"Cleaning? Cleaning my house is how we're going to get through the next ten sessions? Will you make me clean yours next?"

She turned, bracing her hands on the edge of the sink. "Would you leave the house if I said it was?"

I swallowed.

"When was the last time you went for a walk around the block? Or have you been hiding in here since you got back from the hospital?" She chucked the sponge down and walked over to the curtains in the living room. Grabbing a fistful of each side she flung them open. The room was bathed in the harsh morning light.

I winced, slamming my eyes shut against the bright flood of sun into the room.

"When was the last time you opened the front door, walked outside for something other than meeting a delivery man, and did something? Anything?" She stood in front of the window, the sun casting a glow around her body, framing every inch of her.

My train of thought wasn't just gone, it had pulled out of the station and was barreling over a cliff. "Outside?"

"Yes, it's the place where the sun and birds and other people live."

I shrugged. "Recently."

From the arm cross and the toe tap she wasn't buying it. "Perfect. If you've got no problem with leaving, we'll do something outside the house for the next session. Until then, you've got work to do." She pointed her chin toward the sudsy water that was pooling around my feet.

Before going back to the sink, she dug around in her oversized bag and pulled out a speaker.

My hands tightened on the mop. It was the same speaker from that night on the beach. The one we'd sat beside while the sound of the waves and the music rolled over us.

The song that came out this time wasn't slow and melodic, it was fast-paced. Something you could dance to. Or at least, something she could dance to.

Imo mouthed the words and swayed her hips to the beat, sometimes using the sponge as an improvised microphone.

My cheeks twitched, and it seemed the muscles hadn't quite atrophied over the past few months—a smile tugged at my lips as she dragged a sponge across the counter after dumping a pizza box into the trashcan.

We'd gathered three garbage bags full of stuff already and I'd been tasked with dumping them out in the trash bins outside. She'd watched me from the doorway with a cautious gaze, like she expected me to burst into flames the second the sunlight streaked across my skin, or maybe hail a taxi and abandon her in my house. I had half expected something similar, but the fresh air was no longer summer muggy, and the fall crispness it was edging toward felt good.

Back inside, she stood on her tiptoes, wiping a cloth across the top of the fridge. She coughed and sputtered at the dust stampede that rushed across her face, and embarrassment burnt my cheeks. I'd let this place go. My meticulousness was covered over by my three month wallow session, but watching this magical, annoying creature invade my space, bringing light and brightness to my house, made it feel more like a home. Like a place I could do more than just drink under the cover of darkness.

She turned and cleared her throat, catching me staring at her ass, and I sputtered, kicked at the bucket, and kept my head down, mopping.

As she'd said, the citrusy smell made the room feel cleaner.

She opened the windows to let the stale air out. The guys hadn't let me starve, but they weren't neat freaks. My house had become a window into what it would've been like had we all roomed together in college.

I shuddered as I pulled a mystery item out of the couch cushions.

"Is that food?" Imo took a step back from the warped, smooshed greenish brown thing in my hand.

"Do you really want to know?" I chucked it into the trashcan beside me.

"Good point. Wash your hands."

"What's wrong? Worried you'll catch something?" I flexed my fingers in her direction and was met with a smack from the towel she'd had slung over her shoulder. Before I could even think of retaliating, she'd sprinted halfway across the room.

Next, we went through a mountain of mail the guys had set on and under the table by the door.

"This one looks just like you." She held up the last of the letters from an elementary school class. The figure on the page was either a lizard who'd taken up hockey, or a guy who needed a plastic surgeon asap.

"Way to boost my confidence, Imo."

She rolled her eyes. "Like you don't know you're gorgeous." Her hand froze midway to the trash pile.

Gorgeous, hey?

After I dried off and she'd shoved the mop into my hand, we'd kept our distance. Other than my vision being drawn to her ass every time she turned around, the elephant in the room had stayed safely tucked away. We hadn't delved into what happened that night. Not into the way I'd broken down or we'd torn one another's clothes off the second we fell over the threshold of the door. How I'd barely remembered to kick it shut to avoid giving the whole damn block a show and probably get me fined by the homeowners' association. But that didn't mean either of us had forgotten. It would've only be a matter of time before it would all come to a head.

"I can always use a reminder." I leaned closer.

"Without your adoring fans screaming your name in stadiums all over the country, I'm sure you do."

"It's not my life right now, is it?" My words shot out like acid.

She jumped back like she'd been burned. "If we keep working, you'll get there."

"I never said I wanted it. I want to do this to get everyone off my back and leave me alone."

"If you wanted people to leave you alone, you'd have stopped fighting your recovery a long time ago. All you're doing is making it harder for the people you care about to help you."

"People I care about? People like my sister? People like Ford? Or were you talking about you? Was that night back in June your way of helping me?"

"I wondered when you'd want to do this. Let's do it right now." She set the bottle of cleaner down and faced me. "Give it to me." Her fingers motioned me forward.

"Give what to you?"

"Everything rushing through your head about that night and the next morning. I wanted to leave a note, but I couldn't find anything to write on."

"We have these things called phones."

"And I didn't have your number, even after knowing you for five years. I couldn't call my phone from yours to get your number, since it was locked. I'd had a call from Preston's parents about an emergency at the Shack, so I rushed out of here. By the time I dealt with that and could take a breath, I asked Emmett for your number." Her gaze dropped to the floor. "But from what I pieced together, you were at the hospital by then."

Anger and sadness had been my companions that morning, even more than they had in the days after my blow up with Liv. It was part of the reason I'd gone after Ford. But Imo hadn't run away not intending to look back after what had been one of the best nights of my life. Did that mean she'd wanted to continue things then?

"You should've woken me up."

She toyed with her fingers. "Looking back, I can see that. And I'm sorry that you woke up and I wasn't there." Her head lifted and she peered up at me. "Haven't you ever done something you wish you could take back?"

My jaw clenched and I nodded. So many things. How different would my life be—would Liv's life be—if I'd made different choices. Different demands to our parents. Different priorities when it came to playing pro. Different women I'd welcomed into my bed and my life.

"I'll show you a few exercises and then I'll get out of your hair."

I opened my mouth, about to say "don't, stay for a while," but I swallowed the words back. Her apology didn't mean anything had changed between us. For all I knew, the thing she wished she could take back was the whole night, not leaving me in the morning. Yeah. She probably wished she'd bypassed the bar that night and gone straight home. I'd have woken without a clue to where I was the following morning, and with an even bigger crater in my credit card.

When we finished cleaning the rooms, the space felt lighter and brighter. Not that I expected Imo to be the candy striper of physiotherapists, but she knew her stuff. She hadn't been patronizing, only gratingly, annoyingly right.

She'd stuck to her word about what we'd be doing today. Part of the weight had been lifted by moving around and making this place look a bit more like it had before things fell apart. Like some things in the world could be put back to the way they should be. I stared down at my leg. Not me. But I could pretend while she was here. While she was here, there was the tiniest sliver, a barely there voice in the back of my head that whispered maybe...

She walked me through a few exercises I could do to warm up my knee every day.

"A job well done deserves a reward." She pulled some drinks out of the fridge. "Perfect, they're cold enough. Last time I was here, I noticed a particular slant to all the beverages in your fridge. I thought I'd mix it up."

Leaning against the counter, she held up her Root Beer and clinked it to mine. "How are you feeling?" She took a sip.

My knee throbbed, but from disuse, not pain. This was the longest I'd been on my feet in a while, moving around, bending and stretching. "Is my knee supposed to be filled with pulsing fire like there's a gremlin trying to rip it apart?"

"What?" She slammed her can down and dropped in front of me, pushing me back so my ass rested against the stool at the kitchen island.

"Where?" Her hands cradled my lower leg, running her fingers over my skin, tickling the hairs and sending wild thoughts of her on her knees doing way more than checking out my knee. "Is it tender here?" She applied gentle pressure, running her hand higher up the back of my bare leg to my thigh.

Baseball. Praying mantises. Vatican City. Bailey with a pair of pliers.

Only the distractions didn't work and the obvious tent in my shorts became a mountain between us.

Her hands froze. My shin was cradled in the valley of her breasts. My knee inches from her mouth and her fingertips halfway up my thigh.

The tips of my ears were on fire, but I didn't have the words for 'sorry for my boner, but when you're touching me like this my dick is going to take notice'.

She hadn't moved, still frozen on one knee with her hands on my leg.

I choked down a moan when her fingers tightened a fraction of an inch.

My erection stood proud between us like an oblivious tourist.

"It was a joke." The words were stilted and strained. I lifted a hand to touch her cheek.

My words and movement broke her out of the deer in headlights impersonation.

She cleared her throat, and shot back and up from the floor. "Glad to hear it. In that case, we're done for the day." She fumbled through three herky-jerky half steps in three different directions, her gaze bouncing everywhere but at me, before she found her target—her escape. "I'll see you next week and I'll email you some links to the exercises we went over today as a reminder."

Her bag was on her shoulder and she was out the door before I could utter thanks.

Imogen was a dangerous element to introduce to my life.

She made me feel whole when I wasn't.

She made me feel things were possible that weren't.

She made me want things I couldn't have.

16

IMO

"Look at you. Dropping by twice in less than six months. Has a planetary alignment hit or something?" Avery waved me through the double doors leading back to the heart of the bakery.

"No, I had a couple clients cancel, so I wanted to stop by before I headed down the shore."

"So I'm just a time filler to you." Her bottom lip quivered, but her eyes were all smiles.

"Less time filler and more stomach filler. I've been craving everything you have out there in the cases. Are you sure they aren't laced with anything?"

"I'll never tell," she sing-songed, rounding the edge of the thick wood butcher's block-style worktop.

"How are you getting any work done with all these lights around here?" I stepped over the long cables and cords leading to the lights hanging over the counters and workbenches with bowls and baking trays stacked chest high.

Avery wiped her hands on her apron. "It's a bit more than I expected when we first arranged for all this, but there's so little natural light back here that I have to deal with it if I don't want to look like I'm a reanimated corpse."

"This stuff doesn't get in the way?"

"Oh yeah. But it's only here one day out of the week. Jules will be by later today to do our filming. She's so freaking cute, I can't stand it. And talented! Taste this."

As with any visit to Bread & Butter, it wasn't complete until Avery had shoved something into my mouth. But it was always worth it.

"I need you to eat them. I'm a cookie away from slipping into a food coma and dying." She laughed and I cringed.

But I relaxed my shoulders once she carried on with her work. Whenever I was around the Kings and someone mentioned anything related to death, all eyes would swing to me as if waiting for me to burst into tears at any second.

It was another reason I stayed away. I felt like a constant reminder of a terrible tragedy. And I almost felt the need to stay stuck, suspended in that grief stage because with their eyes on me, moving on felt like a betrayal. It got old. I shook my head and helped Avery move some of the trays to the large bakery rack.

Going back to school for physiotherapy had at least been a way I could help people heal, even just strangers in need of someone to get them back on their feet. Once Fern and Charlie had pulled themselves out of their grief, I'd kept up the level of work I'd taken on right after Preston died, but now they didn't need me as much.

All the times they told me I didn't have to come down over the summers hurt, like severing my connection to the life I'd had before. They were his family, but they would have been mine too when Preston and I got married. He'd always be their son and Becca's brother, but who would I be to them? What happened when I eventually found someone to be happy with again? What did happiness even mean? And what happened if I lost it again?

"Summer season is officially finished." Fern flopped into the chair, scooting it back from the table.

Charlie flipped the sign to closed and joined us at the table.

"At least you won't have to make that long drive down anymore."

I smiled and nodded, stacking the napkins.

"What's up, Imogen? Everything okay?" Fern rested her hand on my forehead in a Mom move that nearly brought tears to my eyes. I missed my mom and my dad and Preston. And one day Fern and Charlie might feel weird about having their late son's girlfriend hanging around, and then I'd be alone.

Colm didn't know how lucky he was to have people literally ready to beat down his door to look out for him. That was why my exits from his house were always so urgent. Too many feelings. Too many chances for a misstep—and, man, did I want to step out of line. But what happened to Fern and Charlie then? I couldn't wander in and introduce them to my new boyfriend.

Hi, I know your son is dead, but guess what? I've moved on. You may have been surrogate parents who took care of me once my parents were gone, but your son has been replaced.

Colm wasn't the first client I've had get an erection when we worked together, but he's the first one I've wanted to do something about it with. But that couldn't happen. If he'd wanted to pursue something with me, he wouldn't have ignored my texts. He'd made it more than clear that he wanted nothing to do with me romantically, despite the way his body reacted to me. He hadn't seen daylight in a month, he was just excessively horny. Any woman who'd touched him would have gotten the same reaction.

Once he was out of this and back playing professionally, our sessions together would be forgotten. I'd found him as a wounded bird, and I'd rehab him and set him free.

My baggage wasn't light and I couldn't expect anyone to carry it for me. He'd been through enough. More drama could derail him further. I'd keep it professional. No daydreaming about his hands around my waist with his lips on my neck and his cock sliding into me. A shiver tiptoed down my spine.

"Their first offer was high, but this one was ridiculous."

That snapped me out of my thoughts. "Offer?"

"He didn't tell you?" Fern jerked her thumb at her husband of thirty-two years. "Some developer came around and made an offer on the Shack. Can you believe it?"

A developer? Someone trying to buy the Shack? Knock it down and put up something sparkly and new. Panic seized my chest. "No, what did you say?"

"We've had this place for so long, I don't know what I'd do if we closed up shop. We figured we'd be working here and have our own reserved booth when you and Preston took it over." Charlie got up and flipped his chair upside down on top of the table.

Fern squeezed my hand across the table.

"He left his card. I have a feeling he'll be back."

"Once the summer season's over all the people sniffing around back off. Not many people make it through the off season. I am looking forward to weekend breakfasts only. My old back isn't what it used to be." Charlie stretched up tall before bending back, popping it the whole way. "Ah, that's the stuff."

"You know there are some exercises you could—" I laughed at his narrowed gaze. "Okay, no more advice." Holding up my hands, I backed away.

"Do you want to stay over or are you headed back?" He undid the apron around his waist.

"Headed back. I'll grab my coffee on the way and I have a full tank of gas, so I won't need to stop."

"Be careful out there and call us when you get home."

"I always do."

We finished cleaning up for the night. Inventory and repairs would start next week—even with the bulk of the business being in the summer there was always more than enough to do year round.

Tape for my eyelids would've been handy on the drive back to my apartment. A bigger part of me than I care to admit was okay with falling asleep in my car outside of my building. Dragging myself inside, I'd wanted to lie down on the floor and pass out there. This weekend hadn't been that bad, so why was I dead on my feet?

The drives must finally be getting to me. My shower ended with cold water blasting me on my back. Peeling my face off the tile wall, I rubbed at the imprints of the pattern on my cheek.

I didn't even dry my hair before falling into bed. The rat's nest would be something Morning Imogen would have to deal with.

~

Next time I saw Night Imogen I'd punch her—hard. My hair had a weird, giant crimp to it that wouldn't come out. It was a section that took to worming its way out of my ponytail and sticking straight out from the side of my head.

It also brought on all the comments about how rough of a night I'd had with a few winks and nudges from my jerk co-workers.

"Great session! Keep up your exercises and your progress will go even faster." And the faster I finished this day, the faster I could get back into bed.

My latest client gave me a chagrinned look.

"We'll get you back to marathons before you know it. I promise if you put in the work, it'll happen."

"I'll be sure to put in the time."

Standing by the desk, I scribbled down my notes on his chart. He'd made great progress and it would only be a matter of time before he was back to one hundred percent.

Those were the cases that made my day fly by: the ones where I could get people back to where they'd been and even better, stronger and aware of what they needed to do to maintain their health in the long term. The others, where I had to look into someone's eyes and tell them that this would be their new normal, that we were working to regain only a percentage of their old mobility, strength, or flexibility—those were rough.

Change was hard. I leaned against the wall and closed my eyes, feeling like I was training for my own marathon.

"Long day," a voice came from my left.

I snapped up, pushing off the wall and blinking my eyes like someone had flung a handful of sand into my face.

"Were you sleeping against the wall?" Cecily uncapped her pen with her teeth.

"What? No." I dragged my hand over my face. "Just resting my eyes."

"That's the third time this week. Maybe a vacation is in

order. Tell your boyfriend not to keep you up so late at night."

I flung a stack of towels at her. "I don't have a boyfriend. And if I went on vacation, who'd cover everyone when they were gone?"

"We'd figure it out. Are you done for the day?"

"My schedule is empty. I'm on paperwork duty."

"Hey, Imo."

I jumped, grabbing the front of my chest as my heart thundered at the sudden appearance of an entire human beside me in less than a second.

"Jesus, Bailey. You scared the shit out of me. Where the hell did you come from?"

Her eyes narrowed and her mouth pursed. "It's a benefit of being so short. I'm not seen until I want to be seen. The guys let me know you've finally gotten through to Colm."

My lips stayed sealed. Gotten through to him or given him a way out of facing his real problems, not to mention him being determined not to skate again.

"You're getting him to work out? Stick to a plan?"

"They're probably overselling it. We've met one time. And I didn't get him to comply without flinging a bucket of ice water in his face. I wouldn't say he came along willingly."

"Hmm, ice bucket. I'll add that to the list." She pulled out a small notebook and scribbled down the words. "Anything is better than where we were. My ass is on the line. After the last injury, I made some promises about his comeback. The back-to-back injuries are a double whammy. And I might've given the impression to the higher ups that he's further along in his progress than he is."

For the first time since we walked into the room, her personality didn't fill it to the brim. "Do you think he might be ready by the start of the season?"

He wouldn't even set foot on the ice right now. "He's not there yet, but he's determined to be up to speed by the time the trade window closes." I was glad I'd had so much time to practice lying recently; it made this lie come easier.

"That's months away. I can't hold them off for that long."

"What about the end of the year? Give him until December. He can do it."

She eyed me, but I didn't shrink under her assessing gaze. "I'll see what I can do, but no promises." Dragging her fingers through her hair, she cursed under her breath. "I've never met a bigger bunch of prima donnas in my life. Can I see what you have planned for him?"

I walked her through my unorthodox training regimen for the next nine weeks.

"And you've discussed all of this with him?" She pointed at the calendar and listed activities.

"He was enthusiastic after our initial rocky start."

She made a noise of approval. "This will be enough to get him back to starter shape?"

"If he does the workouts for our days off, it's possible."

"Possible isn't going to cut it. I need him back in condition or he's going to get cut."

"When it comes to my clients, I don't deal in absolutes, so I won't lie to you either. We can never know one hundred percent what will happen."

Her eyes narrowed and she locked her arms across her chest. It felt like she was trying to peel back layers of my skin with her eyes. Then a miracle, the corner of her mouth lifted. "I respect you for not blowing smoke up my ass."

"You seem wound so tight, I don't even think smoke could make it up there."

She barked out a laugh and punched my shoulder.

Wincing, I gritted my teeth, keeping myself from rubbing the sore spot.

"He's in good hands." Her gaze held genuine affection. Under all her bluster, she cared about these guys. She went up another notch in my eyes.

I smiled. "I'm trying my best."

17

COLM

"**A**re you trying to kill me?"

Imo tilted her head to the side and narrowed her gaze. "There are much easier ways."

Springy blue foam blocks and mats covered every inch of the floor. My toes sank into it. Bright fabric hung from a fifty-foot ceiling. The room held the distinct smell of sweat, determination, and disinfectant.

"You have everything you need, Imo?"

"We're good. Thanks for letting us sneak in." She smiled at the sandy-haired guy with a gymnast's build in a tank top and shorts. The guy responded to her thanks by looking at Imogen as though they were at a bar together on their third round of drinks.

I bristled, a possessive streak racing through me. Had she found any other wounded birds at bars since our night together and nursed them back to health with mind-blowing sex? What was his connection to Imogen?

"You're in good hands." They both turned to look at me. Mr. Gymnast extended his hand and I shook it out of ingrained reflex. "Enjoy your PT." He clapped me on the shoulder as Imogen was walking away.

Mr. Gymnast walked behind her and checked out her ass. A long lingering stare—I was surprised it didn't come with a wolf whistle or maybe him getting down on all fours and panting. I squeezed my fists at my sides.

"Hey, Imo check this out." She glanced over her shoulder as he ran across one of the floor mats, twisted into a triple backflip, and landed in a foam pit. Why didn't he run over and hump her leg while he was at it?

She laughed and clapped. "Don't worry, Colm, we're not doing that today."

"Today?"

"Fine, ever. Way to ruin all my fun. Today we're tackling this." A cylinder the size of an industrial soup can sat on its side between her legs.

"A can?"

"Not just a can. We're working on your balance, so we'll also be using this." She grabbed a piece of wood shaped like a miniature surfboard from the floor. Like a horror movie come to life, she set the wood on top of the cylinder and popped up on top, balancing herself. With small corrective motions in either direction, she held her hands out to her sides as it wobbled, trying to buck her.

"You're out of your mind."

"It's easy." She hopped down and motioned me forward.

"Are you trying to reinjure me? Who told you this was a good idea?"

"My physiotherapy degree, and helping over three hundred patients get back on their feet."

"And you put them all up on a death wheel?"

"Most aren't as difficult as you, so we can go the more

traditional route, but you put the conditions in place and here we are."

"There's no fucking way, Imogen."

"We'll start at the wall with a smaller cylinder. You promised me you'd be cooperative. Or I can report back to the guys that you've backed out and they should buy a new game system for your house."

Narrowing my eyes at her with my mouth tight, I bit out one word. "Fine." I'd have much preferred a two-word option.

"I'm happy to see you're looking forward to this as much as I am."

"Let's get this over with. How much are they paying you? I can pay you double."

"This isn't about the money. It's about you getting to where you need to be. Where you deserve to be."

"And where do I deserve to be?"

"On the ice."

Just the words sent a cold shiver down my spine. Rinks used to be a second home for me. Waking up at 4am to get ice time and playing late into the night after school until I had to get Liv home for dinner had been my life. But now that word made my hands clammy and sent bile rushing to the back of my throat.

"I said I'd do your sessions. Nothing about getting back onto the ice."

She laughed, keeping her hands flexed at my sides, like she could take my entire weight if I toppled over.

"What's funny about that?"

Her head shake and continued laugh were like needles under my skin.

"What about any of this is funny?"

"That's almost exactly what Preston said after..." And

her laughter died, the smile falling off her face like she'd dropped her ice cream cone after standing in a three-hour long line.

Preston. Of course. When hadn't her life revolved around Preston? Was that why she'd left that morning? Not only because I was a mess in need of a firehose and Mac truck of ibuprofen, but because she was still in love with him?

"After what?"

"It doesn't matter. But know you're not the first person to be worried about getting back into their normal life after life whips a curveball at them."

She and Preston had been together for so long, they'd been almost like an old married couple from the way Declan and Heath described them. I'd only met Preston once before the accident. I lost my parents, but she'd lost her partner. Was it still hard to be without him? Did she still compare everyone to him? When she was with me, was she wishing she was with him? Had she hoped it was his arms around her? His mouth taking hers and plundering the depths of her desire? Had she worried about calling out his name when I sank into her?

Was that why it had been so easy for her to walk away after our amazing night together? Was that why she was here now? Guilt? Or was it money? An overactive Florence Nightingale syndrome?

"Saint Preston. Canonized and memorialized for eternity," I grumbled, staring straight at the cinderblock wall in front of me, determined to get this balancing thing down.

After five failed attempts, one of which nearly sent me flying on top of Imogen, I got up on the balance board. The knee brace caught on the fabric of my sweatpants, tugging them lower with each rock.

"I'm going to pull these up before the ladies over there get even more of a show." Her hands were on my hips, dragging the soft fabric back up my body. At the same time I reached down to grab them.

My hands landed on top of hers where she'd reached out to help with my balance, but her touch was the ultimate distraction. Her long, soft fingers under mine, pressed against my body.

All the balance I'd achieved evaporated. The board went out from under me and my full body weight crashed to the side, taking Imo with me. I turned as I fell, wrapping my arms around her.

We hit the ground with a thud and a bounce. The spongey floor softened the fall, taking the pain I'd anticipated out of the impact.

"Shit, are you okay?" Imo braced her arms on either side of my waist, scooting down my body toward my knee.

The blood rush was so fast and the sweatpants were so baggy, the tent was inevitable. Could I go a damn day without getting an unwanted erection around her? Was I in eighth grade and going through puberty again?

Jesus I needed to get laid.

Jumping up faster than I'd thought possible after my injury, I avoided eye contact and shoved my hands into my pockets, shooting my hips back as the blood finally left my most problematic appendage.

"Why don't we try some different exercises?" Her gaze bounced to every spot in the whole warehouse-sized room that wasn't near me.

She ran me through a series of exercises and drills. The soft, springy action of the floor kept the harsh impact from jarring my joints too much. Sweat poured down both our faces. She was beside me for most of them, pushing me, goading me, taunting me to get my ass in gear and move it. No wonder she was in such amazing shape.

"I've had seventy-year-old grandmas do this faster than you. Get going, Frost."

With flushed cheeks and stray hairs plastered to the side of her face with sweat, Imo gulped from her water bottle, making that reverberating bottomless pit sound people only made when they'd run a 5k with no water. She'd put in just as much work as me throughout the day, never letting me flag or stop pushing myself.

"Have you talked to Liv lately? Or Ford? Everyone always said you two had a bromance for the ages." She stopped tying her laces and she turned her head, looking at me.

"None of your damn business." Not like the guys hadn't already spilled everything they knew like a piñata at a seven-year-old's birthday.

"Come on. Every time the group got together, you two were always like a group within the group. There were more than a few women that summer who wanted to know if you were gay."

My head snapped up. "Glad we were able to entertain."

"Seriously. Why?"

"Ask the guys. They'll fill you in on all the gory details."

"Other than him dating Liv, the apartment, and the unfortunate intimate moment caught on video, everyone is stumped."

"Shouldn't that be enough?" I began counting on my hand. "The sex tape he *let* someone leak online. Not sharing that my sister's apartment burned down, so I showed up to a pile of smoldering rubble and nearly lost my mind. Him banging my sister when he said he'd protect her. Oh, and I know." I raised a final finger high in the air. "Things tend to get tense when a guy bangs your almost-fiancée." I grabbed my towel. "Are we done?" I needed to get out of that place. Throwing open the doors, my chest was tight and it was hard to breathe even out in the midday sun. My stalk off was stopped by her hand wrapping around my arm and yanking me back toward her.

"He what?" Her eyes were wide like high beams in the dead of night. "Why didn't anyone ever say anything about that?"

"No one knows."

"But—how—"

I cut her sputtering off before she hurt herself. "It's a long story."

"And I drove here." She gestured to her car. "Buckle up, buttercup, I've got all day."

With a grimace, I looked down at my phone and back up to her. Shoving it in my pocket, I trudged to her car.

"Wait. Wait. Wait." She waved her hands in front of her. Droplets of ice cream splattered on the table. Covering her mouth with the back of her hand, she shook her head. "She told you when you were down on one knee?"

I sucked down some of my milkshake, not sure I wanted to relive every moment of my humiliation in front of Imogen. My forehead throbbed as I tried to get the extra thick shake through the straw.

"I'm waiting here. You can't end on that kind of cliffhanger." She shoved at my shoulder.

"Better that than at the altar."

"And Ford wasn't going to tell you? He'd have let you marry her."

"He said she came to him all teary-eyed and freaking out, apologizing and saying she'd never do it again."

"Wow." Imogen set down her spoon and sat back in her chair. "I get why he did it."

"Slept with my girlfriend."

Her gaze narrowed. "No, the reason he wasn't going to tell you. He was trying to protect you. Keep that pain from you. No one wants to see someone they care about in pain."

"What about honesty? He'd have just let me marry someone who'd cheat on me like that?"

She opened and closed her mouth. Lifting her spoon, she pointed it at me. "Touché. So why didn't you want anyone to know you were dating her?"

"Sleeping with the daughter of the owners of your biggest rival team isn't the best way to win friends and influence coaches to get your ass off the bench."

"But no one? You didn't introduce her to anyone? She didn't think it was weird she never met any of your friends."

"Everyone was down here and I was up in Boston. It didn't come up."

"Did she meet Liv?"

"Of course."

"Don't 'of course' me. If she'd never met Ford before that night, it's not out of the realm of possibility she'd never met Liv."

"What did Liv think?"

A shrug. "She thought she was nice enough."

"Do you want to know what I think?" Imo leaned in conspiratorially like she was about to let me in on a heist she'd been cooking up for years.

I leaned in closer. "Not really, but I'm thinking you're going to tell—"

"You knew she wasn't right for you. You felt that it was

off and you didn't want to introduce her to everyone because you knew they'd see it too."

"Or maybe I'd subconsciously been worried Ford would bang another woman I was interested in and ruin that relationship too."

"It happened more than once?" Hot fudge trailed across Imo's chin.

"In college. It wasn't a big deal."

"Dude, you have the worst taste in women."

I leveled my gaze at her. "Or friends." Yanking a napkin out of the holder on the table, I handed it over to her and tapped my chin.

"If you thought he was the problem, then why were you still friends with him after?"

Dragging my hands down my face, I stalled.

"My first hockey try out."

Imo looked up from inspecting her napkin to me. "Are you going to make me pry it out of you or will you just spill it?"

"The other players were out for blood. Making the team meant not just a spot, but scholarships for some people. We were kids, but they were playing like 70s enforcer hockey players and I could feel the bruises blooming under my pads as I was pinned to the boards behind the net. Two of them had me up against the wall, and then out of nowhere the crush of the opposing players was gone."

"Ford was there. Threw down his glove and stick and went after both of them. Hitting them with his bare hands, splitting his knuckles on their helmets. Our team had an open net after he cooled off in the penalty box, but we didn't let them score.

"After that, we were inseparable. He took the penalty for me when it could've cost him his scholarship. He had my back no questions asked because he saw what was happening and knew it was messed up. That kind of loyalty doesn't come around often." I gritted my teeth.

"Isn't that the kind of guy you'd want there for your sister?" Imogen reached across the table.

Dodging her grasp, I lifted my shake to take another blood vessel-bursting sip.

With a soured mood that felt like day-old bile, we ended our adventure for the day with her driving me back to my house. Imogen's words clanged in my ears, repeating until they lost their meaning.

'Isn't that the kind of guy you'd want there for your sister?'

"You think I should be fine with my sister being with Ford?" I blurted out so loudly, Imo jerked at the wheel.

"I think she's an adult and knows what's best for herself."

"Do you have a little sister? Have you been the one taking care of her since she was little?" I snapped. "What the hell would you know about it?"

Her face dropped and I felt like an asshole. "You're right. I wouldn't."

She finished the drive in silence. She parked out front, but she didn't turn the car off, and her fingers tensed on the steering wheel, but she didn't say a word.

I let myself out, but had to duck back in to grab my jacket.

"There will come a time that you push people who care away too hard, and you'll have to deal with the consequences." She took off, leaving me standing there on the curb, the door closed by the force of her acceleration, staring after her retreating car.

18

IMO

"We'd love to have you down for an interview sometime next week. Are you sure you want to leave Philadelphia for our location? I'm sure you get much more interesting patients up there."

I closed the break room door. Times like these I wished I had an actual office, but at the Speedman Clinic I'd have one and possibly my own practice less than fifteen minutes from The Surf Shack.

"I have family down there, so it's closer to them." Becca hadn't been coming back as much since she'd started grad school. Fern and Charlie needed my help even more. That had always been the plan—to move down there and help them with the restaurant. A hold over plan from before, but leaving that behind cratered a pit in my stomach.

"If you're sure." The woman on the other end of the line didn't seem even fifty percent sure.

"Completely sure. Let me know the time and date and I'll be there."

After finishing the call, I slipped my phone into my pocket and walked out of the room and directly into a human wall. Ready to lay into the guys for showing up at my job again, I set my face to scowl and my finger to admonishment.

Strong hands grabbed my arms to right me. "Sorry, Imogen. I didn't think you'd come barreling out of there like there was a fire." He tilted to the side and peered into the break room. "There isn't a fire, is there?" The kind crinkle to the familiar blue eyes evaporated the irritation in my stance.

"No, there's no fire. What are you doing here, Reed?"

He dropped his hands from my arms. "I'm here to see you."

"You're back on my roster? I thought we got everything squared away." I walked to the intake station, scanning my files.

"No, I'm fit as a fiddle." He hit his stomach and the resounding smack certainly pointed in that direction.

"Okay, I'm confused. Why are you here to see me? No flare ups or other issues?" Reed was a firefighter who'd ended up on my client list after a two story fall while fighting an apartment building fire earlier in the year.

His mouth opened and closed and opened again with a low sound coming out. He tapped his fist against his open palm, then wiped them on his pants.

"If it's something you want to talk to a male physio—"

He shrugged with his palms out. "I'm here to ask you out."

Stunned, I exhaled a *huh.*

"I've wanted to for a long time, but I didn't want to do it while we were working together and make things weird. But now that I'm one hundred percent and I've got the okay to head back to the firehouse, I didn't want to miss my chance to take you out, if you're interested."

My lips pinched together at the unmistakable squeaking

of roller chairs being repositioned for the show. I wasn't going to look at them and give them the satisfaction of knowing I knew they were listening.

"That's very sweet of you and I'm glad to hear you'll be back on duty. I know you were worried, but I told you you'd get there. You put in the work and look at you now."

"I can tell by how you're avoiding my question what the answer is."

"My side step was that subtle, huh?"

The corners of his eyes crinkled again. He was a teddy bear of a guy, always up for whatever I threw at him and never fought getting back on his feet, unlike another client I'd been dealing with lately.

"It's okay, I won't make you say it. No one can say I didn't give it a shot?"

This was the second person I'd run from in the past forty-eight hours, but this one didn't deserve it. Peeling away from Colm's house as he stood glowering at me hadn't been one of my proudest moments. There was a chasm between us and I didn't know if I wanted to throw a bridge to get to the other side, if all he wanted to do was hack away at the ropes every time I tried. Did I want to bridge the gap? What did that even mean? Being his friend? Being something more? Other than his 'in my face'—literally most of the time, erections, he didn't do much other than bark and snipe at me like an abandoned dog.

"They can't. I'm sorry."

"Don't be. I brought a lemon Bundt cake I baked. Have a great day, ladies." He waved and walked away.

"And he bakes?! Are you out of your mind? How could you not say yes?" Cecily stared at me in disbelief.

"I'm—"

"If you say busy, I'll scream. You're not busy, you're

pathologically averse to fun. Who else picks up extra shifts like she's not working a second job an hour and a half away?"

"I'm finished for the summer."

"Bull-freaking-shit. What's wrong with you? All these hotties that march in here looking for some Imogen loving and you walk away like they're door-to-door salesmen trying to sell you a vacuum."

"I do not. I'm just not up for dating anyone right now."

"How about banging someone? When was your last date? When did you last get laid? There's going to be cobwebs and moths down there, honey."

"I—" My night with Colm had been the last time I'd slept with anyone. The last time I'd even felt like I could sleep with anyone. He made me want it. He made me want him. Like dusting off an old album you'd thought was scratched and ruined, but it played just right when you set the needle down. And now he hated me—or if he didn't, he was doing an exceptional job of pretending.

Working with him was harder than I expected. I was affected by him in a way I'd thought had been a one-time deal. A night of craziness, but now it was spilling over into my days. The rest of the day passed without any more date invitations, but even more glowering from Cecily. What would she say if she knew I'd gone home with the guy from the bar that night?

The afternoon slipped by in a flurry of paperwork, free weights and padded physiotherapy tables.

My phone buzzed in my bag on my way out to my car. The screen lit up with Fern's name. I jabbed 'accept' and shoved the phone up to my ear. "Fern, what's going on? Is everything okay?"

"Calm down, Imogen. Everything's fine. We're in the city

for a meeting and wanted to take you out to dinner. Are you home?"

"No, I'm not there yet. I'm just leaving work."

"You're just leaving now? So late?"

"Some of my appointments ran over." And I'd taken over half the shift of one of the physiotherapists who'd had to leave early because her kid was sick.

"I can meet you. Just give me the address."

Finding a spot a block away from the Italian restaurant, Tavola, I stepped out of the car and zipped up my jacket. The month was cooling off quicker than usual. It would be a rough winter.

Walking inside, I waved to Fern and Charlie and slipped past the hostess. The two were already seated at a table.

"Why didn't you guys tell me you were coming in? I'd have made reservations for us." I picked up the menu.

"We can handle a dinner reservation on our own." Fern patted my hand.

"How are you? You look tired." Charlie peered at me over his menu, earning a swat from Fern.

"You never say that to a woman," Fern chided.

"It's true. She looks like she'll fall face first into her pasta, if we keep her up too late." He winked at me.

I laughed and went back to scanning the menu. "It's been a busy few weeks."

"And here we thought you'd get a break once the summer was over." Fern sipped her water and stared at me with concern in her eyes.

"How are the repairs and refurbishment going?"

"The usual. Contractors are doing their best to slow things down, but everything is moving along." Charlie slipped his reading glasses into his jacket.

"What meeting were you at up here?"

"It was a meeting with a developer, actually."

My hand slipped off my glass of water, nearly toppling it over. "Developer."

"Remember, we said some people were poking around over the summer? They wanted us to come up to a meeting and we wanted an excuse to see you, so we decided to come."

"How did the presentation go?"

"They're not the right people to take over the Shack." Fern looked up from her menu.

Relief washed over me and I could breathe again.

"I won't say it wasn't tempting, but we've put a lot of work into that place."

"I know you two are stressed about handling things on your own, so I wanted to let you know I'm interviewing for a position at the Speedman Clinic that's opening next year."

"You'd want to leave Philly?" Fern looked shocked and a touch sad.

"It's closer to the shore. Closer to you two, if you needed anything."

"Don't uproot yourself just for us."

"There's not much to uproot." I smiled and shrugged. "It's just me."

The two of them exchanged looks. Our server came and took our orders, and we moved on to chatting about plans for next summer, whether they were going to do their road trip, and when Becca would be back in town.

"If we're lucky, we'll get her to come for Thanksgiving. She's being stubborn about the flights and she doesn't want us to pay for them."

"She'll find a way."

The food was divine. Everything was fresh and flavorful. I packed away way more than I should have. It took all my willpower not to lick the alfredo sauce off the plate. So tempting. The server had had to practically peel my fingers off the dish as I'd reached up to mop up the last of the sauce with my bread when he'd removed my plate.

"Seems you were hungry." Charlie finished his coffee.

I polished off the slice of tiramisu Fern and I had shared. "I guess I was. My appetite has been all over the place lately, maybe this was my body resetting."

Fern rested her hand against my cheek as we stood outside the restaurant.

"You need more rest."

"I know. I swear, I'm getting good sleep. I'm not partying."

Her lips pursed and I could tell she wanted to launch into a mom monologue. Not that I would've been upset to get one, but all that pasta had sent me hurtling toward hibernation.

"As soon as I get home, it's straight into the shower and then bed for me. Don't worry. You two have a safe drive back. I swear, I'm fine."

She hugged me. "You know we worry."

"I know. I'm sorry."

"Don't be sorry. No amount of reassurance will ever keep even that tiny hint of worry away. It's life in the big city, kid." Charlie hugged me and ruffled my hair.

"Drive safely and drop us a message once you get home."

"I will."

The drive to my place didn't take long. Once I was locked inside, I did exactly as I'd told them and crawled into bed with my hair still wet.

The more time I spent with Colm, the more vivid my dreams were. He was getting harder to resist, and his surly brooding did little to stop the magnetized attraction I hadn't been able to shake. But Colm was a problem that I'd have to deal with tomorrow, because tonight, I needed sleep.

After a quick text to Fern, I pulled the sheets up and let sleep claim me within seconds. There was no time to think of Colm or anything else except for the dreams.

19

COLM

I stood outside of the rink with my arms locked across my chest. "What was our deal?"

She looked at me over the roof of the car. "You said no ice."

"I meant no skates. No rink."

"Specifics are important. Let's go." She cocked her head toward the nondescript white block building. "Or are you afraid the hobo chic look you've got going on will get too mussed?"

"I didn't even know these places still existed. The last time I was at one of these was Jenny Stevens' twelfth birthday party." I shoved sweaty palms into my pockets.

The half derelict sign of Roll With It Skate World loomed overhead.

"It'll be fun."

I shot her a look.

"It's part of our agreed workout this week. How about that? You said do your worst, so it's not like you didn't ask for it."

My palms were sweaty and my stomach rolled with each step closer to the doors.

I pulled open the door, and the pungent smell of middle school pepperoni pizza, worn leather, and feet hit me with a blast from the past. The crisp coldness and unmistakable hum of the Zamboni was absent. This wasn't a hockey rink. No ice here. Tension melted away with only a small nudge of my gut, rather than the threatening dry heave that had been kicking at the back of my throat from the second I'd opened the car door. That counted as a step in the right direction.

"You know what that smells like?" She turned to me with a wide smile. The corners of her eyes crinkled like she was a second from a laugh.

More of the tension rolled off my shoulders. "Athlete's foot and a Costco sized box of Pepto Bismol?"

"Fun. Do you remember what that is?" She walked backward, beckoning me forward like she was pulling an imaginary rope.

"Doesn't ring any bells." I crossed my arms over my chest.

Her playfulness and wide smile were so different than most of the times I'd seen her before. She was usually more solemn, her small smile and low words meant to put everyone else at ease as she moved around the room checking in on them each in turn. Even that first time I'd seen her in the hospital, standing in front of Heath and Declan with her arm in a sling and a nasty bruise across her collarbone, she'd leaned in and whispered something to them that I couldn't hear. But their eyes had widened and their choked laughter echoed in the sterile hallway.

She was injured and she'd wanted to make them laugh. Our eyes had locked as she'd looked from side to side, probably checking for someone coming to bust them for having fun in a hospital.

But this Imogen was different. Was this just how she was with all her clients? Loud and boisterous to help them feel less self-conscious? Or was this the real Imogen, with all the pain stripped away?

"Let's go." She tugged on the sleeve of my shirt and I let her pull me along.

We gave the bored teenager in the black and white striped ref shirt our shoe sizes and he handed us two pairs of thirty-year-old skates.

I grabbed both sets of skates, clenching them in my hands to keep them from shaking. My lips and throat were dry. I felt like I hadn't had a drink in days.

"We'll take it slow. I don't expect you to do any grapevines out there."

"Wow, I haven't heard that one in a long time." Some of the tension eased out of my grip. It wasn't until then that I felt Imogen tugging at her pair of skates.

"Sit." She patted the spot beside her on the molded bench with chipped orange coating.

She nudged me, finishing up her laces. The disco lights whirled over the rink and top 40 hits from three decades ago blared through the sound system.

"Let's go, Frost. Get your ass out there."

"And when I bite it and fuck up my knee again, then I'll finally catch a break?"

"Says the trust fund baby with friends and family around him."

"With the dead parents."

"Ditto and throw in a dead fi—boyfriend to boot. You're not milking the sympathy teat anymore. Get the hell up." Her natural ease disappeared and her gaze narrowed.

I glanced over my shoulder, expecting the bucket of ice water. "Let's get this over with."

She ran me through exercises I didn't even know were possible on skates. Again, she tested my balance with single leg movements made trickier by the weight of the roller skate.

Sweat rolled down my back and I glared at her, equally sweaty, bent over and resting her hands on her knees.

"Wasn't there supposed to be some fun in there?"

"You pissed me off, so there's no fun right now."

"Listen, I'm sorry." I skated closer, and she straightened, her defenses up.

I grabbed my ear and tugged on the lobe. "I was an asshole earlier and I'm sorry. You're only trying to help."

Her head jerked back like she'd expected me to knock her over instead of offering an apology.

"Every time I try to talk to you a wall shoots up, except unlike other people's walls it's got rusty spikes with mangled corpses already impaled on them."

"That was vivid."

"You make an impression."

We slowly skated to the half wall around the rink, closer to the day-old popcorn and week-old pizza smell.

"Did you ever think maybe taking the rest of the world on your shoulders is too much pressure for one person?" Imo cocked an eyebrow at me.

"Have *you*? You're here with me, right now, when you could be doing hundreds of other things."

She shrugged. "Not really. If I see a place where I can help, I can't not do it."

I was a compulsion—her inability to walk away from a charity case, no matter how much of a lost cause. Was that the only reason she was here? "Why—"

The doors to the rink burst open and three harried looking adults were followed in by a swarm of kids at least forty deep.

"Field trip. Remember those days?" Imogen smiled at me, hopping up on the rink wall. A real smile this time, not the fake, polite one she'd perfected.

"Those were great times. When the biggest worry was whether or not you'd get to sit next to your best friend or your crush on the bus."

"And you looked forward to pizza day like the best day ever." Her gaze followed the kids as they streaked from the skate counter to the benches. "Things were so much easier back then."

The arrival of a squadron of middle schoolers sent the volume and energy through the roof. Every inch of the rink wall was taken over either by kids clomping in skates, or others whipping around like they'd been born wearing them. It was hard to remember being that young and full of energy. Imogen and I skated slowly, our workout finished, but for some reason we stayed, skating side by side and sometimes singing along with the songs. She knew all the words and so did I. It reminded me of that night on the beach. We could've stayed for hours going through track after track.

A kid sped by and clipped me on his way down, landing with his legs sliding in opposite directions. He bit it hard. Imo and I winced at the *thunk* of his head against the floor. He lay there, staring up at the disco ball decorated ceiling like the floor would open up and swallow him.

"It happens to everyone." Tugging on the leg of my pants, I clenched my jaw, waiting for the shooting pain through my knee. But none came as I crouched beside him, and my skates cooperated and didn't send my ass to the ground. There wasn't any pain, only tightness like an old creaky gate that needed oil. It was like the pain was a habit, my natural expectation that overwhelmed this lesser feeling.

"Is she looking over here?" he whispered out of the side of his mouth.

"Who am I looking for?"

"She's wearing a pink sweater with a bow on the shoulder and she's got black hair like the night's sky."

This kid had it bad. Imogen stood beside me trying to hold in her laughter.

"The night sky, huh?" I scanned the girls along the wall. One girl's gaze kept darting toward our road kill impersonator.

"She looks worried about you, but she's trying to play it cool."

The entire top half of his body shot off the floor. "She is?"

I dropped to my ass on the floor, blocking their view of each other. "She was, but you can't spaz out and run over there. You were trying to impress her with some tricks."

He drew his knees up, wrapping his arms around them. "I thought if I could skate fast around the whole rink and beat the eighth-grade boys that she'd notice me. Now she probably thinks I'm a loser."

Hadn't we all been there? "She doesn't think you're a loser, but if you're trying to impress her, maybe you should talk to her. Throw out that night sky line. Ladies love it when you don't care what anyone else thinks and especially when you compliment them."

"They do?" He looked from me to Imogen for confirmation.

She bent at the waist, bracing her hands above her knees. Her skates wobbled. "They definitely do."

The kid bounced back up and dusted himself off, peering around me to check on whether the coast was clear.

We skated side by side, keeping the steady pace to the beat of the 90s music blasting through the speakers.

"You're pretty good with kids."

I shrugged. "I had to be. You try herding ten girls at a sleepover after someone suggested playing Bloody Mary. Or being the chaperone at a school trip to the aquarium with the known runner from the class."

"Liv was lucky to have you, growing up."

My shoulders did their involuntary thing. "Someone had to do it, but that's not me anymore. I can do whatever the fuck I want."

She zoomed ahead and spun around, skating backward.

"Show off."

Her lips twitched. "What *do* you want? Because the *crazy guy in a bathrobe* routine you were pulling didn't scream 'living his best life.'"

"There's a lot of sh—" We passed the middle schoolers sitting along the rink wall, kicking their skates against the concrete. "Stuff going on."

"All the boozing, sleeping, and not showering is taking up most of your time? Let me see you do another lap." Her body swayed as she took the turn like she'd been on skates her whole life. She raised her arms over her head and spun in a circle, shaking her hips from side to side like she was trying to show me what life had to offer. The whole physiotherapist-therapist act was getting on my nerves. Every opportunity to bring up what had happened between us was shut down immediately.

"It's been an adjustment—not playing."

"A temporary blip. You're making great progress after only three sessions. Imagine what would be possible if you'd sprung for more?" Her eyebrow lifted and she switched from in front to beside me.

And that worried me. If I was completely recovered, as much as you could be with the repaired bone, regrown cartilage and muscle with screws holding it all together, then what excuse did I have? If I ran out of excuses, she'd have me in the parking lot of the practice rink with everyone staring at me expectantly as I puked behind the garbage cans at the entrance and destroyed the last bit of dignity I had left.

Walking in here had been a test of my abilities.

The keys jingled as I tugged them out of the front door. Walking into Colm's house felt as natural as walking into my own apartment now. His threats to find my set of keys hadn't been followed up with anything. We crept toward an uneasy truce even though neither of us was sure where the line was. There were land-mines everywhere—not just his, but mine too.

Every so often, I'd call him out for pushing everyone away. That always seemed to sour his mood.

And he'd hone in on my lack of social life or snipe when I brought up Preston, like the comment was an ugly reminder of something he'd rather forget.

One that soured the mood for both of us was talking about the future. Our interactions were rooted firmly in the present.

Colm's footsteps thudded on the carpeted stairs.

"What the hell did you do?" I kicked the door closed behind me.

He froze mid-step with his eyes wide, looking down at his legs. "Nothing?"

"Then why are you walking like that?"

"Like what?" He came down the last two steps.

"You're pulling your gait to the right. When you came down the steps your body was angled."

He ducked his head.

"Downstairs now." I pointed toward the door off the kitchen.

After session four he'd revealed he had a full gym and physio set up in his basement.

The room didn't smell stale like the first time I'd come down here with him. It was warmer and the distinct smell of sweat hung in the air. He'd been working out.

"Hop up on the table." I patted the blue padded table before going to wash my hands.

"Really, I'm fine."

"Easy way." I grabbed a paper towel drying off my hands. "Or the hard way."

"The joy you take in inflicting pain could make you some serious money, if you didn't have an aversion to black leather."

"How'd you know that's how I get my dates?" Overall, our time together had gotten less contentious, and we could make jokes. He was cooperating more and my stomach no longer knotted before each session preparing for the wrath of Colm. But in some ways that made things harder. When we slipped into this easy teasing banter, the whole reason we were spending time together got harder to remember.

Help him recover. Get him back on the ice. Get Terry her donation. Move to the shore.

"Had many lately?"

I wrapped my hands around his calf, bending his leg at the knee and pushing it toward his chest.

"How many what?" His movements tracked tight to one

side. Too much stress could force overcompensation and strain, if I didn't work that out.

"Dates."

A huff of a laugh burst free from my lips. "No, definitely not."

"You're more of a love them and leave them type, huh?" He maintained his teasing tone, but there was an edge to those words.

"There's always a lot going on. I've been helping Fern and Charlie with the Surf Shack. It doesn't leave a lot of time for a social life. What about you? Are you feeling up for dates?" I rotated his hip, keeping my gaze trained on his knee and not the basketball shorts with a wide open view of his package.

"Dates haven't been on my list of shit to do for the past few months."

"Why not? Now that we've gotten you out of your house, you should try to get back to normal. Go out and have fun. Not too much fun though. Roll onto your side."

He rolled over, breaking his unrelenting gaze. Now that it wasn't filled with animosity and defiance, it was harder to meet it.

Those feelings I'd thought were a fluke or a work of my imagination came roaring back when he looked at me like that. The same way he'd looked at me on the beach and the same way he'd looked at me before I'd drifted off to sleep during our night together. This Colm was dangerous to the tidy plan of my life.

"Make sure your brace is tight enough the next time you do the leg presses. You'll overcompensate and get the stiffness you're feeling now."

"I figured it was soreness because I'd been sitting on my ass for the past few months."

"A little of both, but you need to make sure you're protecting it. Next time you work out, maybe we can video chat to check on your form."

"Or you can come over the next time. If you're not too busy. Nevermind, that was—"

"Of course I will. As long as it's after six during the week. And my weekends are freer now that the Shack is officially in renovation and repair mode."

"How about tomorrow night?"

"That's a perfect idea. Although—if you're dead set on working out, we can do that, but there's this club I thought you might like." I'd push this baby bird out of the nest and back into his life if it was the last thing I did.

His head snapped up and he nodded before I finished. "A club? What club?"

I steered the conversation away from specifics I hadn't figured out yet. I'd have to make some calls, but he didn't seem opposed. That was progress. "Favorite album?" Colm grunted as I drove my elbow into his thigh. The muscle had seized up. Not-so-gentle pressure was a way to release that tension, and keeping him talking without time to think about it would help.

"Don't laugh, but it's the live version of John Mayer's first album. I probably gave my computer thirty viruses to get an actual copy of that one. What about you?"

"The one they aired at like 11am with the white Christmas lights?"

"Yes." He winced when I was a bit overly enthusiastic with my fingers. "No one ever remembers that one."

"He had an infectious energy."

Colm's list of favorite albums matched up well with mine. All the emotional stuff Preston had listened to for my sake, Colm had no trouble admitting he'd crank up the radio and sing it out in the car while drumming on the dashboard.

Our conversation drifted from one place to another.

"You don't have an issue driving all the way down there once a week in shore traffic?"

"I'm used to it at this point. I've been doing it for almost four years. When I went back to school it was easier because I only had one class during the summer to speed up my graduation. It's a little trickier juggling it now."

"So why do you do it?"

"Fern and Charlie are family. They need me."

"You guys are that close, even after…"

"We were close, even before. When my parents died freshman year of college, I was a zombie for a bit. They helped me figure out all the financial stuff. Met with my advisors and handled the funeral. Not many eighteen-year-olds know what the hell they're doing when it comes to choosing their classes, let alone burying two parents."

"I'm glad you had someone there for you. I can't imagine what it must have been like to go through it alone."

"I wasn't. I had Fern and Charlie." They'd stepped in as my surrogate parents immediately, never asking for anything in return. "And Preston." He'd been there to hold me when I felt like the world was turning upside down, and to show me that I hadn't died along with my parents. No one had been there to hold me after he was gone.

"It sounds like they were the perfect team to get you through that." His fingers brushed against mine. It wasn't an accidental touch. There'd been more of those lately. Picking a piece of lint off my scrubs, even invitations for a drink after we finished a session, but that danced tantalizingly close to a line I didn't want to cross. He was a temptation unlike any

I'd met before, and I couldn't let myself entertain the thought of giving in.

"Yeah, they were. You had your own power team too."

This connection between us was hard to keep at bay. Our lives kept intersecting, bringing us to one another when we needed each other most. I wasn't sure what that meant. And I wasn't sure where we went from here. We'd gone from our night together to what we were doing now, and then there was the question of what came after, if anything even did. If everything worked out as I'd planned, I'd be moving. He'd be on the road playing hockey. Maybe all we were meant to have were these brief path crossings when we truly needed them.

"The guys were great." His jaw tightened. "Especially Ford. He helped a lot in those early years. His mom too. They were my surrogate family."

I wouldn't push the topic with him. He needed to fit those pieces together and let go of this box he'd put Liv in. It was the only way their relationship could be mended and his friendship with Ford put back on solid ground.

"How's your leg feeling now?"

He straightened and bent it. "The muscles hurt like hell, but it's not tight like before."

"It's my superpower."

He looked at me with his hands braced on the side of the physiotherapist table. "It's not your only one."

"Enough chit chat, let's get going." I clapped my hands together, rubbing them. "Do you want to try the treadmill?" Innuendo dodge success.

His jaw ticked and he nodded, grabbing the skates off the shelf. The specialty treadmill made for hockey players had blown me away when I'd first stepped into the gym. It was a behemoth, outfitted with a specialty tread to allow the user to skate like they were on the ice.

After nearly an hour of drills on the treadmill sweat was rolling down his back, but there wasn't a huff or puff from him. "You've got great stamina. It looks like you could do this for days. How do you feel?"

"It feels like old times." His smile turned my knees into jelly.

"Let's get you off." My cheeks flamed and Colm tripped on the treadmill, grabbing onto the metal bars to steady himself. "Off the treadmill," I shouted way too loudly in the basement gym. "And see how you feel after a short break." I tapped at the buttons on the display screen to bring the treadmill to a crawl with my entire face lobster red.

Colm side-stepped off with no problems, teetering on the blade of his skates before sitting on the bench beside it with his gaze trained on me the whole time.

Deflect and avert. "At this rate, you'll be back ready to go in a couple weeks. Hell, *now*. We can call Bailey." I was almost giddy in anticipation of him skating again. Really skating, not this basement approximation. Once he was beside the guys on the ice with the crowds cheering his name, he'd see how far he'd come.

We'd done it.

Mopping at his forehead with a towel, he dropped it down beside him. "I can't skate."

"Colm, we just proved it." I held out my hand toward the treadmill he'd dominated for an hour. "You can. You're as close to one hundred percent as you can get without dragging out a microscope and inspecting your individual cells."

"It's not that I don't want to." He hung his head. "I can't."

"When you say *can't*—"

"I mean anytime I try to enter a rink, I start shaking and

feel like I'm dying and puke—in the nearest trashcan if I'm lucky."

Everything clarified like slipping on a brand new pair of glasses. 20/20 vision. He hadn't been avoiding the ice at all. "You've been trying to skate?"

"Every couple weeks I'll think, maybe I'm good now. Maybe I can power through. And then I end up with my head in a trashcan covered with chewed gum and cigarette butts."

"Have you tried—"

"I've gone to different rinks. I've gone at different times of day. I've eaten something before. I've not eaten anything before. Let me tell you, dry heaving isn't fun. Good for the abs, but not fun. I've gone stone cold sober. I've taken a taxi and gone blitzed out of my mind. Every time it's the same damn song."

My heart ached for him. It wasn't that he was being a stubborn asshole, at least not in this area. He'd been trying. I couldn't imagine wanting something so badly, trying it over and over, and failing every time at the one thing your life has revolved around for so long.

"Do the guys know?"

He met my gaze with an 'are you fucking kidding me' look.

"Stupid question." I lifted my hand to touch his shoulder, but pulled back at the last second. "Why don't you tell them?"

"That I'm so fucked up in the head I can't even get on the ice?"

"What do you think they'd do, if you told them?"

"Anything they could to fix it. But what if they can't? What if no one can?" The words were small and full of anguish.

I wrapped my arms around his shoulders, not able to stand by and do nothing as he revealed something so painful and raw. "If you don't try, then what? What's the alternative, Colm? What regret do you want to live with? That you did everything in your power to make it happen and it didn't work, or that you never tried?"

He turned his head, his lips inches from mine.

A shuddering breath rippled through me. The memory of those lips on mine flashed through my mind. I dropped my arms and stepped back.

Why was touching him all over to work on his problem areas so easy? Digging my elbow into his upper thigh until he groaned or setting his knee on my shoulder and pushing his leg forward with my body weight, no problem. But a hand on the shoulder for comfort or a hug, and my body coiled like a snake ready to strike. Like one non-professional touch would be the kerosene-soaked rag on the embers of the attraction between us.

21

COLM

J amming the phone against my ear, I turned my back to the crowd, not feeling in the partying mood. "This is where we're having our PT session?" I stood outside the velvet rope of a club with a line stretched around the block. When she'd given me the location, I'd thought there was a gym or something in the area.

"I told you we were switching things up."

"I figured you meant swimming or something."

"My cab is a block away. Just stay there." She ended the call before I could tell her I'd meet her back at my place.

In fact, I'd love to meet her at my place. Open a bottle of wine, put on a movie neither of us would be watching after the first few minutes and do our own cardio in my bedroom.

The taxi screeched up to the curb and Imogen chucked a few bills into the front seat before hopping out like she thought she'd have to tackle me in the street.

If I'd been chewing gum I'd have choked on it. This outfit showcased a side of Imogen I'd never seen. Her long legs stretched up to the shimmery purple hem of a dress with a halter top showing off her collarbones. The shiny material skimmed her thighs and I couldn't drag my gaze away from her legs. Black ankle boot heels elongated them even more. I was seconds away from drumming on the roof of the taxi to get us out of here and back to my place.

"Thank god, I swore I'd have to chase you down once you realized this was a club."

I gently shook my head to break the trance she'd put me in. I'd seen her naked, felt her naked, but seeing her like this made me want to bundle her up, take her home, and show her off all at the same time.

"You could've given me a heads-up."

"If I'd done that, I'd be standing here all on my own."

"How'd you know I'd dress for the occasion?"

"When aren't you dressed like you're headed to an Abercrombie fashion shoot?" She dragged her fingers down the buttons of my black pea coat and pointed to my shoes.

"And I have a bag of clothes to change into." I gestured to the duffle on my shoulder.

"Even your shitty gym bag is cover model-worthy. Is that Italian leather?" She tugged at the strap over my shoulder. "Don't worry about it. I have a friend on the inside. Well, the outside actually." She winked and took my hand, leading us to the front of the line.

"Murray, I'm calling in that favor."

The burly bouncer with a face made of ninety percent scowl brightened like a kid on Christmas morning the second he spotted Imogen.

His gaze swept up and down her body appreciatively. I clenched my fists at my side.

"Imogen, looking good." They slapped hands and went in for a hug like guys at the gym.

"I clean up every so often."

He chuckled. "Yes, you do. I can't believe this is what you look like out of scrubs."

"Not every day, but tonight's special." She peered over her shoulder, grabbed my hand and tugged me forward.

"Ah, flexing those connections, huh? You're a lucky guy." He extended his hand to me and as much as I didn't want to shake it, I did. "This woman is a miracle worker. Got me back on the door after a couple months of sessions last year."

"How's everything feeling?" She leaned in closer like she could see through the jacket he wore.

"Don't worry, I've been good and doing my exercises every day." He rotated his shoulder, making his bicep bulge against a suit jacket that looked a breath away from exploding like a Hulk comic.

"Stop by if you need a tune-up at some point."

"Will do, Imogen. Head in, I'll let them know you're coming and see if we can get you a table." He lifted the black velvet rope and another bouncer held open the door to let us into the wall of sound masquerading as a club. I pretended not to notice either of them checking out her ass as we walked past. She had no idea what she did to men around her. How could she be completely oblivious to the fact that most would go toe to toe for a dance with her?

But I was here with her tonight. PT session or not, it was my hand on the small of her back, guiding her through the crowds.

She looked over her shoulder with a wide smile, quelling my apprehension.

"What exactly are we doing here?" I raised my voice over the driving music.

"You'll see."

Someone met us at the end of the long hallway and guided us to a row of booths, pointing us to one and plucking the reserved sign off the center.

A waitress came over and Imo ordered us both Shirley Temples.

"I don't get to order my own drink?"

"No. You've had enough to last you for three lifetimes, and I am abstaining because it's a dick move to drink in your friend's face when they're making healthy choices."

"Forcing me into social situations without even the courtesy of lube."

"Caught red-handed. You've been avoiding people. What better test than the crush of human peacocking that is a club."

"You're well versed in club culture?"

"It's fun to people watch."

"I could say the same thing about you."

"What?"

"That you avoid social situations. I'd have thought you'd have shown up in your scrubs."

She ran a hesitant hand over her dress. "I...I didn't think they'd let me in if I did."

So she'd entertained wearing her normal work wear to her not-date with me at a club. "It looks good on you."

Her cheeks flushed. "Thank you. Are you ready to dance?"

Surprised rocked my face. "You want to dance."

"I said nothing about me. I said you. I'll need to keep an eye on your form." Imo looked around. "How about her? Excuse me." She touched the elbow of a woman passing by.

The redhead looked from me to Imogen, her look of

confusion turning to a smile as she raked her gaze up and down my body, stopping on my watch. Were those dollar signs flashing in her eyes? "Yes." She leaned in closer.

"My friend was looking for a dance partner and I thought maybe you'd help him get comfortable out there."

The woman's smile widened.

My blood boiled and my heartrate skyrocketed at being pawned off on some random. Here I'd thought maybe Imogen had had a breakthrough of some sort, the same kind she'd been forcing onto me, but no. Now she was literally looking for someone to rub against me like I gave one shit about being here aside from being here with her.

"Excuse me." I ushered Imogen away before she could break out the sneeze-guard for the Colm buffet.

Finding the closest thing to a quiet spot, I cornered her, my gaze drilling into hers. "Why did you invite me here?"

"We're trying something new."

"Why did you invite me here?"

"To help you have some fun." The corner of her mouth ticked up.

My pulse was throbbing double-time in my ears. "Why did you invite me here?"

The veneer dropped. She dragged her fingers through her hair. "I'm trying to get you back to the old Colm. I want you to see you're still that same guy."

"But I'm not. The old me wouldn't have seen the viper that woman was."

"She seemed perfectly nice."

"And how would you know? She's a complete stranger in a crowded room with dim lighting. Maybe she's a terrible person who cheats on her taxes and steals candy from babies. Maybe she's on the run from the cops. Maybe she jams her finger into the 'close door' button when someone's racing to the elevator.

"The old Colm would've pushed down those warning bells clanging in my ears and looked for her positives. I'd have discounted anything that happened to reinforce what my subconscious was screaming at me by painting a pretty picture of her in my head. Maybe I'd have danced with her tonight, taken her to bed and then out to breakfast the next morning. All the while, creating this fantasy in my head of a perfect life we could have."

Imogen swallowed so loudly I swore I could hear it over the driving music.

"Do you want to know how I know these things?"

One nod.

"Because old Colm did that four times. And I got cheated on each time. Falling for the easy made life a lot harder. But I'm not old fucking Colm anymore. My eyes are open and I'm tired of playing pretend. I'm not the responsible older brother waiting in the wings to swoop in to save Liv. I'm ready to live my life on my terms. I know who I am. And I know who she is and I'm not interested." I braced my arms on either side of her head.

"You don't have to think the worst of everyone. I'm sure there's someone out there who'll be the right one."

"Are you tired of pretending, Imogen?"

Her mouth opened and closed. "I don't know what you mean."

"Bullshit. Are you tired of being this Imogen? The one who's always here for everyone else. Who gives and gives so it's easier to curl up in bed at night and forget. To fade in the blissful darkness of sleep because you're on empty after siphoning off every bit of yourself to everyone all day every day."

"I—"

"It's easier to forget the pain when you're so tired you can barely feel your feet anymore."

"It's not like that." She dropped her gaze.

"Then how is it? Who pushed you, Imo? Who forced you to go back to being the old Imogen?" I ran my finger under her chin, forcing her to meet my gaze.

She licked her lips. "She's gone."

"And so is the old Colm. Who I was then is gone. Just like old you is gone. Show me the new you. Not the woman who takes care of everyone until there's nothing left of her. Show me who you are, Imogen."

"I don't know who I am."

"Then let me help you find her." My lips crashed down on hers.

Her hands shot up to either side of my head, holding me in place as though I could go anywhere.

My hungry, unquenchable need for her overwhelmed me. We were lips, tongues, and teeth trying to peel away the confusion and ache that could only be sated by one another.

I lifted her leg, hooking it high on my hip. My erection ground against the thin fabric separating us. This wasn't quiet, polite, or advisable. We were in a crowded club in a spot barely dark enough for what we were doing, but I didn't care.

The heat at the apex of her thighs ratcheted up the throbbing of my dick. Tonight, I wasn't letting her put that distance between us.

She ground herself against me, locking her leg up even higher and tighter around me. Her moans were swallowed by deepening the kiss. My fingers gripped the hair at the base of her neck.

I rocked my hips against her and in one spectacular

display, she wrapped her arms even tighter around the back of my neck, crying out with her release against my lips.

With glassy eyes, she looked at me with shock painted across her face.

Taking her hand, I pecked her on her lips. "Let's go."

22

COLM

The way she bit her bottom lip while sitting in the back of the taxi sent my heart thundering against my ribs, trying to make a quick escape out the window. She was going through all those thoughts blinking like big caution signs on a dark night saying 'No, don't do this. It's irresponsible. Here are twenty-seven reasons this is a bad idea.' I didn't want to be a bad idea or a mistake in her mind. She sure as hell wasn't one in mine.

Tugging her toward me until she was nearly sitting on my lap, I sealed her parted lips mid-gasp with a kiss. Threading my fingers through her hair, I let my tongue dance along her lips, before delving inside.

I slipped my hand along the side of her thigh, squeezing her supple flesh. Sliding my hand higher, I traced the edges of her panty line with the tips of my fingers.

She moaned into my mouth and I swallowed down her passion, wishing the club had been a hell of a lot closer to my house.

My fingers crept higher, hooking along the thin elastic running along her hip.

Her fingers tightened on the front of my shirt, bunching the fabric between her fingers as her lips hungrily swept over mine. Our tongues danced like our bodies would once we got out of this fucking taxi.

I dragged the fabric down over her hip and swung her legs over mine, lifting her ass off the seat for only a second, but long enough to swoop her panties down over her ass in one smooth motion.

She yelped and broke our kiss, staring back at me wide-eyed.

"Something wrong?" I dragged the fabric held between my fingers down her legs painstakingly slowly, teasing her with each delicious inch.

Her gaze darted to the driver and back to me as her fingers wrapped around my wrist.

My other hand cupped her ass and massaged the supple flesh I couldn't wait to fully explore when we got into my house.

"Don't worry. I'll keep these safe for you." I tugged the panties over the curve of her knee and down over her shoes in one smooth motion.

The taxi driver cleared her throat.

I released my hold on her and shoved the fabric into my pocket.

Now, her pink cheeked glances and slightly mussed hair were a testament to how far away I'd pushed those thoughts out of her mind. That, along with her fingers intertwined with mine. Her pulse drumming against my palm.

She had no trouble putting her hands all over me during one of our sessions, but could still be shy about us exploring one another's bodies. It was an exploration I wouldn't be finished with until I'd committed each inch of her to memory and could discover which spots made her gasp, whimper, and moan.

Her gaze kept darting to the tent in my pants.

"At this point, I'd think you'd be used to it."

With a hasty cash tip to the driver, I hustled Imo out of the taxi.

We burst through the front door like a zombie horde was following us through the streets.

With a mischievous grin over her shoulder, Imogen danced outside of my grasp.

Her laugh made me smile as she took off up the stairs, shedding clothes along the way. I gathered up each piece like the world's most tempting breadcrumbs.

A heel, then another.

Her soft black wrap.

The perfectly formed cups of her light gray bra hung on the railing at the top of the stairs.

I stood silently, trying to find her. She was a stripping Houdini.

Her dress, the one that fit her perfectly, in a heap on the floor in the center of the living room.

My blood thrummed in my veins, pounding harder with each step. I'd been a whisper of fabric away from being inside her less than an hour ago and I was ravenous for her touch.

And that's when I remembered. The bright blue, lacy fabric in my pocket.

She was totally naked.

"Did you want a drink? I was thirsty after that long drive." She stood behind my bar with two glasses held up to her chest like that could hide the unblemished expanse of skin on display. A simple gold chain around her neck was the only thing adorning her body. My mouth watered.

Her smile was barely contained, her shoulders gently shook, fingers flexing against the glass bumping against the surface of the bar.

"Sure, I'll take one, but let me get one of the tumblers from the bottom shelf."

She lifted the carton of juice and tried to take a step back as I crowded her space, but I grabbed onto her butt, pulling her closer and sliding one of the glasses out, rubbing myself against her as I rose.

A perfect gasp shot from her chest and some of the juice spilled, rolling through the valley of her breasts and cascading down her skin.

I licked the sweet syrup off her stomach, before grabbing her leg and hiking it over my shoulder.

She was open to me, wet and ready to be devoured and I was happy to oblige.

With the first lick and suck, she yelped out a curse and grabbed onto the bar.

Cupping her ass, I licked my way down the seam of her pussy. She tasted as good as I remembered. I wanted every last drop.

She tightened her fingers in my hair, tugging at the roots so hard, I could practically hear it being ripped out, but that only spurred me harder. Faster. To give her more to make those cries from her lips even better.

"Please." A keening whine entered her voice. She threw her head back.

I slipped two fingers inside, not bothering to tease her. Plunging them deep I curled them, searching for the spot to make her knees weak.

My cock punched angrily against the front of my jeans, ready to get in on the action, ready for a repeat of our first night together, but I wasn't stopping until she came, no matter how much blood rushed to my dick. Hopefully I wouldn't have to break out the scissors to cut these damned jeans off me.

"Please don't stop, Colm." No doubt in my mind who she was talking to. She tilted her head forward and stared into my eyes. Hers were clear blue and swimming with heady desire and unbridled passion. And I wanted every bit of it.

With a languid tug from my lips, I moved my mouth in unison with my fingers to give her the pleasure she deserved.

Her jaw dropped and her eyes rolled back. Every muscle in her body went rigid, but I held on tight, letting her ride out the cresting wave of her orgasm.

My fingers were kneading her ass like her own personal massage seat.

Trembling, she leaned forward, clutching my head against her chest and shuddering in my arms. Her hands were still in my hair and her pulse pounded with her wrists against my ears.

"You've got an exceptional mouth." She chuckled against my head, sounding just the way I liked, like she'd run a 5k without stopping.

"You've got an exceptional way of making me want to make you come over and over again."

She laughed again and lifted her head from mine. "That's definitely a first for me, as compliments go."

I scooped her up, careful of my knee, but with her weight settled in my arms I felt like I could skate laps around anyone.

She yelped and looped her arms around my neck, burying her face in the crook and peppering it with nibbles and kisses.

We made it as far as the couch. Sometime soon, we'd

have sex in a bed, but today wasn't that day; at least not the first time.

My dick swelled against the front of my jeans as her fingers toyed with the hair at the back of my neck.

I set her down on the couch and her fingers flew to my waistband. She made quick work of the buttons and zipper, and peeked up at me with a mischievous smile as she ran her fingers down over my ass, pushing the jeans down as she went.

"Are you sure you don't want to go to the bedroom?" Her fingers were wrapped around my throbbing dick. She tightened her grip and moved her hand up and down my length. Like I could carry on a conversation while her lips were inches away from my crown.

"Let's not get carr—" A noise escaped my lips as she wrapped her lips around my head and used her tongue to torture me.

"Nope, not happening." I jerked my hips back and pushed her down on the couch, settling myself between her hips before she could protest.

Her fingers squeezed at my back and she lifted her head, watching as I pushed inside her.

I gritted my teeth, trying to keep myself in check. The vise-like grip of her pussy was a masterpiece, and I was seconds away from losing it.

"Colm," she moaned my name, moving one hand to the side of my cheek. "Are you with me?"

I wanted to feel her hand on my skin without anything between us. Staring into her eyes, she seemed to know exactly what I needed.

The depth of her gaze slowed down everything between us, even though our bodies worked frantically, chasing the sexual pleasure building with each thrust. But locked in her gaze, that euphoria reached down deep into me. It wasn't just the physical connection between our bodies that I'd needed, but her seeing me.

Her gaze locked onto mine, letting me know she was there with me the whole time. Our souls were twining around one another, winding together so tightly that even when we weren't touching, the imprint of that touch would last forever.

"I'm with you." I powered into her.

Her back arched off the couch and her eyes fluttered closed before she pulled me down on top of her for a kiss.

I kept thrusting and grinding until she came apart in my arms, moaning and calling out against my lips that she was with me.

That keening cry of hers broke my restraint and I let myself go. Trying to keep my weight off her, I came with spots dancing in front of my eyes. My feelings ping ponged between absolute bliss and excruciating pleasure.

Panting with sweat rolling down the back of my neck, I braced my arms on either side of her.

Her pebbled nipples rubbed against my chest and she stared back at me with a wide smile.

She trailed her fingers down my sweaty neck. "How's the knee?"

Her words cleared some of the sexual fog. I'd had one leg planted on the floor and the other in the back of the couch. As if her words triggered all non-Imogen-focused senses to kick back online, my knee throbbed, angry at being bent that way.

Instead of lifting her and carrying her into the bedroom like I'd have liked, we walked hand in hand.

She fussed over my knee, grabbed my brace and put a moratorium on any more sex involving my legs for the rest of the night, which was fine by me when she climbed on top.

I rolled her nipples and palmed her breasts as she rode me before collapsing onto my chest.

I'd never thought dragging a wet cloth over someone's body could be so sensual, but with Imogen everything was.

Exquisitely ethereal. Even her gentle snores. Every bit of her was a perfection I'd never experienced before.

I'd fucked up a lot in my life, but this felt right. Righter than anything I'd experienced in a long time. I didn't care about the past when I was with her. All I could see was the future. Our future. As a family. Waking up beside her. Candlelit picnics in the middle of my living room floor. Chasing her with the hose while washing my car when I was only looking for an excuse to wet her down and make out pressed against my car. Falling asleep with my arms wrapped around her every night.

She mumbled in her sleep and curled toward me. The gold chain that had been behind her back was now around her front. The hard metal pendant at the end dug into my arm. I shifted and lifted it. A simple silver ring. Preston's. The one thing she hadn't taken off tonight had been another man's ring.

My chest tightened, but then I looked closer. It wasn't a man's ring. It wasn't Preston's. Inside, I looked at the inscription. *For my I, Love Forever P.*

I held onto her tighter. She grumbled and burrowed deeper into my chest. She still wore this ring he'd given her. What did that mean? It had been over five years since he was gone, but he still had a place in her heart. Was there room for me too?

This was about her and me, it had been since the first time I saw her standing in the hospital hallway. Even when I had been surrounded by all those bad memories, her small smile had made the place less cold, scary and overwhelming.

We'd been building to this since the night on the beach, when we'd sat and listened to music with the rolling waves as the backing band in the real world.

She was the one woman that every other woman had been measured against and fallen abysmally short. Maybe that's why I always sucked at finding the right person for me. I knew Imogen was out there, only she was someone else's. But...she wasn't. Not anymore. Maybe now we could belong to each other.

But now I had to convince her that we could have something real. We could be a family. Just the two of us.

I fell asleep with her tucked against my chest, her even breaths fanning across my skin. I'd never thought I'd feel this again. A warm, glowing ball grew in me with each rise and fall of her chest against mine. Home.

23

IMO

Colm woke me throughout the night to eat—it just so happened I was the only thing on the menu. Waking on the verge of a toe-curling, back arching orgasm was definitely a different kind of wake-up call in the pitch black bedroom.

Every muscle ached and sang with a release I hadn't experienced—ever. Sleep dragged us both under when we'd had our fill of one another, only to wake to another round of hands, lips, and—well, another prominent appendage. Sweaty and sated I surrendered to his insatiable appetite until I had to finally call it.

I tapped the bed beside me. "You win. I'm asking for a delay of game until the field can be relined."

He propped himself up on his elbows between my legs. "That mixed a few different sports analogies."

Lifting my head, I glared. "How is my brain supposed to function properly when you're trying to scramble it out of me? My vagina needs a break. Was that a clear enough analogy?" I collapsed against the pillows.

Crawling up my body, peppering my ribs with kisses, he

settled against my side.

"You're not tired?" My eyelids were heavy. His beautiful face was the only thing I could make out through the barely open slits.

"I feel like I've been sleeping for a long time. Now I'm finally awake." He dragged his finger along my shoulder.

"Good for you, but I'm beat. Let's pick this up in the morning." I shoved at his chest and he let me knock him down, flat on the bed. The challenge in the club had broken the invisible line between us that I'd kept trying to reestablish. I'd wanted to reset to a baseline and move within the sphere of our professional relationship. Although it had never been just that. He'd always had a way of seeing through what everyone else took as real.

His gaze was always searching for more. Prodding for what was happening under the surface. Maybe that's why it was so easy for me to sit with him on the beach or know what he needed on our first night together. Because I could do the same thing to him. We were each other's Rosetta Stone, only the secrets we unlocked were the ones we each tried to hide, even from ourselves.

"You're planning on being here, then?" The words were soft and quiet against the top of my head as he held me close.

My heart skipped a beat. I'd hurt him. It was a reminder of my past screw-ups. I yawned, locking his arms around me tighter and snuggling closer against him.

"I can barely move. You'd have to drag me out of the room by my feet to get me out of this bed in the morning." The cooling perspiration and temperature in the room made it easy to be this close to him and he didn't seem to mind. He draped his leg over mine like he was trying to pen me in against the possibility of an escape.

"Good."

Silence and the darkness enveloped me and I didn't feel that normal emptiness and hollowness. I felt warm and safe in Colm's arms. With him there, the dark of night didn't feel nearly as scary and unknown.

The solid warm block against my side shifted. Colm. There wasn't any confusion or moment of panic. Maybe there should've been. He was a client. There were rules about getting involved with people we worked with, but nestled against his side with my cheek pressed against his warm skin, I didn't care.

This felt good. It felt right. It felt like waking up to a day that wouldn't be something I had to push myself through, but could run toward.

"Good morning." He stared down at me, brushing my hair back from my face. Night Imogen had once again put me in bird's nest territory.

His fingertips traced the shell of my ear.

"Morning." How was it my voice sounded like a creaky door and his was like melted butter?

"What time is it?" I squinted at the bright light shining through the window.

"Do you have anywhere to be?" He propped his head up on his elbow and stared down at me.

I flipped through the day in my mental calendar. A blank. "No, nowhere."

"And when was the last time you had one of those?"

I stared up at the ceiling, trying to figure out the last time I'd allowed myself to have a day not jam packed with work, travel, or more work.

A smile spread across my face. "April 23. Spring break my senior year of high school."

He dragged his finger down the front of my shoulder and along the top of the sheet wrapped around my chest. "That's pretty specific and a long time ago."

"My parents took me away for a long weekend. They rented a house on a lake. I woke up early one morning because I was being a pissy teenager. I'd wanted us to go on Spring Break with Preston and his parents, but my parents wanted some time with just us."

Colm's finger stopped its slow methodical torture along my neck and shoulder.

"They knew if Preston and his family were there they'd never see me. So in the morning, I grabbed my phone, a blanket and a book and went exploring. There wasn't any cell reception, which was another reason I was being such a pain. A whole 72 hours without my phone. Why didn't they break out the iron maiden? There was a clearing and I walked into it, trying to find reception and when I looked up from my screen I froze." Sunlight from the window washed over my face like it had the minute I stepped into the clearing. So warm and bright.

"What did you see?" His voice was rougher than before.

"It was a field of flowers. Every color. So many, as far as I could see. They were gorgeous and I forgot about my phone and spent—I don't even know how long, just looking at them. Walking past and letting the petals rub against my fingers. I found a spot, laid out my blanket and read. But every so often, I'd sit up and stare at the beauty around me, not believing it was real. I dragged them back there and made us have a picnic. We stayed until it got dark and the field was taken over by lightning bugs."

"That sounds like a great day."

"It was the best day." I looked over at him. It's these small moments we have to cherish. "And the next day, driving back home we had the accident. The next day, they were gone."

He laced his fingers through mine with a reassuring hold. "I'm glad you got to have the best day with them."

"Me too." I took a deep breath and glanced away. "How's your leg after last night?"

His eyes narrowed for a split second. "I'm not broken, Imo. No soreness. No pain. Nothing out of the ordinary."

"I know you hate that I ask, but it's kind of my job." I looked up at him.

His jaw ticked. "Was this an alternative form of therapy last night?"

I jerked away from him. "What? No."

"Good. If you're not being my physiotherapist right now, then no more talk about my leg. New rule. If we're not in a session, no asking about it at all."

My stomach grumbled like a velociraptor coming down the hallway.

"Looks like I need to get you fed."

I stretched my arms over my head, and the sheet trapped around my chest slipped down an inch.

Colm's gaze shot to the spot like a hawk spotting a school of fish in the ocean.

"But we could have some early morning fun." He yanked the sheet all the way down.

I yelped and scrunched my legs up, only to realize that didn't exactly hide anything.

The brightness of the morning sun lit up the room. It looked so different from the last time I'd been up here. No bottles of alcohol, no discarded clothes, and it smelled like it had the first night I'd been here. He was making so much progress. He was coming back to himself, even if he wouldn't be who he'd been before. He'd be better.

Colm climbed on top of me with his knees on either side of my hips and his arms on either side of my head. Raspberries were the next plan of attack. He blew them against the side of my neck.

I screamed and yelped, pushing at his shoulders and laughing until there were tears in my eyes. His devilish fingers dropped lower to my stomach until a cramp coupled with my intense need to pee sent me into a full on roll complete with an elbow to the side of his head.

"Ah!" He dropped to the bed beside me.

"Oh shit, I'm sorry. So sorry." I tugged his hand away from his face.

He fingered the faint redness at the top of his cheek, which hopefully wouldn't bloom into a black eye. "Bruiser Imogen coming out to play."

"Now you know the consequences of tickling me." A stitch pinched my side. I cupped my hand over it and flipped over swinging my legs over the side of the bed. "Don't mess with the pooch."

He scoffed. "Right, a pooch. Is it where you store rice cakes and water for winter?"

The exact topic a woman wanted to broach naked with a man cut like he was chiseled from granite: her baked goods-induced widening now that fall was here and winter was quickly approaching.

"Not like you're pregnant or anything." Colm laughed.

I opened my mouth to let one out right alongside him, but the word was like the final tumbler clicking into place on a vault I'd never thought I'd open.

The oversized box of tampons I'd bought over the summer that sat unopened.

My mercurial appetite.

My inability to stay awake for long stretches like I used to.

My skyrocketing sensitivity last night.

The joke reply caught in my throat.

"Right?" He turned in the bed, jostling me.

My half-sit on the edge became a full blown drop to the floor. I hadn't had any spotting like I usually did in place of my normal periods.

"Imo?" He dove for me across the mattress as I shifted up and we bumped heads.

"Ow."

Groaning, he grabbed me and hauled me up onto the bed.

I winced, rubbing my head and my ass in a much more painful version of the pat your head, rub your stomach game.

"How's your butt?" Shifting in the bed, he pulled me between his legs.

The possible new reality hung between us, tense and anxiety-inducing. My mouth was dry and the tips of my fingers tingled. "Better than my head."

Tilting my head to the side, Colm inspected my forehead. "There's a red spot and a bump already."

His fingers froze at the mention of bump.

I licked my dry lips and brushed his hair aside, breathing in this last moment between us. "You have one too."

His Adam's apple bobbed. "Are—could you be pregnant?"

24

IMO

I cupped my hand over my stomach. "Things were hectic this summer and I wasn't keeping track." My gaze whipped up to his and I dropped it, staring down at his legs bracketing mine. Whisper quiet, I said the words that could turn our lives upside down. "It's possible."

The words were barely past my lips and he was gone. He'd never moved faster or more nimbly. Snagging some sweatpants from a drawer, he shoved them on, stone-faced.

My stomach knotted. I'd been worrying about entanglements and him wanting something more than I could give, but he looked ready to jump out the nearest window. "You stay, it's your place. I'll go."

He whirled around. "What? No! I'm not running off and neither are you. There's a pharmacy around the corner. I'll pick up a test and we can find out for sure." He crouched down to tie his laces while his head whipped wildly back and forth, scanning the room.

Some of the tightness eased. He wasn't going to run from his own house like it was on fire... until after we got the confirmation.

"As much as I'm sure they wouldn't mind, you might want to put on a shirt first." My attempt at a joke fell flat like a dirty gym towel hitting the floor.

He glanced down at his bare chest, cursed under his breath and grabbed a t-shirt off the top of the pile in his drawer. "I'll be back in ten minutes." Pulling his shirt over his head, he disappeared out of the room.

His footsteps thundered down the stairs and the door slammed seconds later.

My clothes were downstairs and the club dress didn't seem appropriate, given how my morning was going to go. One line or two would change everything.

I could be pregnant. And not just a little pregnant. How far along might I be? Our night together was in June. So— holy shit, that would be more than four months. While most people worked hard for a summer bod, I'd always put on a little weight during summer between funnel cake, diner food, and way too much time in the car. I'd felt rundown as we wrapped up the summer season at the Surf Shack, but had chalked that up to finally allowing myself to slow down long enough to let the exhaustion hit me.

Drawstring pants and elastic waistbands in my scrubs meant I never paid attention to a few pounds one way or the other. I flipped through my mental calendar. I could be in my second trimester.

The gentle slope of my stomach didn't seem so much like diner food and vending machine snacks anymore. A new reality could be seconds from confirmation.

I'd always planned on having kids. When I had envisioned my future, there had always been kids, but then Preston was gone and that vision was snuffed out, replaced by the existence I'd been living for the past few years. The same days had stretched out into an unknown infinity.

Whatever the result, Colm and my relationship would be forever changed. A pregnancy scare wasn't something that blew over without those little thoughts popping up in the back of your head.

I got up and pulled out one of Colm's t-shirts and a pair of shorts with a drawstring.

After I put on the clothes, I looked at myself in the mirror. My normal morning routine was interrupted by needing to keep my pee on the inside until Colm came back, and any distraction seemed like it might help. Standing was a mistake. I sat back down on the edge of the bed and crossed my legs, bouncing with my hands locked on my knees.

The ten minutes could've been an hour for how long it seemed. There was a part of me that imagined him running to the store and then just carrying on past it. Maybe running straight to the airport and hopping on a plane to a place without the complications of Imogen.

Was this his way of bailing? 'Here's a house as a consolation prize. I'm picking up and moving far, far away from you. Please forward my mail.' Just as I was sure I could see a yellow tinge at the bottom of my vision, the front door banged open. Colm burst into the room with two full plastic bags straining against his forearms.

"Did you go grocery shopping?"

"These are all tests." Sweat poured down his face and he panted, swallowing and setting down the bags.

I gaped at the boxes pushing through the plastic and grabbed a handful, cradling them to my chest. Rushing into the bathroom, I dumped them onto the floor. Smiley faces. Plus signs. Two lines. There were so many different types. I picked one and tore into the box with my legs crossed.

Colm stood nearby hovering, looking like he might puke at any moment.

"Get out." I tottered over to the toilet and read the instructions.

He stood in the doorway, leaning in like that constituted out.

"Go before I pee myself and we have to wait until tomorrow to find out."

That got him gone. I scanned the counter and spotted his toothbrush cup. Desperate times.

Three minutes later I was the proud owner of twelve peed on pregnancy tests lined up neatly on the side of the white counter.

My leg bounced up and down, but not from a nearly-bursting bladder this time. How long had it been? Was it time yet for the little pieces of plastic to work their magic? Being in that room alone sent my anxiety skyrocketing. I needed to take a step back and escape.

I flung the door open and walked into the bedroom.

Colm shot up from the bed, looking frazzled and harried like he'd walked through a hurricane. "So...?"

"We have to wait three minutes. I don't know how long it's been. And I used the cup for your toothbrush for the test, so you might want to throw that out."

He nodded, his throat working a mile a minute. Looking down at the bed beside him, he jolted at his phone like it had appeared out of thin air. He plucked it from the bed and tapped the screen, waving it with the three-minute clock counting down.

Three minutes.

"There's another set of tests if you need them." He pointed at the neatly arranged boxes on the nightstand.

"I used twelve, I'm thinking that will give us enough of a

sample size to know the truth." What was wrong with my arms and why did it feel like I'd never crossed them before? Was it left over right or right over left against my chest?

Another nod and darting gaze to the countdown clock. *Two minutes.*

"I don't want you to...I mean I don't expect..." A curse whispered through my lips.

Colm stared at the phone like he was waiting for his life to implode. All his talk about finally figuring out what he wanted to do and no longer feeling like he had to take care of Liv, and now this. All those proclamations about doing whatever the hell he wanted and no longer being responsible for anyone other than himself.

And now the baby clock was ticking on the other side of the bathroom door.

One minute.

"It'll be okay. Whatever happens, it will be okay." He didn't look at me when he said it, like he was talking himself off the ledge of a possibly monumental cliff.

We stood in silence, not knowing what to say. I crossed my arms around my waist.

The chimes sounded and he opened the bathroom door. His deep breath was the only sound other than his muted footsteps.

He made it to the sink first and picked up the first one. "Is a happy face a good or a bad thing?"

I licked my dry lips. "I guess that depends on your point of view." At the other end of the counter, I looked through the tests. Plus sign. Two lines. Other than one with only the slightest hint of a second line, our new reality had been dumped on us like that bucket of ice water.

"Wow." Colm sat on the closed toilet seat I'd abandoned minutes ago. He dropped his head into his hands.

My stomach knots were back—or was that something else? Was it morning sickness? When did you get morning sickness? This explained how I'd crave Avery's baked goodies and then not even want to eat them. My fingers trembled.

"Colm—" I lifted my hand, but dropped it at my side, unsure if he even wanted my touch.

He lifted his head. His nostrils flared and his eyes were watery and red.

"I'm sorry. This doesn't change anything for you. It will be okay." I was a chronic helper. A pathological fixer. A complete and total mess. He deserved better.

His arms shot out and he wrapped them around me, pulling me close. His head rested above my stomach. "It will be okay."

With Tinkerbell light touches, I ran my fingers over his head. His arms tightened around my waist.

Some of the tightness in my chest eased and I dragged my fingers through his hair.

"What are you thinking?"

"It's all too chaotic to hold onto one thought long enough to even tell you."

I wrapped my arms around his head. "This doesn't have to change anything for you. You don't—"

"Don't ruin this moment by telling me that I don't have to be part of our baby's life."

I stepped back, not knowing how you handle the *sorry I accidentally got pregnant after our one night together where you were probably still drunk and emotionally messed up and now I'm at least four months pregnant* talk. "This wasn't something we planned. It's not something *I* planned. I don't want you to think you have to do anything." He was Mr. Responsibility. He was the guy who didn't walk away no matter how much it made sense for him to do it.

He dropped his head between his knees with his hands in his hair.

"Hell, yes, I'm freaking the hell out." He looked up at me with a stricken look and my stomach dropped.

I hadn't even asked the question aloud, but I couldn't exactly blame him for his response. Did I want to be let in on the full conversation going on inside his head?

"You're the only person I've ever had unprotected sex with. It was a fluke and now you're pregnant."

The words were to me, but it was clear that he was talking to himself.

"I've never slept with anyone without protection either."

He jolted like he'd just remembered I was there, and then his eyebrows dipped low. "Anyone."

I wrapped my arms around my stomach and my cheeks heated. "Well, one person." This was going all wrong, although I wasn't sure how a 'surprise, I'm pregnant' announcement was supposed to go.

"Were you on something?"

"Yeah, I was. I am, but nothing is one hundred percent. I'm normally irregular and I'm on the pill, but driving back and forth, I haven't been back of the box on time with everything. I didn't think." Late nights and early mornings. Falling asleep with my shoes on, I hadn't been the best with keeping to my pill at the same time every day, sometimes I'd even forget for a couple days. It wasn't like I'd needed it for pregnancy prevention until him.

"Fuck."

He had that right, and we'd done it again.

I'd opened myself up to him again and this is where it had

led. Instead of finding out on my own and sitting him down for a reasonable conversation where I could lay out my plan and get his input, I was standing in his bathroom with cool tiles under my feet, in his shirt, trying to unscramble my thoughts.

The glass was cracking under my feet and escape was the only option. I darted out of the room and scrambled for my clothes. It wasn't until the front door closed behind me that I realized he'd never even tried to call me back.

Tears rolled down my cheeks in the back of the taxi and all the way back to my apartment. What the hell did I do now?

A baby. Imogen was pregnant. Pregnant with my baby. I was going to be a father.

Holy fuck!

I dragged my hands down my face. In some part of my brain, it registered that she wasn't in the bathroom anymore.

Slowly my brain rebooted itself and stopped being a cloud of people running around screaming and putting out the fires springing up in every corner.

Imogen was gone. How long ago had it been? A few minutes? A couple hours? Was she at home? Was her apartment safe? Did she need anything? Did the baby need anything?

I'd let her go. She'd been trying to talk, but my mouth and lips were dry like I'd been force-fed saltines and cotton balls.

Was this really real? Twenty unopened boxes of pregnancy tests sat on my night stand. After more than ten positive tests, I was pretty sure we had our answer.

The fog in my brain cleared and I saw with laser sharp focus what had happened over the past four months.

My life was a mess. I was a mess, barely piecing things back together and now I was going to be a father. The pressure. The worry. The fear. It all came rushing in hard and fast. But in it was also a light, glowing ball beating like my heart.

Imogen was pregnant with my baby. I was going to be a father.

The connection I'd always felt to her now had a real life expression. A baby. Ten fingers and ten toes. Would they have her smile or mine? Would they inherit the white streak that had struck me and Liv?

Liv was going to be an aunt. Her niece or nephew would call her Aunt Olive, a nickname I'd given her that she hated. I couldn't hold back my smile, but then reality interrupted my Future Colm daydream where everything turned out perfectly and no one had to deal with the bullshit life always lobbed your way.

Liv wasn't talking to me. Or was I not talking to her?

Imogen had walked out of here without another word from me. Did she want me in her life? We'd slept together again, what did that mean? Did she want me to help raise the baby with her? To be with me like I'd wanted to be with her? Or was she still in love with Preston? Her love had been stolen from her five years ago; did that leave me the like of her life because of the baby? Would I always be second in her heart?

A strong knock broke me out of my premature nesting.

I threw the door open.

Ford stood on the doorstep with his hands shoved in his pockets.

Being alone with my thoughts was a dangerous thing right now. The magnitude of a baby made what was going on between me and him seem a hell of a lot smaller.

Holding the door open, I stepped aside, giving him room to come in.

His eyes widened.

"Are you coming in or not?"

He came in with his hands shoved in his pockets.

Tension crackled in the air. The first time we'd willingly been in a room together in a long time.

"How's she doing?"

"She's holding it together. She's trying to pretend this distance between you two isn't getting to her, but I know she's hurting. How are you doing?" He held my gaze, not letting me drop it.

"Fuck."

"Do you still have the bag?" He nodded toward the door leading to my gym.

I huffed. "Yeah."

"Then what are we waiting for?" He held out his arm, waiting to see what I'd do next.

"Why the hell not?" I led him downstairs.

The room was cold, with humidity creeping in through the basement walls even though I'd had it triple water sealed.

Ford lugged the punching bag out of the closet and tossed the gloves to me.

I grabbed the hand wraps, winding them around my hands, in and out between my fingers before securing the end around my wrist. It had been a long time since I'd broken these out. I slipped my hands into the gloves.

Ford hooked the chain at the top of the punching bag to the hook in the ceiling. It was like we'd jumped into a time portal. All the complications life had thrown our way dimmed. I tightened the velcro around my wrist with my teeth and slammed the gloves together.

My hits were tentative. The cold *thwap* of the gloves was swallowed up against the solid black bag.

"You've got more in you than that."

I put a little more power behind my next hook.

Ford held onto the bag, it didn't move an inch.

"Pretend it's my face."

A flood of energy barreled through me, powering up my swing. I connected with the bag and Ford stumbled back. If I'd said I didn't get some extra satisfaction out of that, I'd be lying.

"This can't just be about Liv or hockey. What's going on?" He widened his stance, planting his feet.

Saying it out loud felt like it made it more real. I was going to be a dad. In five months, there'd be a little Colmogen combo out in the world. Sweat beaded on my forehead.

"Imogen's pregnant."

"Did she have some vial of Preston's sperm cryogenically frozen or something?"

I froze mid-punch and glared at him around the bag.

His eyes widened. "Oh shit, it's yours. You and Imogen have been—what? Why didn't anyone say anything?"

"No one knows. We've been discreet."

"Wow. I take it this wasn't planned."

"No."

"How long have you known?"

"What time is it?"

He turned his wrist. "Three."

"Five hours."

"That explains why you invited me in. You're still in shock."

I grunted, taking out my frustrations on the bag in front of me.

"What's the plan?"

"Who said there was a plan?"

He leaned farther out from behind the bag. "There's always a plan with you. It's part of the reason everyone's been so freaked out about you after—well you know. Usually you've got the next five years of your life all sorted out, with alternate plans and *alternate* alternate plans to get to your goal. But you've been aimless."

"Being blindsided will do that to you. Maybe I just realized there was no point in having plans when life never cooperated. What difference does it make?"

"This thing with Imogen. How serious is it?"

I threw a left jab. "No idea. Every time I try to get close, she pushes me away."

"So you don't want this baby?"

"No—yes—I don't know. Have you seen me lately? I'm not exactly father of the year material." That was an understatement—Ford had no idea how messed up I really was.

"I know a certain sister who'd have something to say about that."

"Like adding me to the shittiest parental-fill-in hall of fame? I'll pass."

"She'd never say anything like that about how you raised her. As for how things are going now, maybe she'd have a few choice words, but growing up, she knows, maybe now more than before, how much you sacrificed for her. She's an adult now, though, and she could use a brother more than a father."

"Exactly."

"Stop trying to twist everything into the worst possible scenario."

"And why the hell shouldn't I? What about my life would make me not always default to the worst possible outcome? Maybe my parents are just late for my hockey game? No, they're fighting for their lives on the side of an icy road. Maybe my girlfriend is sensing something is up with me because I'm freaked out about proposing and that's why she's being weird? Nope, she's fucked my best friend and tried to hide it from me. Maybe my sister is nervous about not being able to hack it in med school and that's why she's distant and won't talk to me? Wrong again, she's banging my best friend and giving up on medical school entirely. Oh and that twenty-four hour period where she wasn't answering her phone, was she just avoiding me? No, her god damn apartment burned down and she's nowhere to be found.

"But with Imogen, I'm supposed to believe things will turn out okay? I'm supposed to believe this woman I've had a thing for for nearly half a decade is going to be happy she got pregnant by me when I can barely get her to stay the night? I'm supposed to believe that I'm not the runner-up once again for the heart of a woman I can't stop thinking about. Only this time, my competition is dead. How do I compete with a ghost canonized and revered by everyone who's ever met him? Why the hell would I think I'd be able to matter one bit as much to her as he did? And now we're stacking a kid on top of that. I'll be lucky if I get to see them for alternate weekends. Who'd even want their kid around someone like me? I sure as hell wouldn't." I grimaced, trying to hide from my mountain of screw ups bombarding me in a mental slideshow.

"Are you done with your bullshit pity party?"

"Fuck you." I drove the bag into him.

He stumbled back. "I'm not going to fight you. We both know what happened the last time."

He had to kick me while I was down. Typical. "Get the hell out of my house."

"You invited me in."

"Which means I can uninvite you."

He crossed his arms. "Maybe if you stopped making everything a competition you'd stop setting yourself up for coming in second place. Life is fucked up, and we all have to deal with it. Sometimes our parents suck. Sometimes they're awesome. Sometimes people we love are taken from us too soon. And sometimes we have to figure out how to be happy again without them. You're not the first person to lose someone and you won't be the last, but if you keep up with this pissing match of who matters more or who loves who more, you're going to end up alone and you'll only have yourself to blame. You want me out of your life, that's fine. Then you won't have anyone else to blame for half your problems. But what you need to do is call your sister. She loves you. She misses you. And she's just as stubborn as you, and she'll hold out on admitting it just like you."

I ground my teeth, staring past him.

Ford's footsteps thundered up the stairs and the front door slammed shut.

I threw another punch at the bag before ripping my gloves off and chucking them across the room. I shoved Ford from my mind. My next official session with Imo was supposed to be tomorrow. Would she show up? Our 'official' time had been melding into unofficial, impromptu time over the past few weeks. Usually nothing more than her stopping by to check in on me. I'd been resentful at first, angry that she didn't seem to think I could make it through an entire day without somehow reinjuring myself, but somewhere in there I'd started looking forward to her barging into my house.

But every time I'd tried to tempt her with dinner or a drink, she'd dodged the invitation. Where did things with us stand after last night? She'd been just as hungry for me. She'd stared into my eyes, peeling back the layers and drawing me deeper into her gaze, until I'd been enveloped by her scent, drowning in her touch.

What was she thinking after I'd let her walk out of my house without a word? Would she show up tomorrow? Could I convince her I could be a great dad to the baby? That I could be great to Imo every day of her life?

26

IMO

Numbness. I'd been numb all day. I kept freezing in place, as though I'd sprouted roots. By the third time, I knew I needed something to keep me moving, so I'd driven to the shore to surprise Fern and Charlie.

If they knew something was up, they didn't say anything.

The cooler weather always came to the shore early. My sweater helped hide the bump I was sure had grown in the matter of hours since I'd found out.

Colm had sent me a message, but I hadn't been brave enough to look yet. I'd see him tomorrow for our official session. Were the knots in my stomach about seeing him so soon after the news or was it the baby?

Doctor's appointments. Preparations. Shopping for things babies needed. What did babies need? I was an only child, we hadn't ever had babies around when I was growing up. I had no idea how to do any of this.

I braced myself on the counter and took deep breaths. My hands shook as I took my phone out of my sweatshirt pocket and read Colm's text.

We need to talk. Are you coming tomorrow?

I tapped out my one word reply. *Yes.*

He'd been reveling in his freedom. Slowly trying to figure out who he was without the anvil of responsibility around his neck, and now I'd dropped a baby into his lap. I looked out at Fern and Charlie doing their nightly dance to 'Love Will Keep Us Together'. They were back to their old routine. For the first year or so after Preston had died, I'd clean everything up alone in silence. Sometimes they'd try to help, but other times, they couldn't bring themselves to do it.

What would happen when they found out I was pregnant? Would it bring back terrible memories for them? Make them think of the kids Preston and I were supposed to have had? Would it feel like a betrayal of his memory?

I'd always wanted to have kids, but they'd been locked away in the frozen life I'd lost with Preston. So much of how I'd lived since then had been to preserve the pieces I had left. Fern and Charlie. My work. My aversion to getting involved with anyone.

The doors had been blown off the safety I'd thought I'd found in being alone. Colm had seen the cracks in my armor and pushed past them, never letting me shrink away.

"We shouldn't have stayed open this late into October. The season is long over. It's just us trying to hold onto the last bits of summer." Charlie finished putting the chairs up on the tables and went to get the mop.

"You don't have to keep coming down here." Fern wiped down the diner counter that looked as clean as when I got here.

"The driving helps clear my head and I get in extra cardio going from table to table. Plus, I had an interview with that new physiotherapy center opening ten minutes from here." I wiped down the last of the tables as Fern collected the salt shakers.

"Why would you do that?"

"So I can be closer to you two. Then I can get down here in record time after I'm finished work."

"Imogen—"

"And they're on board with a modified schedule in the summer."

She looked at me with an armful of shakers and gave me a weak smile. "Things are slowing down."

The unexpected snow we'd gotten meant the diner had been slower than usual. Sometimes they could stretch the fall season through to Halloween.

"Not too many tables tonight." She leaned against the counter, more tired than I'd seen her in a while.

"Are you okay, Fern?"

She lifted her head and smiled. "Fine dear, just not getting any younger. We appreciate you coming down to help, but there have got to be more interesting things going on during your nights and weekends, especially now that the summer's over."

"There's no place I'd rather be." I set the salt and pepper down on the counter.

Fern sighed and unscrewed the tops of all the shakers. "Nothing new? Nothing special happening up in the city?" Her words splatted between us like a dirty wash rag.

"No, nothing. I don't have the time." Lifting the other container of salt, I filled the shakers on my side.

"You should. No use being stuck here with two old grouches when you could be out having fun. You can't get your twenties back. Find a guy and have some fun."

I dropped the salt, and a fine spray covered the counter. Rushing for a sponge, I looked over my shoulder. "I have plenty of fun." The evidence of that was chilling out in my uterus as we spoke. My heart rate skipped up and the edges of my vision blurred.

"It seems like all you've done is work for the past five years. You're young and beautiful. I'm sure the guys are lining up around the block to take you out to dinner."

Way more than dinner. Dinner was a rest stop fifty miles back down the highway from where I was. They were nudging me toward maybe dating—what the hell would happen when that turned into a bun in the oven?

"Can you guys handle this? I forgot there's something I need to get back to the city for tonight."

"Imogen—" A sad smile creased her lips.

"It's nothing. I'm just so forgetful lately. Let me know about next weekend."

She nodded. "Of course. Drive safely and text when you get in."

I headed over the bridge, clenching my trembling fingers around the steering wheel. Five years.

The street lights washed over my car in a rhythmic cadence with each passing mile. My eyelids drooped and I jerked my head back, slamming it against the headrest. At least I had an explanation for why I could barely keep my head up sometimes.

The doctor's office had told me they'd get back to me with their next available appointment on the drive down. I'd scrounged in the back office to find a bigger uniform top before Fern and Charlie realized I'd come in. My stomach wasn't going to get any smaller. Maybe it was for the best that they were closing the Shack early. It would give me more time to figure out how to break the news to them.

It was one thing to talk about me dating, but having a baby? How would they handle that news?

All my go-go-go energy had been zapped and I was running on fumes. Usually, I'd stay over with Fern and Charlie and head out at six to make it back to the city in time to meet my first client, but I'd needed my escape.

And tomorrow morning, Colm and I were meeting. He'd thrown out that he wanted to do some work on the weekends to make sure he wasn't pushing himself, but after the news we'd had and his reaction, I wondered whether he'd want to continue with that plan.

Nervous flutters filled my stomach and I couldn't figure out how I'd make it through our sessions in one piece. He was fighting that rising bitterness that came with dedicating yourself to something and finding that you couldn't do it anymore.

When your entire life centered on something, it was hard to make a course correction. I'd had a front row seat to how hockey could consume your life. It took up so much time from when they were little. Waking up before the sun to get to the rink, lugging around so much gear it was hard to walk. That had been his life for as long as he could remember. It was the only way to make it to the elite level Colm had achieved. It was a part of his soul and it was going to end one day no matter what. But that was a hard chasm to jump and sometimes people didn't make it.

I could help him with that. I'd done it before, but I'd almost lost myself. Helping Preston had hurt me, and nearly broken what we'd built together. But there was no one I could talk to about those feelings, not really. He had been sainted and canonized when he died. I'd never told anyone we'd broken up for that brief final month, and it seemed neither had he. The night he'd slipped the ring on my finger hours before our crash would also remain locked away. It wasn't a pain I wanted to visit on anyone else, let alone revisit.

The complicated feelings had been easier to run from than face head-on. His death had erased every bit of his self-ishness and all the screw-ups he'd made like it worked as a giant memory wipe for anyone you'd interacted with prior to death. I loved him, but that didn't mean he'd been perfect.

This time I'd have to keep my guard up because I couldn't put together another broken man only to be left all alone at the end once again. Especially not with a baby. We'd be linked forever now. No matter what happened, he and I were a part of something bigger than ourselves. But a baby was never a way to solve anyone's problems. If anything, this complicated things beyond trying to figure out what was going on between us. Colm needed to figure out what he wanted in life, not try to do the thing he thought was right. I wouldn't be an obligation and I didn't want that for my baby.

The pulsing flash of lights travelled over my car.

My head dipped again. The rhythmic teeth chattering jar of the rumble strip sliced through the brain fog. I jerked the car back to straight, cranked the music, and rolled down the windows, trying to keep the droop out of my eyes. The freezing night air blasted me in my face.

Spotting a rest stop sign, I pulled off the exit and let the gas station attendant fill the tank. New Jersey gas laws for the win. I usually grumbled about waiting for the full-service attendants, but not tonight. He might as well have been an angel sent down from heaven.

A knuckle knock to the window later, I jolted awake. I handed him my cash and pulled into the Wawa attached to the gas station. The hallmark smell of hazelnut coffee mixed with three other flavors and their signature hoagies reached all the way to the gas pumps. I needed coffee. A tub of coffee to swim in, so I could make it home.

Throwing it in park, I zipped my coat and grabbed my gloves. I shoved my hands inside them and pulled on my hat. The fuzzy warmth wrapped around my head. So cozy and comfy. Before I got my coffee, I'd catch a few minutes of shut eye. I rested against the seat, releasing all of the stress weighing me down. It would all still be there when I woke up.

A five-minute cat nap would be all I needed. I set a timer, turned off my car and locked the doors. Five minutes, then I'd get my coffee and get back on the road. Tomorrow I'd figure out what to do with Colm. Tonight I was too damn tired.

Someone needed to oil that leg machine; the knocking was driving me crazy. An insistent knock and bright light streaming through my closed eyelids jolted me awake.

My hands shot to the—*steering wheel?*—and I tried to get my bearings.

"Ma'am. Are you okay?"

An employee in a Wawa hat stood outside my window.

Squeezing my eyes shut, I cleared the fog in my head. I'd been driving home and stopped for gas. My pit stop pushed through the early morning haze. My fingers were tight in the cold and my breath came out in puffs in front of my face.

I glanced at the clock on my dashboard. *Shit!* It was after nine. I'd slept sitting up in my car for almost twelve hours. Between the position and the cold, my muscles ached. I was already in the running for the worst mom of the year.

I rolled down my window a few inches. It was even colder outside. "Hi, sorry. I must have fallen asleep. I'm good though. Thanks."

He eyed me before nodding and heading back into the store.

Running inside, I ducked into the bathroom and then grabbed that coffee I was supposed to get last night.

I pressed the start button, my car kicked on, and I flew back to the highway, keeping just under the speed limit. I cranked the heat, slowly thawing myself out on the way there.

Rush hour traffic had come and gone by the time I got to the city.

There wasn't even time to go home and shower; I'd be a solid hour late by the time I got to Colm's. My busted phone charger taunted me with each mile.

Not the best way to kick off this new chapter of our... whatever this was.

27

COLM

My phone screen dimmed for less than a second and I pushed the button again. The knot in my stomach tightened and those old panicky feelings lapped at the edges of my mind.

The digital clock didn't make a sound, but each passing second reverberated in my head. Fifty-three minutes. I'd been sitting down in my gym waiting for her for over fifty-three minutes. Fifty-four now. As much as I wanted to be pissed, that had died about twelve minutes ago. Was she backing out? Had she decided I wasn't worth the effort? Maybe now that she knew she was pregnant she'd realized she didn't want anything to do with me.

After twenty minutes, when I'd finally broken down to call her and gotten no response, the prickling tiptoes of dread had walked their way up my spine. Liv always thought I was a pain in the ass about her being on time because I was, well, an ass. But lateness tapped into something inside of me that I'd tried to push down and pretend didn't exist in my life anymore.

What if she didn't know how I truly felt about her? And

how I felt about the baby? I still hadn't waded through all those emotions, but my shell-shocked and mute reaction definitely wasn't what I wanted her last memories of me to be.

Scenarios of what might have happened to her ran through my head. What if she had been mugged on the way here? Or had tripped and fallen somewhere and hit her head? All the improbable and fear-inducing ways she could be injured, dying, or dead played in my mind like a progressively dire highlight reel.

I remembered the way I'd kept checking the stands for my parents the night of our last game and how I'd gotten angrier and sadder as each minute of the period ticked down—all the while, they had been fighting for their lives while two separate medi-vac helicopters whisked them to the nearest trauma center.

Only it wasn't them this time, it was Imogen and our baby. The words were still slow to form in my head. A baby. The rest of the guys were all coupled up, so I figured one of them would be first. I'd never thought much about having kids. After taking care of Liv for so long, kids had been pushed back in my mind to after I'd met someone I could share my life with and we'd gotten married, spent time together traveling the world and being a happy couple. Funny how life never turned out the way we planned.

The front door opened and closed. Racing, heavy footsteps streaked across the floor and I squeezed the edge of the weight bench, expecting one of the guys to come rushing down to break the terrible news to me. I wanted to lock the gym door and keep whoever it was out. Short, choppy breaths shook my chest and my nostrils flared. Numbness crept up from my fingers' death grip on the bench.

"Sorry I'm late." Imogen rushed down the steps, her boots catching on the last one. Her recovery was quick and graceful, even as I jumped up to help her. Hair stuck up all over like her hastily thrown-together ponytail couldn't contain her harried mood. Dropping her bag, she wiped sweat from her forehead.

"I know. I know. Let me wash my hands and we can get started. I'm sure you have things to do." She dropped her wooly hat on top of her bag and jerked down the zipper to her coat.

I was on the way to her before I could even think. Relief slammed into me like a tsunami, nearly knocking me off my feet. I swayed, locking my knees to keep upright. She was here. "You're okay."

My fingers tingled, needing to touch her and hold her, make sure she was really safe and okay.

"Stiff muscles, but other than that I'm good. It was a long night at the Shack and I fell asleep at the Wawa on the Expressway." She let out a nervous laugh, and her words felt like ice cubes being injected into my veins.

I spun her around, gripping her shoulders. She stared at me wide-eyed.

"You slept in a gas station parking lot."

She cracked a weak smile and shrugged. "Not on purpose. My back is not thanking me right now. I was tired. I fell asleep."

"In the middle of the night in a place where who knows what could've happened to you or the baby." My fingers tightened around her arms. How was she not getting how dangerous this was? How anything could've happened to her? To both of them? In a blink they could've been gone. A random ice patch in the road, some drunk asshole in oncoming traffic, a fallen branch, there were so many things that might have taken her from me. Taken them from me.

"But it didn't." She lifted her arms and jerked them down, breaking my grip. "I'm an adult. I can take care of myself. Sorry for being late and worrying you, but it's none of your business where I sleep."

My heart made a frantic sprint in my chest. "None of my business." My lips were numb. "You were almost an hour late."

"I've been getting to and from the shore for over five years. I'm not your responsibility. You don't need to keep tabs on me." She turned on the water and shoved her hands under the warm spray. "You'll still get in the full session." Grabbing a towel, she wiped at her hands like they'd done her wrong.

I wedged myself between her and the sink. Her words sent my blood pounding even harder in my veins. "You think I give a shit about our session." My breaths were choppy and frantic. "After our night and the test." Was it getting darker in here? Did I need to check the lights?

"Hey." She reached up and touched the side of my face, gazing into my eyes. The light in her eyes flickered from annoyance to concern to understanding. Her other hand rested on my chest. "I'm okay. I'm right here."

Enveloping her in my arms, I squeezed her tight. My chest crushed against hers and my heart tried to make an imprint with its thundering pace. "You're here. You're okay." My voice was shaky. Tackling my physiotherapist, possibly now girlfriend, definitely soon to be mother of my baby wasn't exactly the unaffected and dispassionate vibe I'd professed we'd be able to keep up when we started all this. "I was sitting here thinking of all the things that might've happened to you."

She wriggled her arms and for a second I thought she was trying to push me away, but I wasn't ready to let go yet. Her fingers sunk into my hair, scraping against my scalp and sending shivers down my spine. She cradled my head against her shoulder with her lips pressed against my ear.

Without a word, she seemed to know exactly what I needed. Her steady, rhythmic breaths dropped to the crook of my neck where her head fit perfectly. The gentle brush of her fingers through my hair kept time with her breath.

I stood with my arms around her, feeling her breathe. My grip loosened after a time, it could've been five minutes or five hours, but slowly my heart stopped pounding and I pushed each of those vivid nightmares back into the chest at the back of my mind where those things I couldn't bear to think about were locked away.

I disengaged my arms from around her like a rusty vault door. "Sorry." Ducking my head, I avoided her gaze. Not exactly the best way to show her I was a together guy who she could count on—losing my shit because she was an hour late.

She bent her knees to catch my gaze. "I get it." Her fingers ran along my arm and captured my hand. An energy pulsed between us. The same one I'd felt that night on the beach and the night in the bathroom and that night in the club. She'd managed to break through the walls I'd erected around myself to protect me from what inevitably happened to the people I cared about. It seemed to be a thing with us.

"But don't think you're getting out of what I have in store for you today." It was a wry smile. One that told me she didn't see me any differently after what had just happened and she wasn't going to cut me any slack. Even after the way I'd let her walk out of here, she was still trying to remain professional.

"No special treatment for the heart attack you almost gave me?"

"You're young, you can handle it," she called out over her shoulder.

"About yesterday..."

"We don't have to talk about it. I get that it was a shock to you. Let's tackle one problem at a time." She turned away from me, rushing back to the sink.

I came up behind her and braced my arms on either side of her. "Only, I don't think it's a problem."

"But you—"

"Were shocked. I had always thought of kids as being a far off thing for me. I hadn't thought it would happen any time soon."

"Neither did I." She dropped her head, exposing the nape of her neck to me.

"But that doesn't mean I'm upset about it."

Her body went rigid and I let her escape the cage of my arms.

She rested her back against the counter and crossed her arms over her chest. "What are you saying?"

"I'm saying, I'm ready to have this baby with you. Anything you need, it's yours."

"You're just getting back on your feet. You were talking about how excited you were to live your life without needing to worry about Liv anymore. And you're just okay with this?" She eyed me like she expected me to yell 'psych' and run away.

"The best laid plans, Imo. Was it what I expected was in store for me? No. But now I can think straight, and all I've wanted to do is tell you that I'm in."

She bit her lip. "Let's talk when we're finished." A stall

technique. I'd allow it. Not like I hadn't needed time to get my head around this whole thing.

Our session was more of the same, but my gaze kept drifting to the razor thin strip of exposed skin whenever she'd reach high over her head. The gentle curve of her stomach that held a little piece of us both. Strands of her hair fell around her face as the hastily done-up ponytail slowly failed to stand up to a routine of lifting and pushing.

I curled my fingers around the weight bar instead of running my fingers down the curve of her neck. What would she want long-term with a broken hockey player? I was even more determined to get back on the ice now. I'd show her this wouldn't kill my determination to return to the ice and be the kind of guy she could be proud to be with, that our baby could be proud to have as a dad. A hockey player who went out on his own terms, not as a washed up, broken failure.

Gritting my teeth, I pushed on for three more reps after Imogen called it.

Keeping her fingers away from mine, she guided the bar back to its resting spot. "We're done for today."

I couldn't get over how one hour with her could transform my world and make the scary difficult things seem less so. Maybe I should try again. The possibility that I'd be able to skate this time was tempting. I'd never had motivation like this before.

I got up, bracing my hands on the bar. Funny how the tables had turned. For a long time I'd been hoping for a doctor to show up and tell me it was all over. I was done. Now I wanted to get back out there. Finish out my career on my terms. Be someone my kid could be proud of. Make Imogen proud and show myself I could do it.

"They have a game in three days." I dragged my hands through my hair, interlocking them on the back of my head.

"You're ready, Colm. You can do this." Her fingers brushed against my chest.

My heart thundered, not from the workout she'd put me through, but from the way her fingers tightened against the fabric of my shirt.

"Thank you for telling me how you really feel about all this."

That wasn't half of what I felt for her, but I could take my time. Patience hadn't always been one of my strong suits, but I'd exercise it in spades, if it meant she'd keep touching me.

"There's one other thing I wanted to try this morning, but I wasn't sure you'd be up for it." She trailed her fingers along the physiotherapist table with small measured steps.

This was going to be bad. Was she going to make me run steps until I puked? Maybe put me on roller skates?

"Rip it off like a Band-Aid. What were you thinking?" I braced myself for the worst.

Her gaze fluttered to mine as she closed the gap between us. With both hands on the sides of my head, she dragged my mouth to hers.

Dipping my knee, I grabbed her ass, lifting her and setting her down on the padded table.

Our hands made quick work of my sweats and her scrubs. Off and discarded in record time, flung over my shoulder never to be seen again, if I had my way.

She wrapped her sock covered feet around my back, digging her heels into my ass urging me forward.

I didn't need an invitation any louder than that. Bracing my hands on either side of her and dipping my head, I captured her nipple with my lips and teeth, teasing it as I canted my hips and sunk into her in one long, slow thrust that drew a moan from both of us.

The sounds of our grinding, urgent thrusts were countered by the squeaking of the table. I prayed it wouldn't collapse, because even that might not have deterred me from wringing every last hungry moan from her body.

She tightened around me until it teetered on the edge of painful. It wasn't long after that the electric shocks of pleasure ricocheted through every cell. I collapsed before remembering to brace my weight.

I brushed back a strand of hair from her face. "I'm up for that workout any day you want to run me through the gauntlet."

28

IMO

Our pretense of client and physiotherapist had ripped away the second he'd wrapped his trembling arms around me when I'd arrived. The warm, floating feeling was back inside me as though it had never left, despite yesterday's anxiety and the night in my car, blanketed by the muscled weight of Colm.

Even through my protests, he carried me up two flights of stairs. I let it slide because he seemed to need to prove to himself that he could do it. We fell into bed and made the most of it, only getting out when the delivery man showed up with our Chinese food. I hadn't had a day this lazy in a long time. Getting used to this could be dangerous.

We listened to music, debating which James Bay album was his best. There might have been a cooling off period after some intense disagreement. Colm's room didn't feel like the makeshift cell like he'd turned it into when I'd first come to work with him. It was cozy.

He never seemed to go more than a few minutes without a touch, a caress or pulling me onto his lap. I'd forgotten what this felt like. I let myself feel the pang in my chest that

I'd kept at bay for a long time. This was what it felt like to be with someone. Really with them. It was the small moments that seemed so insignificant, but when you looked back on them, they were the ones that you yearned for most.

I wrapped my arms around his bare chest and sank into his hold. It had been so long since it felt this natural to relax in someone else's arms. He tapped into a part of me I'd thought wouldn't ever want to emerge again. I drifted away on the tide of sleep, pulling further and further away from the worries of the day.

"Sleep, Imo."

"You were talking."

He let his fingertips brush down my face, starting from my forehead and trailing down over my eyelids, closing each one, before caressing my lips and down my chin. "It's nothing important. Get some rest."

The silence of the room wasn't overwhelming or empty like it usually was during my nights. It was filled with Colm's warm embrace, steady heartbeat, and the calm that settled over us like a cocoon.

~

"Good morning." His lips brushed against my cheek.

"Morning." My groggy, sleep laden voice was nowhere near as smooth as his, which had no right to sound that good this early in the morning. "What time is it?"

"After ten."

I rolled over in the circle of his arms. "I can't remember the last time I slept this late. You really wore me out." Grinning, I pushed myself up. Morning breath be damned. His soft, yet firm lips were my new favorite morning snack.

With a hooded gaze, he squeezed my ass, before giving it

a gentle swat. "We can't get started with that again, not yet anyway. Are you up for breakfast? I can make waffles or French toast. There's bacon and eggs too." He let go of me and swung his legs to his side of the bed.

"You cook?" I scooted up to the headboard, dragging the sheet with me.

"Our mornings haven't exactly started conventionally, so I haven't had a chance to flex my skills before. Why do you seem surprised?" He tugged open the dresser drawers and pulled out a pair of gray sweatpants.

No freaking fair. "Not many guys whip up full breakfasts on the fly. I'd imagine that number is even smaller for pro athletes."

"Don't let the jars of toenail clippings fool you. I'm fairly domesticated. I had a hungry teenager to take care of, and she was only going to let me get away with cereal for so long." He smiled, but there was a touch of sadness to his reminiscing about growing up with Liv.

"Waffles sound perfect. Can I help?"

"If you want to eat, you'd better." He leaned down and kissed me on the tip of my nose.

I got out of bed and Colm handed me one of his shirts. "No pants?"

"You won't need them." His lazy smirk made my mouth water.

The heated floor kept my feet toasty even without socks.

Together we were wearing the perfect outfit. His gray sweatpants hung low on his hips and the white t-shirt hit me at mid-thigh.

He poured me a big glass of orange juice and began pulling everything out of the fridge.

I downed the ice cold drink and felt a flutter. My hand shot to my stomach and a gasp escaped my lips.

"What's wrong? What happened?" He threw down everything in his hands and was in front of me, his gaze bouncing from my eyes to my stomach.

He cupped my cheek. "Was it the baby?"

"I—I think so."

He glanced at the orange juice and back to me. "Sometimes when you drink something cold, it can get the baby's attention."

I tilted my head. "How do you know that?"

His cheeks pinked up. "I've been reading up since I found out. Can I?" He nodded toward my stomach.

It only felt a little silly that after he'd literally peeled my underwear off with his teeth, he'd worry about touching my stomach.

"Of course."

He flexed his hand before settling it over my t-shirt-covered bulge. He was gentle, as though his moves might scare the baby off like a school of fish.

We stood in silence, awaiting the movement that had stopped me in my tracks. I picked up the glass of orange juice and took another hearty gulp. It was more than a flutter this time, but I couldn't tell if he could feel it too.

His wide-eyed gaze met mine for confirmation.

I nodded and he sucked in a breath and dropped to one knee in front of me, protecting his recovering leg the way I'd always gotten on his case to. "I can feel the little bean. They're so small." His voice was full of awe and there was a sheen to his eyes.

I ran my fingers along his bearded chin. "It's amazing."

"You're amazing." He placed a reverent kiss on my stomach and wrapped one arm around my back, pulling me closer. "Thank you."

"No thanks required." I laughed and cupped his cheek.

We were frozen in time, living in this perfect moment of pure unbridled happiness. It was a moment we both knew never lasted forever and could be ripped away without notice. I swallowed past the lump in my throat and my nostrils flared. *Do not cry, Imo. Don't you dare freaking cry.*

Colm let go of my waist and got up from the floor. "Let's get you two fed."

We worked together in the kitchen, moving in unison, always handing over what the other person needed before they asked for it, like we couldn't stop being aware of one another. The smells made my stomach rumble—it was probably shaking the bean like an earthquake.

"My first doctor's appointment is at the end of the week. Did you want to come?"

He looked up from his plate. "Of course. I can take you. Pick you up from your apartment and we can go together."

"That's okay. It's in the hospital across from the rehab center; I can walk across the street and meet you."

"I could pick you up from work and we can walk together."

"You don't have to do that, really. I can meet you there."

He nodded, but didn't look altogether happy about me making the twenty-yard walk all on my own. "You're right. I'll meet you." He shoveled a forkful of food into his mouth with a big smile that didn't reach his eyes.

We cleaned up and he disappeared as I turned on the dishwasher. Heading back to the bedroom, I spotted the bathroom light on.

Standing in front of the mirror, he stared back at his reflection with a handful of shaving cream. Lifting his hand, he covered the hair with the fluffy white mixture.

"Do you want me to help?" He turned to me with a shaving cream-covered beard, and his gaze flicked between the old-fashioned razor and me. "I promise I won't nick you." I entered the bathroom and hopped up onto the counter in front of him. A part of me was sad to see the beard go. The soft rub of it against my skin and between my thighs, but this was a big step to him. A return to something he'd thought he'd lost. I'd be sad to see it go, but not that he was reclaiming a part of himself he felt was gone forever.

He nodded, held out the blade to me, and moved between my parted legs.

Turning on the water, I tugged up the stopper for the sink.

I stared into his eyes, before breaking the connection and lifting the blade to his cheek. Keeping my hand steady, I dragged it down, careful of the pressure, slowly revealing the old Colm one stroke at a time.

His hips settled against my spread legs, the nudge of his growing erection pressing against his sweat pants and to my naked core.

I dipped the razor into the warm water and went back to his face. There was no sound in the room other than the gentle scrape of the sharpened metal against his skin, droplets of water hitting the small pool in the sink, and our combined breath.

Down his cheek. Around his chin. His upper lip. He held my gaze. The look in his eyes was like the one he'd had that first time we sat listening to music on the beach. Not the bitter one I'd run up against over the past couple months, or the one who'd taken me like a man who'd lost everything, but like the smiling guy who only wanted to cheer me up. The one who made my heart race for totally different reasons than the Colm I'd met again later.

But I loved them both. An internal jolt rocked me at those words. I loved them both. Only I didn't mean Colm and Preston. It was Colm—then and now. Two sides of the same coin and I'd given my heart to them both for completely different reasons.

My hand dropped away from his face and I lifted the towel from around his neck to gently wipe away the remnants of the shaving cream.

"How's it look?" He stared into my eyes like he was peeling away the layers of my soul, flaying me with a raw emotional energy that threatened to overpower me.

Lifting my hand, I wiped away the last of the cream on his earlobe. "You look like the old Colm." I forced the words past my lips, unable to say more.

He shoved down his sweats with one hand and pushed inside of me in one smooth motion, not stopping until he was fully seated, stretching and opening me like only he could. Every nerve ending came alive like I'd been attached to a live wire.

I held onto him with my arms wrapped around his back. My face rubbed against the newly clean shaven cheek.

He buried his head in the crook of my neck.

This wasn't the furious coming together that seemed to have conquered every sense I had, but it was overwhelming nonetheless.

He ground against me like even an inch of separation was too much. Each rub sent shockwaves through my clit.

Wrapping my legs around his back, I pulled him closer. His thundering heartbeat drummed against my chest.

"More," I moaned against his skin. Every cell was singing and I was blissed out like never before.

Snaking one hand up my back, he gripped my hair at the back of my neck, before retreating and slamming back into me. The force and power sent an explosive orgasm ricocheting through me, every cell hanging on for dear life as the sensory overload threatened to shut me down.

I threw my head back and screamed out his name.

His hungry kisses peppered my shoulders and neck. He tightened his hold on me, expanding inside of me as he came.

We clung to each other, breathing through the comedown from the all-consuming energy between us.

"Does that count as second breakfast?" I ran the back of my hand across his smooth cheek.

"Nope, I didn't get to eat you, so it doesn't count as a meal." He trailed his fingers up and down my spine.

Neither of us let go, content to be in one another's arms and cocooned in this perfect moment.

"Move in with me." His head jerked back and he stared into my eyes, brushing the sweaty hair back from my face.

My lips parted, but the words stalled. "I—we can't."

"Do you have an ankle monitor I don't know about? Why can't you? Why can't we? You're going to have my baby. I want you here with me."

Every part of me wanted to scream out *yes* and fling my arms around his neck. But it was all so new. We had a future together, in some form, but we hadn't really even dated and he wanted me to move in? Why was he asking now?

He loosened his arms and dropped one hand to my stomach. "The two of you."

The baby. This was that good guy thing of his. He was pulling himself out of a period of recovery. He'd have a lot to focus on once he was back on the team. He needed to focus on himself—at least for a bit. Now wasn't the time to add whatever it was we were doing on top of trying to figure out being new parents.

I t hadn't taken much convincing to get her to stay. Our breakfast had turned into lunch, which flowed into dinner. It was a day like the one I'd wanted to have after our first night together. It was one I'd hoped we'd have even more of in the future. Today, things had been different.

She'd been different. She'd scraped away the beard I'd been hiding behind, chiseled at the walls I'd erected around my heart and let hers down for a fraction of a second. Then I'd asked her to move in with me.

It was a stupid move, but I wanted this every day. I wanted her sitting on the edge of the sink, watching me shave every morning. But then I did what I always did. I jumped eight steps ahead, pushing things too hard too fast. *Take a breather, Frost.*

I tugged down the sheet covering her and stared at the gentle curve of her stomach. She was in the second trimester now, but the bump was still small. Inside her was a piece of her and me that would forever link us.

Every dream I'd had about her for the last five years was

coming true in a way I'd never imagined. We'd made something beautiful together and I'd get to meet him or her in four or five months.

Calls needed to be made. We'd go to the best doctors and the best hospital. Normally, setting foot in a hospital sent my stomach roiling, but it would be different this time.

All those ideas I thrown out about not needing to take responsibility for anyone had been me trying to brush aside a hole in my life. Aimless and without any direction, I'd have done whatever I needed to cope, but this was with Imogen. We could be parents together.

A ring. I needed to buy a ring. I'd been ready to marry her that night on the beach, why the hell wouldn't I want to do it now? Back then I would've been a guy who didn't know any better, but now I did. I'd gone through the relationship gauntlet, disregarding my instincts, and it had been a disaster every time. I'd convinced myself things couldn't be this easy. I couldn't feel a connection to someone and be drawn to them and know they were the right person for me.

Only it wasn't crazy, because here we were years later and she still made me feel the same way. Hell, I felt even better than before, and now she felt the same—and she was pregnant. It was the universe finally giving me a break; I couldn't second-guess this now. How would I get her to see that too?

Slow down, Colm. This was what got me in trouble before, skipping ahead of where we currently were. At this point, I was happy when she was still in my bed when I woke up—were we ready for a step that big?

She'd pushed me hard to regain what I'd lost. But taking that next step, getting back on the ice, scared the shit out of me. Maybe, if I could show her that everything had worked and I was back to being that guy, she wouldn't be so freaked out about making things serious between us. Making this real.

The father of her child wouldn't be a washed up, unreliable, reclusive mess of a hockey player. I'd do everything right by her. She was different than any woman I'd been with before and I was different now. The mistakes of my past wouldn't be the mistakes of my future. I'd have a better future with her.

Wrapped around her, I knew what I needed to do. The step I'd need to make to set everything back on track. Breathing in her scent, I let it wash away the worries and strengthen my resolve.

I crept downstairs and grabbed my phone. Scrolling through months of notifications, I found our group chat. It hadn't been used in a while. They'd probably created one without me.

Me: Guys, I need your help.

Their replies poured in like they'd been waiting for me to ask all this time. How'd I get so lucky as to have friends like these? They'd stuck by me when I didn't deserve it one bit.

Emmett: When?

Declan: Where?

Heath: Who?

We hammered out the details in minutes. Ford stayed silent, but I couldn't blame him after the way things had ended last time. I needed to talk to Liv.

I sent him another message. His reply came more slowly, but at least he replied. It was more than I'd done.

Gathering up my gear, I sent Imogen a message and let her know where and when to meet me. Then I steeled myself for what came next. My palms were sweaty, slipping off the door handle as I stepped out of my house. The entire drive, my stomach threatened to revolt. There were so many things I'd fucked up in the past year and I'd start making amends today.

The long walk down the apartment hallway sent **déjà vu** racing through my head. Only this time I wasn't racing to the same door, pounding on it thinking the worst. But I was prepared for it.

My knuckles rapped against the wood.

"Why'd you want me to—" The words died on the tip of her tongue and Liv stared back at me with fury blazing in her eyes. "What do you want?" Her fingers tightened on the door.

"I came to talk."

"Now you want to talk. Now you show up." She shoved at my chest. "Why didn't you answer any of my calls? Or texts?" Each word accompanied by another shove.

"Because I'm an asshole."

Her eyes widened.

"Quit hitting him." Ford came up behind her and wrapped his arms around her, tugging her into his apartment. Their apartment. "Come in."

"Are you in on this?" She glared up at him.

"He's here. Let that be enough for now."

Liv jerked her arms down and out of his grip. "Fine. Talk. I'm going to go sharpen the knives."

True to her word, she jerked open one of the drawers and grabbed a knife and sharpening stone. No one could say I'd helped raise a pushover. The metal scrape of the knife was the only sound in the loft apartment.

"I've been an asshole."

"You said that already. I'm going to need more." She drove the blade down over the stone.

Ford sat on the chair at the kitchen table.

I sighed. "And I was wrong."

A pointed glare from Liv.

"You're your own person and I should've respected your choices. It's not up to me to dictate how you live your life."

The metal clattered to the stone. "I get you being upset we lied." A brief flash of guilt shot across her face. "And if I'd known you were coming back early I'd have never said not to tell you about the fire. I knew you'd overreact and I didn't want you to worry when you were finishing up your rehab and I was completely safe."

"That was a mature and considerate thing to do."

She picked up another knife. "Don't patronize me."

"I'm not." I held up my hands, palms out. "I'm not patronizing you."

"And I know the little video didn't help things." Her cheeks flushed.

I winced, trying to scrub the memory from my mind. If mental bleach were a thing I'd be the first in line at the store.

"Let's never talk about that again."

"Deal." The word shot out of her mouth and she set down the knives.

"So why are you here now? What made you show up out of the blue?"

I dragged my hands over my face. "A lot's been going on."

She rounded the kitchen counter. "Is everything okay?"

"Things are good. Great even, but...I couldn't take this next step in my life without setting things right with you. I should've done this a long time ago."

"No shit," Ford mumbled under his breath.

"What's changed?" Liv walked around the breakfast bar and leaned against one of the chairs. "Why has your obsession with me going to med school and not ruining my life changed?" She put 'ruin' in air quotes.

I stared out the large industrial windows to the morning sky outside. "After that first night at the hospital, I didn't let you come back."

Her head jerked back at my abrupt change in topic.

"It scared the shit out of me. Being behind the nurses' station, coloring and drinking those tiny cranberry juice cups, waiting for them to get out of surgery was a hell of a lot different than seeing them both in those beds." She ran her hands up and down her arms. "But you went for the two days they were there."

I nodded. The cold, disinfectant-filled rooms and hallways were different when I wasn't showing up there to retrieve something from my parents in between them scrubbing into surgery, or needing them to sign a permission slip. The nurses were used to me, I melded into the scenery.

"There was a woman in the ICU along with them. The nurses never talked loud enough for most people to hear, but they'd still talk, and the residents were the worst. They never shut up, always trying to show off."

"And you wanted me to be one of them?"

I tilted my head, giving her a sad smile.

"They were going over the charts and the full patient history. It was a mom. Presented with some insane issues. She was scheduled for surgery for the day after Mom and Dad got into the accident."

Her room had been beside Dad's. When the residents did their rounds, wheeling around their laptops, they were pissed. Several had chosen their residencies to work with one or both of my parents. That they were lying in the hospital beds instead seemed like nothing more than an inconvenience to half of them.

"Mom was going to perform the surgery, but they had to call someone else in. Transporting her to another hospital wasn't going to happen. She wouldn't make it.

"They did the surgery and wheeled her back into the room. One of the residents talked about her chances where I could hear. They were slim to none. A matter of hours. He said if Mom had been the one at the helm of the surgery, she'd have had a fighting chance. Maybe a fifteen or twenty percent chance of recovering."

"Colm, no one can know that."

"Her husband had visited her every day, staying for the whole day like me. We kept running into one another at the coffee machine or cafeteria with that shell-shocked look we always saw people wearing. But after the attending explained things, he left. I thought maybe he couldn't deal with it, but he came back an hour later." I brushed the tears off my face. "He had three little kids with him. They couldn't have been more than six. They were so little. They reminded me of when I'd push you on the tire swing in the backyard."

Liv held onto my hand.

"And they had little cards they'd made her. I saw them walk by and I could hear them talking to her. They kept telling her they loved her so much and asking when she was coming home and—" My chest ached and I caught the emotions rising in me like a drowning tide. "The dad asked one of the nurses to wait with the kids and broke down in the pantry across from Mom and Dad's room."

"Colm, that's terrible. I'm sure that wasn't easy."

"It was my fault."

"What? No."

"If I hadn't bitched about them coming to the game, they'd have been in surgery that day. How many other people were lost because they weren't there?"

"The other doctors said she'd have only have had a fifteen or twenty percent chance even if Mom and Dad had been there."

"Every little bit matters. Those kids had to grow up without a mom. They never got to hold her hand again or make her silly cards or shitty macaroni ornaments. And our parents were gone. I stole that chance from them. I took them away from you. The med school fixation, I don't even know." I wiped my nose on the sleeve of my shirt. "Maybe I felt like it was righting a wrong or something? A way to repair some of the damage I'd done by taking two doctors from the world. I was trying to give one back."

Liv wrapped her arms around my neck and squeezed me tight. "No one can predict the future. Not even you, you big doofus. You've been dealing with this all this time? Carrying this burden that was never yours to bear? We all make choices. We all screw things up, but you can't take the blame for the fifty things that come down the line after that. It's not your fault. You were the best parent I could've ever had. And I'm sorry you had to carry this with you, but that's the kind of shitty obliviousness kids are best at." She let out a watery laugh.

I followed along with that. "I didn't mean to throw all that out there. I came to tell you I'm sorry and I was wrong."

"I'm glad you told me everything. No one should have to feel that way. You were an amazing dad, Colm. You took care of me and I appreciate every sacrifice. The opening for an amazing dad was filled and is now closed. But the role of awesome big brother is wide open and yours, if you want it."

"That I can do. I might need some pointers every so often."

"Don't worry." Ford came up and held out his hand. "I've got you covered."

I grasped it and he tugged me up for a hug.

30

IMO

"We'll get back to you as soon as we have the final numbers for the new clinic. Are you sure you wouldn't rather stay in Philly? We have an office in Center City, not far from your current location. State of the art facility with interesting and challenging patients. Our new practice by the shore will mainly cater to the over 60s. Run of the mill hip and knee recoveries."

"Yes, of course." The rightness of this decision ticked down each day, but walking away scared me. Walking away from this job meant walking to what? Colm and I hadn't even figured out us, and now there would be a baby stacked on top of that question mark in our lives.

What if he was traded to a team on the other side of the country? What if he didn't want to shoulder the responsibility of fatherhood after already being that guy for as long as he'd remembered? What if he spiraled again?

I pulled up to the rink, not sure why Colm had told me to meet him here. There were a few cars in the parking lot. The practice rink in Jersey wasn't anywhere near as flashy as the stadium. Hell, from the outside it was barely a step above the Roll With It Skate World, but at least the sign wasn't missing any letters.

The door handle was cold, and I zipped my jacket up all the way. Rinks in the winter were always colder than outside. I'd forgotten. It had been so long since I'd been to one. Leaving Colm's place this morning knowing I was going to an interview had made the toast he'd left for me harder to choke down.

Waking up beside him had become the norm after my late arrival for our session. We'd clung to one another that day and the next. The pattern came so easily it scared me. I'd leave to go to work and come back to his house. When I needed to go to my apartment to pick up some clothes and other things, he'd come with me.

It felt weird to have him in my space. For so long, there'd been no one in my place besides me. He walked around, looking at things, running a finger along the framed pictures of me with Fern and Charlie. Me and Becca. The Kings and I at a backyard barbecue last spring. And a picture of me and Preston. I was sitting on his lap looking up at him adoringly. Colm lingered, staring at the picture.

He'd been quiet on the drive back to his place and he'd stripped me in record time once the front door closed. This time it wasn't fast and hungry. He made love to me like he wanted to brand an imprint on my soul and I wasn't sure he'd failed.

Our situation threw tangled on top of complicated. How much of this was real and how much of it was a product of Colm's need to do the right thing and step up to the responsibilities life threw at him? Could he pull those two things apart or had they become so intertwined, they were now one and the same?

The rhythmic sound of skates and sticks hitting the ice

filled the tunnel as I walked farther into the rink. There wasn't a full roster, but there were more than a handful of guys on the ice.

Their jerseys flapped against their bodies as they whipped around the ice, keeping low with sticks in their hands.

Colm skated by, smiling. He grabbed his helmet off the ledge by the box and shoved it on his head.

A breakthrough. After all the anguish he'd shouldered about letting his team down, he'd done it. Tears flooded my eyes, but we were both all smiles now. I rushed forward, right up against the glass, to watch him fly.

He spotted me and waved, changing directions in a split second. His movement was perfection. Fluid, not an ounce of stiffness. Instead of banging into the boards to stop, he used his hands to slow himself and leaned over the halfway in front of the bench box.

"You made it."

"Have you ever known me to not show up?"

His gaze roamed my face, searching, like I somehow looked different when he was standing on the ice. "No, you always show." Sweat rolled down his face and he was panting.

"How long have you been here?"

"Four hours. The guys came with me and have been helping me get back up to speed."

"Four!" My voice boomed in the rink. "That's insane. You're pushing yourself too fast."

His grin widened and he stared back at me in that way that made me feel like he'd never looked at another woman before. Sparks of electricity pulsed along my skin. "It took me nearly two hours to put my skate on the ice. I've only been skating for two hours out of the four. The guys..." He looked over his shoulder. "They came through."

"Of course, we did." Declan slammed into the wall beside him. "How could he ever doubt us, Imo?" Declan shook his head and jerked his thumb in Colm's direction.

"I have no idea, Declan. He's stubborn sometimes."

"Understatement of the year. How are you doing?" He leaned forward, planting a very sweaty kiss on my cheek.

"I'm good. Even better now that this one is out there with you guys." I held out my hands toward Colm, presentation-style.

"He looks good, doesn't he?" Declan leaned onto the rink ledge.

"He's right here."

"Get your asses back out here. We've got a lot of work to do." Emmett's hands were cupped around his mouth, recalling them both to the game.

"Got to go." Colm lifted himself with his hands and kissed me. It wasn't a peck on the cheek like Declan's, but a full on someone dump a bucket of water on us kiss, complete with his gloved hand on the back of my head.

More than a couple heads turned on the ice.

I sat and watched him, thinking about that declarative kiss and what it would mean to the group dynamics. How would everyone feel about that?

Sitting in the molded plastic seat, I shoved my hands in my pockets and kept my eyes on the ice. He was lightning fast and didn't miss a beat. If I hadn't known how hard he'd worked, I'd have thought he'd never had a day off.

A few of the rookies took to the ice, probably drawn by the fact that some of their hockey heroes were out there. Colm huddled up with one or two doling out advice, pointing to different spots on the ice and coaching them through breakaways or other moves. He was in the zone. Being out there with his team breathed even more life into him and my heart glowed.

I could see myself there with a little baby watching his or her dad out on the ice, doing the thing he loved and kicking ass at it.

Movement in the stands from the other side of the rink caught my eye.

Bailey sat halfway up with her gaze trained on the ice.

I made my way over and sat beside her.

"How's he doing?" She didn't take her eyes off Colm.

"You can see for yourself. He hasn't missed a beat."

"Shit, I was hoping you wouldn't say that." Bailey tugged on her ponytail, giving herself a temporary facelift.

"You were the one who's been riding his ass to get back on the ice. You were the one who practically blackmailed me to get me to work with him. I figured you'd be doing cartwheels in the stands."

She dragged her hands down her face. "I have, but I've been fighting the tide of the higher ups. They've got young healthy kids coming from all over the world to play. They're itching for the cup this season more than ever. The owners wanted better results last season, and with Colm in the mix, I knew we had a shot. He's a killer player, I knew that from the first day I spotted him, but he's had two back-to-back injuries, and this is a young man's game run by old assholes." She glared up at the currently empty owner's box.

"They want to end his contract."

Out on the ice, Colm whipped by. The lineup of pucks didn't stand a chance with him. Ford was in the net, but Colm still snuck three by that brick wall of a goalie. His laughter carried across the vast open space. He spotted the two of us sitting together and raised his gloved hand in a wave.

I waved back numbly. Bailey's wave was like she was a lifelike animatronic figure.

Bile rushed to the back of my throat. "He's worked so hard."

"I can see that. You act like I didn't see his grifter impersonation a couple months ago. Fuck!" She threw down her notepad. "If he'd been like this a couple months ago, maybe things would be different now. I don't know." Misery radiated from her voice.

A couple months ago. What if I hadn't run the first time the guys asked? What if I'd volunteered to help him and get him in shape? The what-ifs stacked up into a mountain of regret.

"Is it a done deal?" I tore my gaze away from him to her.

She let out a deflated sigh. "No, it's not, but once that chatter starts, the wheels are in motion. Trust me, I'd much rather have another Colm on this team than some of the colossal dickheads coming up right now, but they don't tell me everything. If they're striking deals, I might not know about it until the ink is dry. My hands are tied at a certain point."

"How long until you'll know for sure?"

"Maybe a week." She shrugged. "Maybe a month. Maybe it doesn't happen."

"It will destroy him."

"He's made it this far. He's walking and skating. Some guys don't even get that."

"You saw him before. This could kick him right back down into that place again." I grabbed onto her arm. "Don't tell him today. Look at how happy he is. Trust me when I say he needed today. Don't take it away from him."

He took the helmet off and whipped his hair around, splashing sweat on the other guys. His smile from twenty rows away was blinding.

"Once you know, call me and I'll help prepare him."

Bailey picked up her notebook and stood. "What a fucking nightmare."

31

COLM

My skates hit the solid floor of ice beneath me. A part of me had been reawakened when I finally made it onto the ice. Declan, Emmett, Heath, and Ford had stood beside me for the nearly two hours it took to get me up on my skates.

"If you'd told us this was your problem before, we'd have strapped you to a backboard and carried you out here and skated you around a bit to get you comfortable." Heath leaned against the Plexiglas wall of the box.

My head was between my knees and I choked back the vomit threatening to paint the floor.

"It's been like this since the accident?" Declan crouched in front of me.

"Every time I've tried to skate. This is the furthest I've made it."

Emmett clapped me on the shoulder. "We'll take that win."

"You don't have to do it all today." Ford sat beside me. "We can come back as many times as you need us to."

They were the best friends—no, family—a person could ask for. "Thanks for being here."

"We'd have been here a lot sooner, if you hadn't been doing your Grumpy Cat routine all summer. Are we skating or not?" Heath had a way of deflating the tension in most situations.

On shaky legs I stood, pushing down all the fears about what might happen out there. Imogen was on her way. I'd given her the address and told her to be here in another hour and a half. She was my failsafe, in case I tried to chicken out. I could do this. I needed her to see me out here, whole and unafraid.

"Just a step out there." It was more to myself than anyone else.

"One step, then we reassess." Declan shoved his skates on.

I don't know how long I stood at the open half door to the ice. Five minutes? Twenty minutes? But no one made a sound. No one forced me out there.

My fingers tightened on the wooden ledge and I lowered my skate to the ice. Holding on like it was my first time out there, my foot connected and slid forward an inch. My body corrected, and, like slipping on an old pair of shoes, I was upright without thinking about what came next.

Another step onto the ice with both feet under me. I stood, breathing in the freezing rink air. It filled my lungs and the sights and sounds were sharper. All the blood pumping in my ears had drowned out the familiarity of this place.

This was my second home. My only home when I'd had none to go back to.

Another step. And another. Without a word the guys were

beside me. We took the lap together in our old formation with me at the front. They slowed a bit as I got closer to the still-open door to the team bench, but I blew past it and they came up behind me, letting me take the lead. A fiery energy coursed through my veins. I was back with my team, the friends I'd tried to push away, but were so damn stubborn they hadn't let me. And I'd never loved them more for it.

We'd skated like that for the next hour. They took their cues from me and kept up the gentle pressure of not letting me psych myself out. And then Imogen arrived.

The look on her face like I was walking on water out here warmed my heart. Pride radiated from her gaze and I wanted that from her every day, all day. I wanted to see that she was proud of what I'd done and who I was. It would take some work to mend all the fences I'd wrecked, but—I looked over my shoulder at Ford—I was getting there.

I hadn't been able to hold back from kissing Imo. We'd never set rules for what we were or decided who to tell or not tell, but I didn't want anyone to question what she meant to me.

Ford knew she was pregnant, so it hadn't come as a surprise to him, but he was as tight-lipped as Heath was loose, so he hadn't mentioned it to anyone yet.

There would be questions in the locker room once we finished on the ice. Bailey popped in for a second, but she was gone with little more than a wave. At least she'd peel that *Reserved for Colm* label off the ball vise I was sure she had in her office.

"How are you feeling?" Heath grabbed his water bottle and squirted it into his mouth. Some ran down his chin, joining the rest of the sweat covering his face and neck. "You know I was busting your balls to make you laugh, right?"

"Of course, man. You always know the exact wrong thing

to say at the exact right time."

Heath held out his arms wide and skated backward. "Damn right. It's my super power."

"What is? Man buns and saying inappropriate things?" Emmett skated behind him and locked his arm around Heath's neck.

"My hair is amazing," Heath wheezed before shoving Emmett away.

"Enough screwing around. We've got a center to get back on the ice." Declan knocked his stick against their helmets.

Some of the rookies showed up a bit later. Their awe only added to the confidence boost I'd gotten from not puking once out here.

I was sweaty and tired, and I'd never felt better. It was like oiling up an old creaky gate.

We wrapped up practice and I searched the stands for Imogen. She stood by the tunnel to the locker room with a smile that didn't reach her eyes. It wasn't the wide infectious one she'd worn when she showed up and saw me on the ice. This one was capped with shuttered eyes and a porcelain finish.

"You okay?" I climbed out of the box and shook off my gloves, letting them fall to the ground.

I cupped her cheek and searched her eyes for the answer.

"I'm good. Only a little tired." She clasped her hands in front of her and dropped her head.

"Some of that is probably my fault?" I ducked, trying to catch her gaze.

She nodded.

"Let's get you two out of here. It'll take me five minutes to change."

Then a noise I hadn't heard since the jungle gym in the

sixth grade broke through the connection I'd been trying to forge with Imogen.

"Colm and Imo sitting in the tree. K-I-S-S-I-N-G. First comes love, then comes marriage, then comes a baby in a baby carriage."

Imo's head shot up, her wide-eyed gaze shooting past me.

"Heath, enough," I called out over my shoulder. The guys filed past, leaving us behind.

"Did you—"

"I haven't told anyone. I figured we'd do that together. You know they're going to go out and buy a hockey onesie the second they know."

"It might be a girl."

"Never stopped Liv from slapping on a pair of skates." I held onto Imo's arms, soaking up the small smile on her lips. I didn't care how big it was, only that it was real.

The curve of her lips grew even bigger and brighter. "You're right."

"I'll be right back. Don't go anywhere."

"Don't worry. I have no place else to be."

I jogged back to the locker room, ready for the world's fastest shower and change in history. The door flew open and I was blindsided by a part tackle, part hug, lifting me off my feet.

"Careful. We don't need someone else getting hurt."

Emmett set me down on my feet. "You and Imogen?" His grin was megawatt wide. "Does Avery know?"

"I don't know."

"Oh man, if I know something before Avery, she's going to lose it." He rubbed his hands together.

"How long has it been going on?" Declan tugged his jersey over his head.

"It's still new, so we're taking it slow."

Heath yanked his skates off. "I didn't think slow was in your vocabulary. You're always like, 'hello ma'am, very nice to meet you on our first date. Would you like to move in with me? Perhaps an international vacation while we wait for the movers to pack up your belongings. Have you met my little sister yet?'"

I threw my sweaty jersey at him, hitting him as he rambled into the next part where I got their name tattooed on my chest.

"For the record, I have no tattoos."

"That we know of." Heath lifted an eyebrow.

"She's waiting for me. Yes, Imo and I are dating. No, there's no wedding planned." I left out that I'd already asked her to move in with me; those were extenuating circumstances. And the part where I'd already checked in with a few jewelers around town to see what they had in stock. There was nothing wrong with being prepared, and if the right moment presented itself, maybe...

"We're glad you two finally pulled the pin on that sexual tension grenade." Emmett wrapped a towel around his waist.

"It was almost as bad as Liv and Ford." An avalanche of dirty towels cascaded over Heath.

All eyes swung to me. My fists clenched in the reflexive way they had since I'd found out about the two of them, but I took a deep breath. Her crush had been pretty obvious, looking back on it. I let out a laugh. It was a little strained, but I was still a little new to being okay with the two of them being a couple.

Every shoulder relaxed and chatter filled the room again. Making sure I didn't still reek, I went out to find Imo pacing and biting her bottom lip.

"What's wrong?"

She straightened and let her lip fall free of her teeth. It was plump and wet and I couldn't hold back. I wrapped my arms around her and dropped a kiss on her lips.

"Nothing's wrong."

I ran my fingers along her cheek. "You looked worried."

"No."

"Are you sure?"

She wrapped her fingers around mine and leaned into my arms.

"Completely."

Those moments when she let me in—really let me in, holding my gaze and giving me everything I'd hoped for—made it hard to imagine anything before her. And I didn't want to experience anything after her.

"I still don't get how you can eat that when it's so cold out."

She licked her way around the cone. Her tongue was proving too much of a temptation, and I readjusted myself as I walked. "It's never too cold for ice cream. Especially not coffee ice cream with chocolate jimmies. Where are we going anyway?"

"It's a surprise."

Her gaze narrowed. "You're not going to take me to some sex club, are you?"

"That's exactly where I'd want to take my five months-pregnant girlfriend. A sex club."

"Damn."

I stumbled over her softly spoken word.

She peered over at me, smiling with ice cream drying on her nose.

I liked where this was going. "Arrangements can be made. Just say when."

"Maybe in a year or so when I'm trying to rediscover my wild side."

"Your wish is my command."

We turned the corner. The marquee ahead of us was lit up with warm, glowing bulbs.

"We're here."

Looking up from her ice cream, Imo's eyes widened. She looked from me to the sign and back to me. "Are you serious?" Her ice cream forgotten, she dumped it into the nearest trashcan.

"James Bay. James Bay is here? In Philly, today?"

"From the sign it sure looks that way."

"Do we have tickets?"

I pulled the printout of our tickets from my coat pocket.

"Holy shit. Let's go." She pulled the folded pieces of paper out of my hands and dragged me by my coat cuff. Her excitement was infectious and I swore I'd pay for James Bay to fly over from the UK every month if I could keep getting this reaction out of her. A few calls were all it had taken—that, and the promise of a sold out show, even if I needed to buy out every seat on my own. Even with such late notice of this exceptionally late addition to a tour that had been over for months, I'd only had to buy half.

But watching Imogen sing along to every word was worth all the money. Seeing her giddy and nearly bouncing in her seat after each song finished made everything else fade away. I'd gotten on the ice. I was listening to James Bay with the woman who had made everything possible. And our little one was safe and sound. This was a perfect day.

I felt untouchable.

32

IMO

The night after Colm's first skate had been magical. We were front row center with James Bay only a few feet away. After each song break, I'd look over at Colm and that leaden weight of the knowledge I had settled heavier on my chest. What could I say? How could I fix this?

I didn't have any more answers the next day at work, and the flipping and kicking had become more pronounced and was no longer mistakable for an upset stomach. "We've got an appointment Wednesday afternoon, if that works for you."

"Yes, perfect. Thank you." I ended the call and shoved the phone into my bag. Rushing out of work, I saw that I wasn't the last to leave for the day. That was a new development. I hopped into my car and headed straight to Colm's place. For the past week that had been my natural destination. Colm's house.

It was crazy that his house was where I wanted to go after work. Sometimes he'd pick me up and we'd go to my place, but it always felt a bit cramped compared to his. Plus, his kitchen was much better, and wow, did he ever know his way around it.

He'd asked me to move in with him. He hadn't brought it up since that day, but the question lingered in my head. Moving in with him was a big step. I snorted. Not like having his baby didn't also fall into that category. But packing up my apartment and unpacking those boxes would change things in a way even a baby wouldn't.

It would mean we were in a relationship. Were we already? Our time together straddled a no-man's land neither of us wanted to define. Defining it made it real. It made it something that could end.

Bailey hadn't gotten back to me about what the final decision was on Colm re-joining the team. She said she'd try her best, but what happened if they didn't let him back on? How would he handle that? I hadn't mentioned it to him— why bring it up if there hadn't been a decision yet? Once we knew the new lay of the land, then we could adapt and rework his plan.

There were so many decisions that needed to be made.

I'd gotten an earlier appointment, which would mean that his badgering me about whether I was okay might ease up a bit. The stack of baby books on his side of the bed grew by another volume every day.

His side of the bed.

I parked in front of his house and hopped out. My bag vibrated. I fished around and found my phone ready to tell him I was already here.

Speedman Clinic flashed up on the screen. My heart sped up.

"Hello." I glanced up at the house and turned my back to the door, covering my other ear from the sounds of the street around me.

"Imogen?"

"Yes?"

"This is Mary, we spoke late last week."

"Yes."

"I wanted to call to congratulate you. We have the final date for when the clinic will be ready. June is our opening date, which would be three months after your due date, right?"

"That's right."

"We could bring you on as a consultant during your maternity leave, if you need the insurance, or you can stay with your old job. But we'd love to have you stop by a couple times a month to make sure everything at the clinic will be to your specifications once it's ready. Dr. Speedman is excited to have you on board, and we were even able to swing a pay bump. It would be great if you could come down to the Center City office to complete the paperwork."

I turned and stared up at the brownstone.

"Hello?"

"Yes, sorry. I'll come down later this week."

"This is great news, right? You do still want the position?"

"Of course. Sorry, I'm outside and it's a bit noisy."

"We can go over all the details when you stop by."

I ended the call. The happy dance feeling didn't come over me. After a year of searching, I finally had a job that would be perfect for me. A location close to Fern and Charlie. More money. Flexible hours. And none of it felt right.

My earlier excitement at seeing Colm leached away with each step closer. How would I tell him about my plan?

I opened the door. The curtains were drawn and Colm sat at the counter with a tumbler of amber liquid in his hand. He spun it against the granite countertop, scraping and screeching with each turn. "The coach called me for a meeting today."

My stomach dropped. "I'm so sorry. I know how much you wanted back on the team. Bailey said she'd do everything she could to get them to reconsider."

His head shot up. "How much I wanted back on the team? Are you saying they're not going to let me back on the team?"

The pit in my stomach morphed into a yawning abyss and I was being dragged down to the bottom. "You said you had a meeting with the coach today."

"He called me for a meeting today. It's in an hour."

He slid off the stool. "Did Bailey tell you they were booting me from the team?"

My mouth opened and a small sound echoed in the silent room. "She said they had a hot new recruit and were going to take you off the roster." My shoulders slumped.

"When did she tell you?"

"The day you invited me to the rink."

"You've known since then and you didn't think I could use a heads-up?"

"She said she'd do everything she could to stop it from happening."

"How about giving me the information about *my* future? You think you know the best way to handle it or the best way I should deal with it?" The muscles in his neck tightened.

"It wasn't a sure thing."

"You should've told me."

"And lose all the progress you'd made? Anything deviates from the plan and you're ready to shut out the world and find your answers in the bottom of a bottle."

"Do you think you being pregnant has been part of the

plan? You don't think that's stressed me the fuck out? But have I shut out the world? No, I've been sticking to my recovery plan. I've been working my ass off. I got out on the ice because I wanted to prove it to myself. I wanted to prove it to you."

"And you did it. Whether you get back on the team or not, you did it."

"With you lying to me the whole time."

"That's not true."

"You were going to let me walk into the building and straight into an ambush."

"Bailey said she'd tell me once the decision was made. I only found out a couple days ago. I thought we had more time."

My phone's shrill ring escaped my bag.

"Who is it?"

I glanced at the screen. "Bailey."

He plucked the phone out of my hand and jabbed at it.

"Sorry, Bailey, Imogen isn't here right now. You don't need to give her the warning about me being cut from the team. I already know you've been hiding that from me. Save your fucking sorry. The two of you were the perfect good cop, bad cop, weren't you?" His searing gaze swung to mine. "Let's make sure Colm doesn't go crazy when he finds out. Get him out of the house and skating again, at least he won't continue to be a shut-in."

I shook my head. "It wasn't like that."

"How was it then?"

My mouth opened and closed.

"You know what, save it. Both of you." He ended the call and tossed the phone back to me.

I fumbled, nearly dropping it.

"Get out."

"Colm—"

"You've done your job. I'm not broken anymore. Thanks for the help."

"Maybe there's something that can be done. A deal or something temporary."

"I don't need any more of your solutions, Imogen. Congratu-fucking-lations, you've fixed up another hockey player. I'm sure it felt good to mend another baby bird. You patched me up just like you did your dead boyfriend."

I flinched. "That's not fair."

"We know better than anyone that life isn't fucking fair, Imogen. But I thought you'd at least have been upfront with me. Were you upfront with Preston? Did he get the same treatment you gave me?"

"Stop." Tears burned in my eyes.

"Was it your secret treatment that took Preston from absolute mess to full sainthood?"

"Don't do this."

"Don't do what? Was this why you didn't want to move in with me? You were hedging? Biding your time until you could collect your check and leave? Damn, this baby must've been a real inconvenience." Sarcasm and vengeful-ness dripped from each word.

My hands shot to the growing bump under my sweater. "Don't you fucking dare!" Anger shoved the sadness down and threatened to boil over. "This was never about anything other than getting you better. It wasn't about money or the baby or Preston. You've got this fixation on him."

"One of us does."

"This is about us."

"There is no us. I've been so stupid, tiptoeing around you and trying not to scare you off, easing you into a relationship. I shouldn't have to beg for that. But, hey, the joke's on me! You never wanted it in the first place."

"Can't you see why? You cut off your sister and shut out your best friend because they didn't fit into the boxes you put them in. You're always so sure you know the exact right thing for everyone else's life."

He slow clapped in front of my face. "Welcome to the damn club. What did you just do to me? You had to swoop in to 'fix' me." He put his fingers up into air quotes.

"Or you'd still be drowning yourself in the bottom of a bottle."

"There *you* go again, knowing what's best for everyone else. At least I'm upfront when I tell someone what I think. I don't go behind their back, making backroom deals. And for what?"

"There was no ulterior motive. None. All I wanted to do was help." Confusion crowded out the maelstrom of emotions. How the hell had the conversation gone here?

"Saint Imogen has come down from her perch to huddle with the unwashed masses."

"Screw you! All I was trying to do was make you see what you could have and stop sabotaging yourself left and right," I shouted, getting straight in his face. My cheeks were burning, and a curtain of rage clouded my vision. "You're the most self-important asshole, only ever thinking about yourself. You don't give a shit about anyone else around you, because if you did, you'd have pulled yourself together for them even if you couldn't muster up the courage for yourself. Instead I literally had to waterboard you out of bed to stop your damn pity party."

Our gazes were locked, both of us panting like we'd run a two-minute mile.

"You made me want it." The words barely made it past

his clenched teeth. "You made me hungry to get back on the ice and play for the team that doesn't even fucking want me." The flicker of pain in his eyes was gone in a snap. The muscles in his neck strained. "Story of my life. I don't know what the hell I was thinking. Girlfriends, fiancées, now you. Always hung up on someone else. I'm not going to do that anymore. You go ahead and raise our kid with the ghost of your dead boyfriend and get the hell out of my house." He said it in a low boiling rage that sent a streak of guilt and fear that I'd fucked everything up racing down my spine.

I fled the house, slamming the door behind me and jumping into my car with tears streaming down my face.

In front of my building, I dropped my head to the steering wheel, trying to catch my breath as the sobs wrenched all the air from my lungs. It hurt. I wrapped my arms around my stomach, letting loose everything I'd kept bundled up inside. Tears streamed down my face for every sleepless night all alone. Every date night spent alone in my apartment. Every day I'd yearned for someone to touch me like I'd dreamed of being touched. Not just someone. Colm.

I'd thought we could be a family. I'd thought I could finally start over again, but that was a lie, and the pain made it hard to breathe. My head ached, throbbing as I flung myself into my bed. I curled up into a ball and pulled the blankets over my head. Maybe I'd wake up and it would all have been a terrible nightmare.

Why hadn't I told him? Why had I kept that information from him? Because I'd thought he'd react this way, lashing out. Or I'd feared he would. Or maybe I'd hoped he would to shatter the infancy of our relationship before I'd gotten in too deep, but I'd been wrong. It was already way too late for that.

33

COLM

Staring at the bottle of gin on the counter, I lifted it to pour into my glass, but slammed it down before the first drop hit the bottom of the tumbler. The shatter was the first signal that it hadn't filled my glass to the brim. Glass shards and splinters littered the ground and the pungent smell of alcohol pushed the lemon fresh scent away.

I dropped my head into my hands. What had I done? I'd been paralyzed by that same rooted-to-the-floor haze that had overcome me when Imo and I discovered she was pregnant. When my hands finally unclenched, the muscles screamed in agony.

Sitting at the counter with my drink before she came in was meant to be part celebration and part mourning. Once I was back on the team, we'd still have over sixty games to play. It would be weeks on the road by bus and plane, crisscrossing the country. And it meant I'd go stretches without seeing Imo.

At least that's what I'd thought, until Imo dropped the bomb that had turned the plan in my head into ash. There wouldn't be a need to charter a plane to get back to her faster. Or warn the Coach that when Imo went into labor I was on a plane, even if we were in the middle of a period. That worry had been in vain.

I was done. Kicked off the team. I made the long walk to my execution in a haze. The glass dumped into the trashcan. Mopping the floor. The drive to the stadium. Everything was on autopilot as I drove to the end of my career.

Part of me wished I was still unable to walk into the rink. I'd much rather have been puking in the trashcan outside the entrance right now. Then being cut would have felt like a relief.

Squaring my shoulders, I walked in trying to figure out what the hell would happen when this was all over. It's what I'd wanted, wasn't it? To stay holed up in my house and drown my sorrows? But Imogen had peeled back the layers of my insecurity and hadn't let it happen.

If I'd gotten off my ass and poured myself into my rehab and told the guys earlier what was going on with me, maybe I could've salvaged this. Now I had to face my fate.

My anger at her had been misdirected. It wasn't unjustified—she'd lied when I'd asked her what was wrong at the rink—but I was equally pissed at myself for letting an opportunity some people would kill for slip through my fingers.

I stood outside the door to the Coach's office with my fingers wrapped around my knees, squeezing until my fingers ached.

The door swung open.

Instead of the coach coming out to sit me down for the shutdown, Emmett, Heath, Declan, and Ford filed out.

"What the hell are you guys doing here?"

"Making a deal."

"What? What kind of deal?"

"That's enough, you've all done enough. Let me talk to him," Coach's gruff voice barked out from the office.

Emmett knocked his fist into my shoulder. "We've got your back."

I went inside, standing with my hands locked in front of me.

Coach eyed me. The grim set to his jaw contrasted with the fury in his eyes. "Quite some friends you have there."

I kept my lips locked.

He slammed a manila folder down on the desk. "You get one chance. You're going head to head in a scrimmage. You against your trade. You win, you're back on the team. You lose, we part ways with no hard feelings."

I stumbled forward opening my mouth, but no sound came out for what felt like minutes. "Why?"

With his arms crossed over his chest, he stood from his chair. "They threatened to walk." His jaw popped as he rounded the desk.

"They—"

"Said they'd walk away from their multiyear, multimillion dollar contracts, if I didn't give you a chance to keep your spot on the team." He squeezed his forehead and let out a long sigh. "I'll give you a shot at your spot, Frost. Normally, I don't take kindly to ultimatums, but damn if it isn't four of my veteran starters. I've never seen it before in my thirty years of coaching. The damnedest thing. You've got some friends most people would kill for."

They'd all stood by me through more than I deserved.

"They're my family, Coach." Pride in them and their willingness to sacrifice everything they'd worked on for me filled my voice. I'd never be able to repay them.

He huffed. "You get one shot. Maybe you pull it off, maybe you don't. Either way I get my winning team back."

"Thank you, Coach, you won't be sorry."

His growl was my dismissal. I'd walked in ready to accept my fate, to stand there while he gave me my walking papers, but I'd been given a reprieve. A stay of execution.

The hallway was empty. I jogged to the exit, throwing the stadium doors open. Only a few cars dotted the parking lot, but four figures stood beside Emmett's SUV.

"Anyone want to grab a beer? I've got plenty of beer at my place. Burgers too," Declan said before anyone could say anything. "You coming, Colm?"

I stopped short, my throat so tight I could barely breathe. When I nodded, he smiled. "Get in. We'll come back for the cars later."

We piled into the SUV like the old days back in high school. Heath and Declan fought for the front seat next to Emmett. Ford and I got straight into the back, taking over the third row and half the second.

Our drive over to Declan's house was filled with old school music from our senior year and conversations about nothing. Their next game. A new recipe Avery was trying.

"Is no one going to talk about how you all are the biggest bunch of boneheads? Threatening to walk for me? You've put everything into your hockey careers. What were you thinking?"

"There are more important things than hockey. At this point, we have enough money." Emmett looked at me in the rearview mirror. "All we have left are the people in our lives who make it worth living. You've worked your ass off to get back into shape to get back on the team. You deserved a shot."

"Life's short. You know that better than anyone. We've

got your back. We've been saying that from the beginning. And if you'd told us about your little ice fright, we'd have strapped you to the front of a Zamboni and gotten your ass out there, puke or not."

"It was my idea." Heath grinned at me from the other side of the second row. "I ran the stats for the four of us and showed Coach that he couldn't afford an entire collapse of his starting line." Heath interlocked his fingers, cracking them in front of him. "We're indispensable when we band together."

"I'm glad Imo called us or we wouldn't have even known." Emmett glanced into the rearview mirror. Our gazes met and he raised his eyebrow.

Her name was a flare of hope. She'd called them. After how I'd treated her, she'd called them and made sure they'd be here for me.

"Why the hell didn't you tell us?" He waved a hand behind his seat until it connected with my leg with a weak smack. "We could've headed this off before you got called down here."

"Imo called you?

I'd thrown her out of my house. The mother of my child. No wonder she kept things from me and seemed so hesitant about letting me into her heart. The awful shit I'd said to her when I lashed out came back to me.

I'd fucked this up beyond comprehension.

34

IMO

The throbbing in my head had lasted since I'd left his house three days ago. And my new little passenger meant no ibuprofen for me. Talk about a kick in the teeth after the day I'd already had.

Colm: We need to talk.

A single text the night after he'd thrown me out. I'd been tempted to shut off my phone, but what if Fern or Charlie needed me? Instead, I'd blocked his number and vowed to message him back when looking at his name didn't bring tears to my eyes. So far, no dice.

That afternoon replayed through my head at least ten times a day. His anger—no his rage, directed squarely at me. It came from an even deeper and darker place than he'd been in the night I'd found him standing on top of a bar.

He'd been blindsided by a fear he'd been wrestling with since I walked into his bedroom-turned-cave. My anger at him had transformed into a dull throb once the numbness wore off. I'd screwed things up. Why had I felt like I couldn't tell him what Bailey said to me? Because I was afraid he'd react the way he had or because I didn't trust that what we were doing was real? I'd never hesitated to tell Preston anything, but with him I wouldn't have had to! He'd have...

I tripped over that thought. A stutter step in my mind. Preston. We'd known each other for so long sometimes we didn't need words to know what the other was thinking. There weren't any secrets or surprises. We'd been together through every trial, every heartache, every celebration. Our lives had been so deeply intertwined it was hard to know where his experiences began and mine ended.

But things were different now. I was different and so was Colm. The uncertainty of navigating a relationship with him had kept me even more guarded. What kind of relationship were we even building? I hadn't really made space for Colm in my future either.

I'd gotten that call from the Speedman Clinic, and they were fine with my salary request, maternity leave, and anything else I needed. It seemed not many people wanted to set up a new clinic in an area that was sleepy for nine months out of the year.

Fern and Charlie needed me nearby. How would he deal with that? Would my relationship with them be a constant reminder of Preston until he couldn't take it anymore and broke things off? What would happen when he found out I was moving? My decision wasn't made and it was harder to imagine with each passing day, but this had been what I'd wanted and worked for since I started working as a physiotherapist. It also hadn't escaped me that Fern and Charlie were getting older, and this practice could let me help them, too.

No one had responded to my all-hands text to the Kings, and I couldn't say I wasn't dying to know what had happened, but they'd tell me when they figured things out. The hope that they could do something was a reach, for sure, but what other option had I had? Bailey hadn't been able to do anything.

All Colm's hard work and he'd thought it wasn't worth anything now.

I'd dragged myself out of bed and into work, not nearly ready, but knowing it was better than sitting at home all alone.

The day went by at a snail's pace. I kept up my smile for my patients, giving them just as much encouragement as before, but more than one had asked me if I was okay.

"Imogen, there's a delivery for you." Cecily walked in, peering around the corner toward the entrance.

"Can you sign for it and I'll pick it up when I'm finished with this file?" I took a bite of my sandwich, happy that at least my appetite had recovered in jean-splitting fashion.

"You act like this happens every day."

"Please just sign for it."

She shook her head and left. A few minutes later, droplets of water splattered onto my file folder. A vase bursting with flowers plopped down right in front of me. They were roses, but not red ones. It wasn't a lovers' bouquet. It was bright and multicolored, with some shades I hadn't even realized roses came in. Cecily leaned against the desk, whipping a small card back and forth against her palm. "Aren't they gorgeous?"

"They're pretty." And from Colm.

"Don't you want me to read the card?"

"No, it's okay. Just give it to me." I didn't need flowers from Colm. His guilty conscience must be nagging at him, telling him what he did was wrong. It was, but that didn't mean he wasn't right that we were better off apart.

"You've been holding out on me."

"I haven't. Leave it here." I tapped the empty spot on the desk beyond the roses bumping into my head.

"Then who is sending you flowers?" She dangled the card in front of my face.

"No one."

"So, no one called up a flower shop, gave them your name, wrote out this card, and paid for the delivery."

"Yes." I grabbed for the card.

She danced away from my grasping hands. "If it's from no one, then that means you won't mind if I read this card."

My chair shot back, banging into the desk behind me as I rushed after her.

"Dear Imo, you deserve better." Her broad smile dropped like a deflating cake. "C." She looked from me back to the card. "Who is this?"

I took her momentary distraction to snatch it out of her hand and stared at the writing. "No one. A friend." The word tasted stale on my tongue.

It was in his handwriting. He hadn't placed the order online or over the phone. He'd sent these himself. I deserve better. Than what? How he'd treated me? How I'm living my life? Than how he'd reacted yesterday? My mind went into overdrive.

The next day, I sat in the small break room at lunch, not wanting to hang in the cafeteria around so many people.

Cecily nearly overshot the doorway. Her rubber soles squeaking on the linoleum floor, she grabbed onto the doorjamb to steady herself. "You have another delivery." She was out of breath and a little sweaty.

More flowers? My stomach went into a triple backflip. "Leave it at the desk, I'll pick it up. And don't touch the card." I pointed an accusatory finger at her.

"I think you're going to have to come to it."

Eyeing her like I needed to keep a hold of my purse, I set down my pen and sandwich and followed her out from behind the desk. Before I made it to the door, the floral scent nearly overpowered me. Unsure I wanted to round the corner, I peeked and my jaw dropped.

Vase upon vase of multicolored bouquets lined the hallway. Tears sprung to my eyes. Pinks, oranges, whites, creams, blues, reds and yellows. The entire space looked like a destination wedding locale rather than the overworked hallway to a physiotherapy center in need of serious renovations. No, it looked like a field of flowers, a bed so thick you could lie on it.

Men in green jackets and hats walked in with even more roses, daisies, orchids, sunflowers, tulips, peonies, and others I couldn't even name, setting them down on any gaps on the floor. One set walked out through the double doors and another set of men replaced them.

"Someone's been holding out on me." Cecily tapped the card against her chin before holding it out for me. "A friend?"

"Are you Imogen Walsh?" He read my name off the clipboard in his hand.

"Yes."

"Can you sign here?" Sliding a pen from the top of the board, he handed it to me.

Scribbling my name, I stared at the card still in my hand.

"Open it."

I jumped, forgetting I had an audience.

"Here you are pretending you don't ever date and you're elbow deep in insanely expensive floral arrangements from a mystery man."

My fingers shook as I slid the card out of the envelope.

I'm sorry. More sorry than you could ever know. You deserve the best day every day. C

Sorry about our night together? About the new connection between us? For how he'd lost it on me? Like it did whenever the smell of flowers was so strong, I remembered that day and how badly it started and how magical it had been by that night.

"They're from a friend."

"A friend who spent a few thousand dollars on flowers? I need more friends like that." She crouched, sniffing the roses and not so slyly sliding a couple vases into the locker room.

The complications of this back and forth between me and Colm was driving me crazy. What would happen when the baby arrived?

Every patient that day got a beautiful bouquet. The guys took them home for their girlfriends or wives—hell, even for themselves. Who didn't love a fresh flower arrangement? All the women were giddy about their physiotherapy parting gift and asked if it would be a normal thing. We let them know it was a one-time special treat from a generous donor.

At the end of the day, I slammed my locker shut, the thought of facing my apartment alone knotting my stomach.

The elevator rattled up to my floor and the doors opened. At the end of my hallway, a figure stood with his back against the wall and one knee bent with his foot propped up. If he'd been standing here for a long time that could aggravate his knee.

Part of me wanted to jab my finger into the elevator button and leave, maybe never come back, but it wasn't like I could run from him for long. I cupped my hand over my stomach.

We had to figure out how we'd work together as co-parents and give this baby the best chance at a great life.

He spotted me and my chance for escape evaporated. Pushing off the wall, he shoved his hands into his pockets, watching my approach. "Hey."

"Hi." I swallowed against the boulder in my throat.

"How are you?"

"I'm okay." I fidgeted with the strap on my bag. "How are you?"

"Honestly? I feel like shit. It's hard for me to sleep." He ran his fingers through his hair. There were heavy bags under his eyes. It looked like my Hail Mary to the Kings to help out with the situation hadn't worked.

"Once the new future without hockey settles into your brain, you'll adapt. You did it before, you can do it again."

"You think this is about hockey?"

I met his gaze.

"Did you get my flowers?"

"Yes. Thank you. It was a nice gesture, but—"

"I didn't think that would fix anything I did. Reverse anything I said." He slammed his eyes shut before opening them. I could see the war going on inside him. The internal ass kicking had been going on for a while from the looks of it.

"It was a thank you for being you. For calling the guys. For not letting me stop you from helping." His eyes dropped.

I'd gone back and forth on whether to let them know. It wasn't like they wouldn't have found out one way or another, but being vulnerable had never been Colm's strong suit. He was the protector. He was the one looking out for others. I'd made my attempt and failed. I thought the guys might be able to get through to him.

"You don't have to thank me for that. I thought they'd

want to know, and that maybe they could do something about it." Helplessness at this awkwardness between us filled the space around us.

"They did. They all said they'd walk." He said it with awe in his voice. "In the middle of a season where we haven't lost a game. With their million dollar contracts on the line, they said they'd leave it all behind if Coach didn't give me my spot on the team."

My smile was automatic. "It worked?"

"No. But the coach is letting me play my potential replacement for my spot."

He'd made it through his trial by fire and would at least get a chance to reclaim his position. "I'm glad they were there for you." I turned away from him. "Thank you for stopping by." One look over my shoulder was all I could risk.

These feelings were too much and confusing at the same time. I shoved my key into the doorknob and turned the handle, moments away from my escape.

"You scare me, Imo." The soft words were spoken when I was a step over the threshold.

35

COLM

"It's hard for me to depend on other people. And outside of a small circle of people, it's not easy for me to trust."

She nodded. "Everyone has a past that shapes who they are."

"Only, I don't want that to define me anymore. I want to stop looking at what's behind me and start looking at what's in front of me." She looked at me then, not in a shrewd or calculating way, but probing, like she didn't believe the realness of those words.

"Colm, we don't have to—"

"What I said to you. Those words still ring in my ears. I don't expect you to forgive me, but I want you to know that I know it was wrong and it won't happen again." I didn't shield or hide my pain. She needed to know I meant it and that I'd been up night after night since the door slammed behind her. "How I treated you." I squeezed my eyes shut and shook my head. "I've had a lot of regrets in my life, but that's at the top of the list."

"You were upset."

"Stop being so understanding. If I'd heard someone else talk to you like I did, I'd have laid them out. Well, I'd have made sure I wasn't wearing skates and both my feet were firmly planted on the ground, but I'd have knocked at least a few teeth loose. It shouldn't have happened."

"I'm sorry I kept that from you. I didn't even know how to say it. You'd just gotten onto the ice. You were so happy and then Bailey blurted that out and everything went sideways. I didn't know how to fix it."

"You can't fix everything, Imo." I lifted my hand tentatively, giving her plenty of time to get out of the way.

She let me cup her cheek, leaning into my touch. The fear clawing at my chest that I'd ruined what we'd been building ratcheted down to an angry scrape.

"Trust me, I know." She looked up at me with a mirthless smile. It reached deep down into my soul and ached for all she'd been through. I wished I could have protected her from the loss and harshness of the world, but it wasn't like I'd been able to protect myself either. I could only hope to be a shield for her from any thieves of happiness she encountered in the future. If she let me.

"Thank you for coming." She pulled my hand from the side of her face and held it in hers. "It seems like it all worked out in the end." A pat to the back of the hand. Was that it and she'd send me away?

"It didn't all work out."

Her head snapped up with a bewildered gaze.

"How can you think I'm happy about the way things went with us? About how they are now."

"There never was an us."

"My point exactly. I know I've got some shit to figure out. The team shrink will get a chance to poke around in here for a bit." I tapped the side of my head. "Maybe if I'd gone that way in the first place, they'd have gotten me back on the ice sooner and you'd have never been in the same position you were in."

"And you wouldn't have needed me." Her fingers tightened around mine for a half a breath.

"I'll always need you, Imo." I covered our combined hands with mine.

"Come in." She reversed her hold and led me into her apartment. Setting down her bag, she looked over her shoulder at me.

How had I lived without her? How had I thought what I'd felt before was love? Every glance, every smile, every touch was a gift with Imo. And I still didn't believe I was lucky enough to receive it.

Her cozy apartment. The one we hadn't even spent a night in. She always came to my place with the ten foot ceilings and crown molding, but her place was just like she was. It made you instantly feel at home, like you'd immediately know where the silverware and towels were.

"Did you want a drink? I have tea or coffee. There's water and some juices." She squinted and scratched the side of her head, backing up to the kitchen. "I'm not sure what kind, but I know I have some."

"Stop trying to take care of me. We need to talk." I followed her.

Her audible swallow brought a smile to my face. It wasn't just men who hated those words.

"Let me get you something." She opened the cabinet, hiding her face.

"You don't—"

"I know I don't, but I want to." When she peeked back at me her shirt lifted, showing off a band of skin. The small rounded bump made my heartrate triple.

"Cranberry juice. I think I have some." She clutched the cups to her chest.

Cutting off her stalling technique, I plucked both cups out of her grasp and poured a glass for her and water for me. I set it down in front of her on the coffee table. Picking the chair diagonally from her, I hovered on the edge of my seat, trying to figure out the best way to say this.

"What did you want to talk about?"

"Us."

She nodded with the glass still up to her mouth, biding her time. After the world's longest sip, she held the glass in her hands, letting her fingers dance across it.

"I'm back on the team now."

Her whole demeanor changed. Straight back, full smile. Had there ever been someone happier for another person?

"Which means I'll be on the road a lot."

Her head dipped a little. Trained on my knee.

"It would make me feel a lot better if you moved into my place. Your place is great. I love it. It's got everything you need and I know it's your home, but my house also has everything you need. Plus, it's closer to the hospital and your job. There's a full security system and I can have cameras installed. When I'm away, it'll drive me crazy if I think of you needing to walk five blocks to find parking."

"What would that mean for us?"

"Whatever you want it to mean. If you want to stay in a guest room, that's fine. We can get the nursery together and get things ready for the baby. But I want to be there with you as much as possible. I don't want to miss a thing."

"And I don't want you to miss a thing. I don't want to take anything from you."

"I never thought you did, but I want you to know I'm a dependable guy. I can be the one you lean on and can count on to get anything you need. I've got sixty games to play over the next six months, but I'll jump on a train, rent a car, charter a plane—whatever I have to do to get back whenever you need me. That is, if everything goes the way I hope at my team trial. If not, you'll have me around a lot more."

Did I even want to win the scrimmage? If I said screw it and ducked out now...she'd never let it go and neither would the guys.

"We'll be fine. You don't have to worry about us."

Her stomach was so much bigger now. "The baby's the size of an eggplant."

"And she or he's happy to hear your voice."

My body jerked forward.

She lifted my hand and rested it on her stomach. "They're going wild hearing you after only a few days apart."

It brought tears to my eyes. Would this be the reception every time I came home from the road? The baby jumping around like mad to hear my voice?

"That's amazing."

"I like to think so. When do you have the big game?"

"Tomorrow." The pressure against my hand moved up and down against her belly.

She shot up. "Tomorrow! What are you doing here? You need to sleep. You need to clear your mind of everything except getting back on the team."

"I couldn't think about anything but what I did." I ran my hand along the side of her neck.

Her lips parted. "You need to sleep." One look over her shoulder. "Do you want to sleep here?"

I tugged her closer.

"Only sleeping. You need your rest, but trying to get you out of here and back to your house would be a trial, I can already sense it." She toyed with the buttons of my shirt.

"I'd love to sleep here with you."

"Only sleep."

I held up my two fingers in front of my chest. "Scout's honor."

"I don't have anything for you to sleep in."

Somehow that made me feel better. That she didn't have a drawer filled with Preston's clothes like he was still there.

"I have a bag in the car and all my gear."

"Were you angling for a sleepover?"

"No, I'm just always prepared."

"Were you even a Boy Scout?"

I laughed. "No, but I know the motto."

She turned me toward the door and gave me a push. "The keys are in my purse. I'm going to change the sheets."

Unclipping the keys from her purse, I walked down the hall to the elevator. It wasn't until I was on the way back that I realized she'd never given me an answer about moving in.

By the time I got back upstairs, she was asleep in bed. Her soft snores and the blankets peeled back on my side of the bed in invitation hit me harder than I thought it would.

Kicking off my shoes, I unbuckled my pants, keeping my gaze on her the whole time. This could be my life. This could be our life, if she let it.

Calls to the jewelers would have to happen in the morning. Whether I made it back on the team or not tomorrow we'd have something to celebrate. I'd show her I was serious about being there for her and never letting her down. And she'd make me the happiest man in the world. All she had to do was say yes.

36

IMO

The stands weren't filled, but there were more people there than I expected. It seemed word had gotten around about the friendly match for Colm's spot on the team. It would be a sudden death one period game. If someone scored that was it. If there was no score at the end of the one period, then the coaches would make the call based off game play.

It was a closed session. Only those affiliated with the team.

When I walked in, Bailey had her gaze riveted on the ice.

"If that fuckface screws this up for me I'm going to murder him."

"Are you talking about Colm?"

Her forehead banged off the glass and she turned around, looking at me with wide eyes.

"No." She gritted her teeth, her gaze shooting over my shoulder at the moving building walking past me and onto the ice.

"Is that the guy?" I talked out of the side of my mouth as the huge guy shoved the helmet down over his head.

"Yes." Bailey's jaw popped. "Viktor."

Like he'd heard his name on the wind, he turned to where Bailey and I stood and smirked at her, waving like they were old friends.

She let out a noise that made me afraid she'd climb over the glass and punch him in the mouth.

Where Colm was refined and pristine, this guy looked like he'd rolled out from under a car and hadn't cleaned the grease from his hands. Meanness radiated off him and sent a shot of fear down my spine. The rest of his chosen team took the ice behind him.

I'd tried to talk to Bailey again, but she kept yanking on her ponytail and half growled at me that she wouldn't be any good to talk to until after the period.

Emmett, Heath, Declan, and Colm skated out together. Ford was already in goal. They'd found a sixth, Beckett, a rookie and he was suited up out there, skating along with them like they'd been doing it for years.

"Are these seats taken?" Avery smiled at me with her coat buttoned tight around her waist.

"Is there something you forgot to tell me?" I poked at her stomach.

She smiled and poked at my bump. "Seems I'm not the only one."

"Things have been a *little* busy over the past couple months."

"You don't say." She dropped into the seat beside me. "Congratulations, Imo. I'm so happy for you both." Her arms wrapped around me and she squeezed me as tight as she could with the armrest between us.

"I didn't know you were coming."

"Like we'd miss it."

"We?"

She rested her elbow on the armrest and pointed over my shoulder with a huge grin on her face.

At the end of the row, Mak, Kara, and Liv stood with gift bags covered in pink and blue balloons. Apparently, everyone knew.

They squealed, *shh*ed and served up enough tight hugs to make me regret the large bottle of water I'd downed before we got there.

Each of the guys skated by and raised their sticks at us.

Before anyone could say anything more, the buzzer blasted and the puck was dropped. Even with everything happening on the ice, I could still feel the four of them looking at me. Liv leaned over Mak and sent out her own sign language version of 'oh my god I'm so excited I'm going to be an aunt. I can't believe you didn't tell me. I can't wait to buy everything for the baby.'

She had *very* expressive hands.

My leg bounced up and down with my hands on my stomach, sending Colm good vibes from the two of us. The play wasn't laid back or chill at all for a 'friendly'. Two careers hung in the balance and everyone played like it was their own spot on the team at stake.

The refs were also lax with the calls. I slammed my eyes shut with each slam against the boards. Not just Colm, but all the Kings. The last thing we wanted was for any one of them to end up with an injury.

Every slap of the puck by the opposing team sent my heart leaping for my throat. Possession changed too quickly, and it was hard to see who had the puck. Each play turned into a blur of bodies, everyone throwing their weight into the player beside him to change the tide of the game.

Each minute of the period ticked down. Both sides took

a minute or so to feel one another out and gauge how hard the period was going to be.

By the way the Kings banded together, slamming guys against the board, no one was taking this lightly.

The one Bailey called Viktor gunned for Colm. After one slam that bordered on a tackle, Colm shoved him away and wiped at his nose. The bright red was visible even from here.

Down ringside, Bailey slammed her hand against the glass, yelling and stabbing her finger in Viktor's direction. He lifted his stick in her direction and blew her a kiss.

That's when she boosted herself, clambering for the top of the glass. Someone grabbed her from behind and hauled her off into the tunnel.

A whistle blew and a time out was called. Ford came out of the goal and clanked helmets with Colm. They all huddled up with their arms around one another, heads bowed deep in concentration.

Liv touched my arm. "You know he'd been through a lot, right?"

I dragged my gaze away from the ice. "We all have."

"Yes, but he's my only brother."

"And you're his only sister."

"He deserves to be happy." A sadness beyond her years clouded her eyes.

"I know." My chest tightened. I didn't want to be another wave of bad news to the Frost family.

A whistle blast sliced through the frigid air and everyone was back into position. The Kings were in possession of the puck.

Colm passed the puck back to Declan like he didn't want his chance. Declan pushed ahead with Heath and Colm covering him and took the shot. Everyone held their breath.

My fingers tightened around the armrest. The small black disk slid across the ice, hitting the tip of the goalie's skate. He blocked it—barely.

Emmett had the puck and took it to half ice, passing it to Colm. Without pausing for more than a fraction of a second, he whipped back his arms and followed through. The puck moved so fast, skittering across the ice, I could barely make it out.

I held my breath and grabbed onto Mak and Avery's arms. Their suppressed yelps were the only thing I could hear except the pounding in my ears.

The back of the net shook and the light on top flashed on, spinning around signaling a goal.

I was on my feet, screaming until I was hoarse, jumping up and down with Avery, Mak, and Kara around me. Liv out-yelled us all, though, even jumping up on the arms of her seat, throwing her fists in the air.

For a second, she seemed poised to launch herself down the few rows to rink side and skate across the ice in her heels.

He'd done it. The relief was absolute. Complete and total, so keen it brought tears to my eyes. The tension that had wound so tightly in me since my first conversation with Bailey evaporated, and my whole body felt light. I floated down the stairs to the half door the guys would exit the ice from.

The last of the tension melted away and a giddy happiness overtook me. I bounced on the balls of my feet, eager to see him. Hold his face in my hands and kiss him, not caring that anyone else saw.

A sliver of me was sad he'd be on the road so much; I'd heard the stories from Mak, Avery, and Kara, but I would be okay. But the rest of me cheered that he'd done the thing so many others hadn't been able to do. He'd overcome his injury and everything inside his head that kept him from his destiny on the ice.

Maybe staying at his house wouldn't be so bad. Slowly, we could move forward, ease everyone into whatever we decided we'd become. Everyone already knew there was a baby on the way, and it wasn't like they didn't understand how that had happened. No birds and the bees session required, but how would they feel about me with Colm, really? What thoughts would be swirling in their heads? Would they have to deal with what that meant for their memories of Preston?

Colm tore at his chin strap and ripped his helmet off, chucking it onto the ice and skated toward me. The remnants of blood stained the skin around his nose.

A chill raced down my spine like I'd been doused with ice water. Bile rushed for my throat. The accident. *Looking over at Preston with scratches and cuts all over. Blood dripping into my eyes, the seatbelt digging into my shoulder. Pushing my hands off the roof of the car that was now under me.*

My chest tightened and it was hard to breathe.

Stepping off the ice, Colm was swallowed by a pile up of the Kings and other players from his team that was all congratulations and flailing limbs.

The part of me that hadn't been pulled into the tunnel vision of my nightmare cringed at the rough jostling, but this was what I'd prepared him for. My breaths came out choppy and strained as he emerged from the pile of players. There were so many people now. Everyone in the whole rink had converged on this one spot.

Colm looked at me, his whole body relaxing like he'd exhaled a long breath. He turned to Emmett who hesitated before handing him something. Colm clasped it in both hands and walked toward me, that hockey player gait balancing on the blade of his skates.

His uniform was soaked through, sweat dripped off his hair. "I'm glad everyone is here." I looked around at small group assembled around us and jerked when I saw that Fern and Charlie were amongst all the smiling faces with hints of confusion in their eyes. What were they doing here?

I turned back to Colm and braced my hand on Mak's arm as Colm dropped to one knee in front of me.

My breath left my lungs like I'd been kicked in the chest. A wheeze escaped my lips.

"Imogen Marie Walsh, this time I wanted to do it right. Your happiness is my happiness. I've never met someone who is more loving and caring and I want to spend the rest of my life with you. Will you do me the honor of being my wife?" He opened the ring box, but all I could see was the dented and scraped metal of the ring the police officer had found and handed to me the night of Colm's first offhand proposal.

Radio static filled my ears and brain, switching back and forth between this moment and the night that Preston had knelt in front of me the same way. I couldn't catch my breath. Blood still ringed Colm's nostril. Fern and Charlie were still here. I backed away one step. Tears welled in my eyes.

Another step back and Colm's smile dropped. I backed right up into someone and didn't stop my push for escape.

Colm's hands wavered as he stood. He said my name, his voice uncertain and full of so much sadness. Some part of me knew I was another person not choosing him, but I couldn't breathe. I was in the hospital room all over again. I was in the car crash. Preston had proposed to me and died, what if the same thing happened to Colm? What if I was cursed or bad luck or something? All these moments were compressed so tightly in my chest I expected a rib to break.

I punched a hole through the crowd with my insistent retreat through the familiar faces gawking at my display, but I couldn't stop myself. My entire body shook, trembling as this past and future I'd been trying to outrun collided spectacularly.

Colm stared after me with a sheen to his eyes and defeat in his posture. Emmett laid a hand on his shoulder. I was causing this pain. That was my last view of him before I took off. Someone called my name. More voices joined the chorus of "Imogen," but I was gone. Bolting for the exit, I slammed into a sweaty wall.

Hands were braced on my arms, but I tore them out of his hold. If I hadn't been on the verge of losing my shit, I'd have kneed him in the groin. Viktor. He'd emerged from a doorway still on his skates. Bailey came out after him, flush faced and panting. Her eyes widened as they collided with mine.

She called out my name too, but I kept running. Pushing on the long metal bar across the glass door, I escaped into the daylight and climbed in my car with trembling hands.

I drove, not stopping until I made it to my destination. What had I done? Who had I just lost?

37

COLM

She left. I proposed and she ran away like I'd menaced her with a twelve-inch knife instead of a ring.

The look in her eyes had been one of abject horror.

Surrounded by my friends and family, I'd watched the woman I love run away, barely stopping on her mad dash to the exit. A brief flash of light filled the end of the tunnel as she made it to the door. And then darkness.

Emmett kept his hand on my shoulder. Declan joined him on the other side. Everyone looked at me like I might collapse at any second. But it wasn't my body I worried about. That had been repaired and rebuilt, better than ever. It was my heart that lay shattered in my chest with the shards jammed into my ribs.

Had I thought the rejection hurt before? It had nothing on this.

"Let's get you changed."

"We'll be back."

The mood of the crowd nosedived into embarrassed somberness. It wasn't like anyone had died, right? Except for my imagined picture of a life with Imogen as my wife. But the embarrassment couldn't slice through the pain. I welcomed the numbness that invaded me, blocking out everything else around me.

No looks of pity to dodge when you were already drowning in self-loathing.

"Colm." Liv grabbed onto my hand.

"It's okay, Liv. Don't worry." The words were wooden. My reflex words I'd always said to reassure her.

"It's us against the world, right?" She searched my face for a response.

But there was no response. I had to hold it together because falling apart here and now...I might never get back up. Imogen had pieced me together and shattered me in a matter of months.

I couldn't think about the future. About our child. All I wanted to do was get out of my gear, take a shower and go home.

Coach came up and begrudgingly shook my hand. He said something about no selfishness on the ice and needing my ass to be at practice in two days.

I nodded on autopilot. Emmett, Declan, Heath, and Ford corralled me into the locker room, letting me know the next step of what I needed to do. Oh, take off my jersey. Take off my skates. Get undressed and get a towel. A bar of soap was shoved into my hand. Showering? How strange. Had I done any of this before? It all felt alien. Was this an out of body experience?

The urge to maintain this fog with a bottle of whiskey was strong, but I wouldn't do it. I couldn't hide from this pain forever. And I needed to be there for my team. And for my child, whenever he or she was born.

How far would Imogen run? How much would she push me away? Would she let me be a father?

In the shower, under the spray of the water, I rested my forehead against the cold tile and let the tears fall. I could give myself this moment to fall apart and then I needed to get my shit together. I'd used up my lifetime supply of wallowing.

Leaving the shower, no one had to tell me to dry off or get dressed, but I didn't miss their worried glances.

"I'm okay, guys."

They exchanged looks, waiting for my beard to sprout and a bathrobe to appear out of thin air.

"I'll be okay. I just need some time. And your help, if I haven't burned through enough of that to last a lifetime."

Without another word, the group hug slammed into me. A wall of the best friends anyone could ever have. The family I hadn't been lucky enough to be born into, but one I loved just as much as blood.

"We're here for you, whatever you need." Declan pulled his head from under Ford's arm.

The arms relaxed and everyone took a step back.

"You don't need to ask, of course." Emmett clapped me on the shoulder. "What do you want me to do with the ring?"

I swallowed and breathed deeply through my nose. "Can you hold onto it for a little bit?"

He nodded, face full of understanding. He'd held onto a ring for Avery, the woman who owned his heart, for way longer than I'd held onto mine.

Ford put both his hands on my shoulders and stared into my eyes. "You deserve the love you've been searching for, and you'll find it. Don't let this stop you from opening up that big heart of yours. You tried to pretend it wasn't there for a while, but we all knew the truth." He thumped his fist against the center of my chest.

"Thanks, man." I choked out the words with the rising swell of feelings making it hard to keep my emotions in check.

"This probably isn't the right time, but I ordered a massive cookie cake to celebrate. What should I do with it?" Heath offered a half smile and shrug.

A tight laugh burst from my mouth. Count on Heath to cut through the room's tension with the promise of an over-sized, slightly under-baked chocolate chip cookie from B&B.

"Let's eat the damn thing."

We filed out of the locker room to the waiting few people left. Avery, Mak, Kara, and Liv. Crushing emotions flared in my chest and burned in the back of my nose at their eyes staring back at me.

Liv flung herself at me with red-ringed eyes. She wrapped her arms around me and squeezed me tighter than I would have thought possible for someone with her small stature.

I hugged her back. I was used to being the one doing the comforting, not the one being comforted. But my baby sister had taught me so much about life already.

"It will be okay. She's scared and once she realizes what she did, she'll be back." She didn't mean it in a vindictive or snarky way. Her voice was full of pain and understanding beyond her years. "I'm sure she's confused and she just needs to work through everything in her head. Some people take too much on themselves and give so hard they bleed themselves dry. And sometimes that gets so overwhelming they snap and do things they wouldn't normally do." She tilted her head with a small smirk. "Give her some time, big bro."

"I want to believe you're right." I stared down the long abandoned exit. Was Imo safe? Was the baby safe? Where had she gone? How long would she run?

I'd thought I'd learned not to hope for happy endings, but I'd been stupid to think I wouldn't imagine one with her. I'd gotten ahead of myself once again, scared Imo off, and possibly ruined any chance I'd had with her forever.

A frantic blur of activity. After the last five months, being back on the road was a blast of insane intensity. It was a fire-hose of sights and sounds and people, but I wasn't going to hide away from everything and everyone. Going back to that screwed up place wasn't going to fix anything. I'd wanted back on the team and here I was.

Lugging my bag off the team bus for what felt like the twentieth time that day, I walked through the lobby with the rest of the team. A squadron of suited hotel employees escorted us to our floor and helped everyone into their rooms.

I sat on the edge of my bed, staring down at my hands. Was any of this real? Did any of it matter? For so long it had been the only thing I could think about, and I'd been afraid I'd never do it again. Now, here I was, and we'd won every game since I'd been back, but it felt hollow.

Each time I picked up my phone, I flicked to my contacts. Imo's smiling face was the first one in my favorites. The stricken look in her eyes when I'd gotten down on one knee had kept me up at night, staring at the ceiling and wondering if she'd ever cared about me half as much as I cared about her. As much as I loved her.

Out on the ice everything else outside the stadium faded

away and for a couple of hours, I poured myself into the game. I pushed myself harder than I ever had to make sure I didn't let them down.

And the second the adrenaline crash hit in the shower after the game, her face would fill the blankness of my mind.

A knock on my door broke through the quicksand I was treading through. Right on time.

I grabbed my key off the dresser and opened the door.

The four of them stood in the hallway like sentries after each game, ready to make sure I ate and didn't sit in my room staring at the blank wall until I passed out.

Ushered into a private dining room, we ordered bad food and drinks. The beers arrived first and we all grabbed one.

We'd adopted Emmett's old Avery rule when it came to Imogen. If anyone brought her up, I'd leave the room, so they learned not to.

"Three more days until I can sleep in my own bed." Declan stretched his arms overhead, cracking his back. "You'd think these hotels would have beds that were more comfortable."

"It's not their fault you're incapable of sleeping without Mak." Heath grinned and gulped from his bottle.

Declan picked at the label on his bottle, muttering something about how good she smelled.

The ache in my chest didn't stop me from being happy that he'd found his other half in a woman who he'd sworn to hate during our senior year of high school.

"Do you remember that last party our senior year at Rittenhouse?"

Everyone's gaze swung to me. While I hadn't fought their

dinner invitations, I hadn't been a conversational savant since we'd all gone back on the road.

"You mean the one where you and Ford bailed because Liv showed up with her other thirteen-year-old friends? The one I left early to make out with that hot student teacher? The one where Mak and Declan had their monster throw down? The one where Emmett broke up with Avery and shattered his front door? That one?" Heath drained his bottle.

The guys stared at him, slack-jawed.

Heath looked up as it dawned on him that no one else was talking. "What? We had a few parties that year, I wanted to make sure I had the right one."

"Yes, that one." I broke the tense silence. "But before all that happened. We figured it would be our last night all together. We'd go away to college and hoped we'd make it to the pros, but never imagined we'd all be together like this again."

"Well, for you and Ford, we knew that was a given." Emmett chuckled, finishing off his beer.

"Even that wasn't a guarantee. But I wanted to say thank you all for being here. You guys are my family and you've been there for me even when I didn't deserve it."

"It's what we do." Ford leaned over and clinked his bottle to mine.

Our food arrived. Burgers and fries. A plate of nachos for the center of the table. None of us were looking for anything other than comfort food. The rest of the night was quiet and over early. The guys all wanted to go back to their rooms to call their better halves.

I lay in my bed and stared up at the ceiling with my hands behind my head.

I hadn't messaged Imogen since the day she'd run, not wanting to freak her out even more. I'd been lied to, used for my money and cheated on, but nothing hurt more than watching her back away from me after I'd shared a piece of my heart with her and asked her to exchange a piece of hers in return. But I'd be there for her and our child, even if that meant I needed to stay hands-off until she was ready to talk. As much as I wanted to show up at her apartment and demand that she speak to me, I couldn't force her to love me. All I could do was make sure I was the best father I could be and give them both whatever they needed. It would kill me seeing her and not being able to touch her, but I needed to stay strong and find a new future for myself without her.

38

IMO

They'd found me on the beach in my favorite spot. The spot where Colm and I had sat that night. Without a word, they'd brought me back to the house I'd felt was my home for so many years.

That had been...five days ago...no, maybe it had been a week. Time slowed down and sped up, slipping away and lingering all at once.

As much as I'd wanted to be the same Imo that Fern and Charlie had always known and counted on, never showing the cracks and splinters, I couldn't scrounge up the energy to keep the charade going. Curled up in a ball in Becca's bedroom, I ate whenever they brought me food, and went to the bathroom when the baby decided to turn my bladder into their own trampoline, but I couldn't do more than that.

Walking away from Colm had been like ripping out a vital organ, but everything about that day had been amplified, shining a spotlight on everything in my past and the wounds I'd thought had healed, but never had.

"Imogen, can you come down?" Charlie called up the

stairs, not giving me the excuse of staying upstairs any longer.

My toes hit the cold wooden floor and I hugged my arms around myself as I walked down the stairs. They busied themselves at the stove, taking boxes out of the cabinets. I sat in the chair pulled out at the kitchen table and waited. Instead of staying in Preston's room like I always did, they'd put me in Becca's. Like they didn't even want me in his room anymore after everything that had happened.

Eventually, Charlie and Fern sat across from me at the kitchen table. My stomach knotted, the tension so heavy it made it hard to lift my head.

Fern covered my hand with hers. "We have some news for you." Her voice was soft and gentle, but the worry shone through.

That made me feel even worse for upsetting her. I kept my head down.

Charlie set a cup of hot chocolate with marshmallows in front of me. The thick richness of it had always been a go-to on cold winter nights.

"Thank you." I slid my hands from under Fern's and wrapped them around the mug.

Her sigh, coupled with the disgruntled scrape of Charlie's chair, sent waves of sadness rolling through me. I felt like an intruder, an unwanted guest who'd ruined a happy family portrait.

I glanced at the one hanging on the wall in the living room. The five of us standing together a year after my parents died. It was like losing them all over again.

"You don't like it?" Charlie caught my eye.

I offered up a meek smile and took a sip, burning my lips, but not caring. "You said you had news." Would they tell me to pack my bags? That I'd forgotten Preston and it was time to move on?

"You have some of your own too." She nodded toward my stomach.

The baggy clothes were gone. The only thing I had in the drawers at their house were my summer clothes. Becca's sweatshirt was tight around my midsection.

Dropping my hands into my lap, I cradled my stomach.

"How far along are you?"

"Six months."

I would have sworn there was a thud from the way their jaws dropped.

"But you're so small! I'd have thought you were barely out of your first trimester."

"No, I'm almost two thirds of the way there." The flutters weren't so much butterfly wings anymore. Movement rippled in my stomach like a reassurance from the baby that they were still there.

"Is this why Colm proposed? Because you're pregnant?"

Hyperventilating had never been something I understood. You breathe. We all do. It's a fact of life. How could you not just breathe normally? Through the injuries, hospital stays, and funerals I'd never had anything close to a panic attack, but this question sent me on a spiral.

Tears flooded my eyes and my shoulders shook as I tried to keep it all inside.

Fern was out of her seat, holding onto me. Her shhs and the gentle touch of her hands across my hair made it even worse. I couldn't breathe, choked by my emotions and tears. I'd lost so much, and just when I thought I couldn't lose anymore, I was on the verge of losing them too.

"Yes. No. I don't know." Tears flooded my eyes. God I hated being a weepy mess. I could count on my hands the number of times I'd let them see me cry before all this. "It's all so hard. Moving on without Preston here. We were supposed to do all these things together and now we can't. But doing them with someone else—it's hard because I feel like I'm losing him again. Leaving those pieces of him behind and moving on. I was supposed to be *your* daughter-in-law."

"Sweetie." She pulled back and cupped my cheeks, tilting my head up to look into my eyes. "You'll never be our daughter-in-law."

I didn't think anything could hurt more than what I'd been through, but those words reached inside of me, plumbing the depths of my deepest fears and bringing them to life. I couldn't catch my breath. My eyes slammed shut.

She smoothed my hair from my face. "I need you to know that, Imogen. You'll never be our daughter-in-law, but you'll always be our daughter."

I looked back at her with tears blinding me.

"Your parents loved you. And we love you. Not because you were Preston's girlfriend, and not because he planned on marrying you, but because you're our family and nothing will ever change that. Not hundreds or thousands of miles, not time, not a baby, and not you finding love with someone else. We want that for you. He'd want that for you. You can't keep living in this holding pattern circling a life you'll never have. That life died when he did."

They exchanged worried looks as I tried to pull myself together.

Letting out a shaky breath, I dried my face with the handkerchief Charlie held out for me.

"Sorry."

"Don't ever be sorry, Imo. You've always been so good at keeping everyone else afloat and making sure they were okay, but now you need to do it for yourself. And we're going to try to do that for you now.

"The news we have for you is that we're leaving."

Confusion creased my face. They never left for more than a few days in the winter. Day trips, sure, and sometimes long weekends traveling around the area, but this sounded different. "For the winter?"

She shrugged. "We're not sure yet. But we're going to head out to California to stay with Becca for a while. See the sights. A long road trip. We've never done one before, and we always thought we'd do it once we retired, but then we figured why not now? We never know what tomorrow will bring."

"What about The Shack?" Panic edged closer.

"That's the other part of our news. We've had several offers to buy it. Some of them tempting, but we know you wanted to move down here, so if you want it, it's yours."

"Mine?"

"If that's what you really want, we'll sign it over to you and you can have it. There's enough cash flow to hire a manager, so you wouldn't have to be here every day. But, Imogen, sweetheart." She cupped my cheeks. "Is that the life you want to live? You've lost more than anyone should at your age. I can't imagine what that's been like for you."

Her fingers brushed at the tears on my cheeks. "Every day is a gift. I don't want you to miss out on the possibility of even more in your future. A future that isn't only about your little one, but about you. Do you want to keep living a life that died with Preston? Or do you want to start something new with someone who obviously loves you? I know it's scary. I know it's hard. But you're strong. Stronger than any of us have deserved.

"We will support you no matter what you choose. We'll

love you no matter what you choose. But you need to decide how you want to live your life. Do you want to be looking back at what you've lost, or moving toward what you can create?"

I swallowed hard. "What if things don't work out between us?"

"How do any of us know?" Charlie rapped his knuckles on the table with a chuckle. "At least you tried."

"What if he hates me and he never wants to see me again?"

"I'm sure that's not the case." Fern shook her head in that all-knowing Mom way.

"What if something terrible happens to him?" My voice cracked and my nostrils flared. "What if I lose him too?" Even saying the words felt like an invitation, like I was opening the door to something that would end me. I'd tried to protect myself from it, but somehow, I couldn't stop these feelings for him. I couldn't keep myself from falling for him and that brought with it the scary reality of life.

"Do you wish you'd never met Preston? That you hadn't gone to that seventh-grade dance with him? That you hadn't been there for him when no one else could reach him?" Fern wore a warm smile, but the tears glittered in her eyes.

"No, never." Every minute was worth it, even with all the pain that came after.

"You can't live your life afraid of what you might lose, because then you'll never embrace everything you have to gain, and those are the memories that make it worth it."

Charlie set down another cup of hot chocolate.

"Good night, kid. We're here for you, if you need us." He kissed me on the top of my head and the two of them went upstairs.

I sat at the table with only the ticking of the grandfather

clock in the living room to keep me company—that and my thoughts.

Colm had been so hurt. He'd been through so much. He'd had Liv with him, but that had its own pressure. An eighteen-year-old taking care of a teenager. But he'd opened his heart to me after everything he'd been through.

That night I lay in Becca's bed, staring up at the ceiling. The gentle flutters in my stomach were a comfort, reminding me that I wasn't completely alone. No matter what, I'd have this baby. Our baby. Colm would be in my life regardless of my choice, but letting him into my heart...that opened the door to another round of loss. Was I ready to make that choice? Could I handle everything that came with truly being with him?

Swinging my legs over the side of the bed, I ran my fingers along the fine chain around my neck. I'd worn it for so long, I'd forgotten it was there half the time. Lifting the gold over my head, I held the band in my palm. He'd proposed to me even though I'd slept next to him every night with this around my neck.

There was so much good that came with letting him in. The way he looked at me, lighting my soul on fire. How his touch made it hard to breathe. The way he never let me shield the parts of myself that no one else even knew were hidden.

I squeezed the ring tightly in my palm so hard the edges dug into my skin. Staring at the gold band, I re-read the inscription, running my finger across the etched words. I love you too, Preston, and always will. But it was time to embrace my future as fiercely as I had my past. I pressed my lips to the still warm metal and let the necklace slip from my hand and into my bag.

Did he still want to be with me after the lies and the way I'd hurt him? Could he forgive me?

I rolled over and grabbed my phone. Starting my first ever group text, I took a deep breath.

Me: Hey, I need your help.

39

COLM

"Did we really have to do the walking tour of the city? All the pictures are posted online." I shoved my hands into the pockets of my coat. Even my gloves weren't enough to ward off the winter wind whipping through the gaps in the buildings.

"You know you can't buy a house from a picture."

The guys were doing everything they could to keep me out of the house during our two days back home. Dinners at their houses, even forcing me to cook for them—not that I minded. It felt good to have voices other than my own rattling around in between my four walls.

Deliveries kept arriving for the nursery. I'd grab them and put them up in the room I'd had painted green. Once I worked up the courage, I'd call Imogen and see where she wanted me to put everything.

We switched from walking strung across the sidewalk to single file as a couple walked toward us. They both wore matching bright red scarves. Like every other time I saw a couple together, I thought of Imogen. There had been radio silence since the rink. Not a word from her.

Even with how much it hurt, I'd sent her a letter from my lawyer about how I hoped things would go once the baby arrived. Split time as much as possible and I'd give her anything she needed to be happy, even if it wasn't me. She could hire as much help as she wanted. I didn't want her to feel like she had to start working right after the baby was born.

And as much as it would hurt not to lie beside Imogen and hold our baby together, I wanted her to be happy. I'd just hoped she would be happy with me. But I wasn't going to be that guy. Not the second string who she stayed with because she didn't have a choice, or felt like it was the right thing to do.

Avery would probably let me know when Imo went into labor. The messiness of this situation wasn't lost on me. I'd had her. For a short time, we'd been happy.

Could I even blame her? I hadn't screamed dating, let alone marriage material. When she showed up at my house after our night together, I'd thrown her out. If Liv had shown up with a guy like me, I'd have told her to run the other way. Which meant my hypocrisy with the Liv/Ford situation wasn't lost on me.

Maybe some time alone would be better. Talking to the team shrink, I'd seen how so many of my patterns had been self-sabotage at its finest.

The crisp winter air made walking in and out of these houses a pain in the ass. My lips and skin felt raw from the temperature shifts. A couple walked down the street toward us with their arms linked. The guys fell back to give them room to pass.

As they passed, they pulled their arms from behind their backs. Instead of ducking for cover, my eyebrows dipped as they held out two roses. One was pink and the other orange. I stepped aside for whoever those were meant for, but they turned as I did, holding them out to me.

I glanced to the side at the guys who shrugged.

"No thanks."

"They're for you."

"I don't have any cash."

"They're free." They shoved the de-thorned roses into my hand and took off. I glanced behind me. Turning around, three more people walked toward us with roses in their hands.

What the hell was going on?

The four guys behind me could barely suppress their smiles. Something was up. Was this their way of cheering me up? Random strangers giving me flowers? They'd have been better off making it passersby with shots—or, if they were trying to keep me from getting blind drunk, at least some of Avery's cookies from Bread & Butter. With the work-outs we'd been doing this season, it wasn't like I couldn't afford to eat a few cookies. Maybe that was the approach I should take, since I'd limited myself to a beer with the guys over dinner. Stuffing my face with baked goods: why hadn't I thought of that before?

We turned the corner and I stopped. No one banged into my back, so they'd been ready for this.

The street had been cordoned off and transformed. Flowers covered the ground like a heavy blanket, and at the end of a path was Imogen.

Her black hat and coat looked out of place in the center of so many vibrant colors. She wore her hair braided over her shoulder. The end peeked out from the collar of her coat, which couldn't hide her bump, even at this distance. That swell was where she was keeping our little one safe.

That didn't explain why she was standing in the middle of the road.

From the second I'd turned the corner, her gaze had locked onto mine. Her gloved hands fiddled in front of her, but she didn't move from her spot.

"I think she wants to talk to you," Heath leaned over, whispering in my ear.

Passersby watched, whipping their phones out to record everything. Like all of them, I didn't have a clue what was going on.

Someone cleared their throat and nudged at my back.

I stumbled forward, feeling like I had taking my first steps out of the hospital bed back in May. Only I wasn't walking toward a black hole of a future.

40

IMO

I was so sweaty. Under my coat, I was twenty percent clammy and one hundred percent scared out of my mind that this wouldn't work.

Declan had shared his live location with me, so the little dot neared the corner he'd turn before he saw me. He stopped and my stomach balloon-animaled itself into a poodle. I got a kick in return for my anxiety-induced stomach twister. "We've got this, kid."

When I'd told the guys of my idea, no one had questioned my sanity, but now that I stood here with chapped cheeks and fearful hope in my chest, I questioned it. Was this the way I should have done this?

Would he turn around and go the other way? Had I had one too many chances? Was this too over the top? Maybe I'd gone about this the wrong way. Dozens of strangers were milling about to watch the pregnant lady humiliate herself.

Slowly, at a rate that seemed crafted to increase my anxiety, he walked toward me. The second he hit the first row of flowers, the music started.

His head snapped up. Need the Sun to Break. I'd come

to think of it as our song. When I'd asked Heath for some music, I hadn't expected an entire city choir to come streaming out of the doorway of a building beside us, lining up and serenading us.

My jaw hung open as I looked at the spectacle with trembling hands. Taking a deep breath, I refocused on Colm. In for a penny...

"Fancy meeting you here."

My half-smile and attempt at a joke dive-bombed like a ravenous seagull at a freshly made batch of fries.

His eyes bored into mine. "What's going on? What is all this?" He ducked his head in a whisper, leaning closer to me.

The sounds of the city were covered over by the shutter sounds of phones, and whispers from everyone watching. More people had walked over from neighboring streets, probably lured by the irresistible sounds of James Bay being sung by nearly two hundred people.

I reach down to the basket behind me and held out the paper plate covered with another one. My black coat was slowly being covered by a fine dusting of powdered sugar picked up by the wind.

He lifted the plate and his eyebrows dipped.

"Funnel cake?"

"I remember how much you liked it whenever you came into the Shack. You'd get the mini funnel cakes almost every afternoon. They could use a little time in the oven, but I wanted you to have them."

"You did all this." He spread his arms wide in a half circle. "To give me funnel cake?"

There had to be at least a couple hundred people lining the streets now. They edged close to the flower blanket that surrounded us.

"I needed you to know how I feel."

"And this was the way you wanted to do it?"

"This was the way I needed to do it. In the middle of winter, you're a field of flowers. With you, when I wake up in your arms, I'm never thinking about what I've lost, but only what I have to look forward to. And I wanted to say this out here in front of everyone."

Wobbling for a second, I got down on my knee. My coat tightened around my midsection, pulling against the bump that seemed to have grown even bigger overnight. With hundreds of people surrounding us and the James Bay that had been sung on repeat coming to a close, I opened the ring box.

The passing cars sounded so much louder now that the singing had ended. My blood pounded in my veins and my cheeks flushed as he stared down at me with eyes so wide, I was tempted to see if there was a car barreling toward me from behind. Swallowing past the weight lodged in my throat, I forced out the words in a rush.

"You've asked me a question twice and I thought it was only fair that I do the asking this time. Colm Alexander Frost, will you do me the honor of spending the rest of your life with me?"

He looked down at me like I'd asked him to Bonnie and Clyde our way across the country one bank at a time.

Swallowing against the tightness in my chest, I stared up at him with the ring box in my hand. I wasn't sure how this whole *proposing to the guy* thing went. When I'd asked Emmett about it, I wasn't sure how to take it when he'd said Colm had asked him to hold onto it for him. Did he not want it near him? Was I supposed to buy one for him?

Was it hot out here? My hands seemed to be sweating as I held up the box.

"I'm sorry about last week. I—I wasn't ready then, but

I'm ready now."

"What if I'm not ready?"

I dropped my hands and stared up at him.

His lips thinned into a hard line and he helped me up. Unease rippled through the crowd.

"We need to talk."

The pained and embarrassed expressions didn't touch me; it was the fear that I'd finally lost something, thrown it away instead of having it taken from me, that sent my stomach into free-fall. I let him lead me away from the crowd, not sure where we were going, but anywhere seemed better than staying in the middle of a street covered in the evidence of my failed proposal.

Bursting through a glass door, he whirled around, running his fingers through his hair. The smell of chocolate and coffee filled the air. A barista behind the counter stared back at me. My cheeks burned from the sudden change in temperature.

"What the hell were you thinking, doing something like that?"

"I..." My mouth opened and closed, but no sound came out. The ring box was still in my hand.

"I don't hear from you for a week after you walk away, and now you just spring this on me? No, hey Colm. No, can we talk? My favorite James Bay song and flowers and you think I'm going to jump up and down waiting for you to slide the ring on my finger?"

"I wasn't sure how it worked." I cringed. "I figured you'd slide it onto mine." This wasn't at all how I'd thought it would go.

"You disappear for a week, Imogen, and then surprise! 'Will you marry me?' What was your reaction when I did that? What do you think my answer should be?"

41

COLM

S he'd gotten down on her knees in the middle of the cold street in November to propose to me? It had taken me at least a solid ten seconds to understand what was going on when she held up the ring box. Ten seconds might as well be an eternity with hundreds of people staring. It was like being out on the ice when we're one goal down, and I'm in possession of the puck and the entire stadium is watching me.

Only they weren't watching because a two-hundred-pound guy was racing after me trying to take my head off. They were watching because the woman who I'd thought would never feel for me the way I felt about her was kneeling in the middle of a flower garden, backed by a full choir singing the song that seemed to be the theme of our relationship, and asking me to marry her.

The light from the glass door behind her backlit her, as though a movie director had put us in this spot for the perfect shot.

"Another chance is all I can ask. You don't have to say yes, but I wanted you to know I was serious. I'm not going to run away scared again. Holding you at arm's length has been one of the hardest things I've ever done, and I was an idiot to do it. I love you." She wiped at her nose with the back of her hand. "Sorry to be such a mess."

"Give me the ring." I held out my hand, letting my foot tap as her head shot down to it like she'd just realized it was there.

She set it down in my hand like she was afraid my touch would burn her.

"How long were you out there?" I shoved the ring into my pocket.

Her body seemed to deflate like a week-old balloon.

"An hour, maybe," she said absently, keeping her gaze on the center of my chest.

"What have you been doing this past week?"

"Honestly?" Her clear blue gaze collided with mine.

"I wouldn't have asked if I didn't want to know."

"Crying. Trying to figure out what I wanted my life to look like and what kind of person did I want to be."

"Did you come to any conclusions?"

"I did. Fern and Charlie offered to sign the Surf Shack over to me. And I got a job at the Speedman Clinic, a new rehab and physiotherapy clinic in Ocean City. But—"

"If you're planning this great escape from the city, then why are you here proposing?" My heart stuttered. And I wish I hadn't asked the question.

"You didn't let me finish." The corner of her mouth lifted.

"Finish." I crossed my arms over my chest, trying to keep my heartrate under control. It was pounding like we were in a sudden-death shootout after running for three periods straight.

She looked down at her gloved hands. "I had a choice to

make about what kind of life I wanted to live and who I wanted to let into my heart. I could follow the path I've always been on and do everything I could to protect myself. Continue to keep my circle small, never letting myself live out of fear of what I might lose."

Her throat worked up and down. "Or I could take a chance that the man who'd made me feel alive for the first time in years would be worth the risk. That opening my heart to you wasn't opening me up to more potential loss, but to a love I hadn't experienced before. You're the most challenging, infuriating, stubborn, kind, caring, loving, and sexiest guy I've ever met." The way her voice softened with those last ones, and the lick of desire when she said 'sexiest' made a thrill rush up my spine.

"I could say a lot of the same things about you." Stepping closer, I tugged her gloves off her hands. "Losing you was one of the hardest things I've ever done. Letting you walk—well, almost run away from me—it scared me, Imogen." I cupped her cheek. "Because I knew you were it for me. This hasn't been like any relationship I've had before. We weren't even official, but spending the rest of my life with you was everything I'd ever dreamed of, and the thought of losing that scared me even more than never playing hockey again."

"I'm sorry."

I silenced her with a kiss. All the sadness and hollowness melted away with the touch of her lips against mine. The tip of her nose was still cold, but I'd sure as hell warm her up. She looped her arms around my neck and held me close, like she never wanted me to let go, and I wouldn't now that she'd shown me that our hearts sung the same tune.

A round of applause and whooping broke through our moment.

We turned our faces and met the gazes of the coffee shop customers. They'd had a front row view of the outdoor proposal through the large glass window, and we'd given them a much more satisfying encore.

Imogen buried her face in my chest, holding onto the lapels of my coat.

"You're embarrassed by this? You were outside with a full choir singing our song and you weren't this embarrassed."

"Does she still get the ring?" a woman called out through cupped hands.

"That depends." I spoke to the woman, but kept my eyes on Imogen.

"On what?" Imogen looked up at me with her full pink lips still flushed from my kisses.

"How long do you plan on wearing it?" I slipped the box out of my pocket.

"And what if my answer is for as long as you love me?"

"Then I hope you're okay with forever."

I sank down to my knee and opened the box. "Imogen Marie Walsh—"

"Yes!" She flung herself at me, peppering my face with kisses.

"I didn't even get to dramatically open the box or anything. I didn't ask the question."

"And I didn't want to wait another second."

"You got me there." Standing, I slipped the ring onto her finger.

Applause filled the coffee shop. The door behind us opened and everyone piled in. Declan, Heath, Emmett, and Ford. Liv, Mak, Kara, and Avery came in behind them, exchanging hugs and kisses with everyone.

The choir arranged themselves in the doorway and

along the front of the shop to sing our song again. I covered coffee for everyone for the rest of the day.

Imogen and I slow danced surrounded by our friends and family. Holding onto her hand, I loved the solid edge of the ring pressing against my fingers, and I couldn't wait to have one of my own as a reminder that my heart was out there walking, living and breathing in the world and lying beside me each night.

It was non-stop laughter, talking, and music. We received congratulations from strangers, hockey fans, music fans, and people who loved good old-fashioned public displays of affection.

In the taxi, Imogen's eyes drooped and she rested her head against my chest. Resting my head on top of hers, I'd never been happier. We were going home.

42

IMO

We said goodbye to everyone and promised to come by Emmett and Avery's house for a double baby shower. It was time I stopped putting so much distance between myself and the people I loved and who loved me right back.

In the back of the car, I leaned against Colm, feeling his steady heartbeat under my touch. There was still so much life to live and I needed him to know everything about me and my past.

"I know you're going to say you don't need it, but I want to explain what happened that day at the rink. It wasn't just about us. It was also about Preston." I entwined my fingers with Colm's.

His body stiffened slightly before relaxing under my touch. "You were both each other's first and only. I get that."

"I wasn't his first and only."

"I thought you guys dated since middle school?"

"We did."

"Was he sleeping around in elementary school? Sweet talking girls with juice boxes?"

"No. It was in college."

"He ch—"

"We were taking a break."

I laughed at the look he gave me.

"A real one. Right after his diagnosis. He lost it and I get it. The life he thought he was going to live died when we left the cardiologist's office. Everything he'd worked for disappeared in an instant. And I was a reminder of that."

He ran his thumb across my cheek. The tiny circles of the rough pad of his thumb anchored me in the present.

"He was crazy to let you go."

"People do crazy things when they're hurting and afraid. They sometimes hurt the people they love most. It's not ever okay, but I understand it."

Colm kissed the side of my head and held onto my shoulder.

"But things were great after that. He did everything he needed to do to keep playing and do the surgery after the season ended. They were still running tests and making sure they had it all right."

"Then he had his accident."

"Yes, and on the night of the accident," my voice cracked. "He proposed."

Colm's eyes widened. "No one ever said anything."

"No one knew. Only Avery, and I swore her to silence."

"That night on the beach?" I tilted my head to look at him through my watery gaze. "After you asked me and I freaked out? The police were at the Surf Shack earlier. They'd found my ring. I hadn't wanted to wear it that night because it was so cold and my gloves were on, so I sat it on the dashboard to admire it. I didn't even see the car that hit us coming. I was staring at the ring."

"Why didn't you tell anyone?"

"What would've been the point? Everyone was worried initially. The time never seemed right and he was getting better, so we thought we'd wait until we could tell everyone once he was out of the hospital without the cloud of the stress of accident hanging over us. And then—" I lifted my shoulders and breathed through the burn in my nostrils. "I didn't want to take another piece of his future away from his parents by telling them."

"So you kept this with you all this time."

"I'm not the best when it comes to burdening other people with my issues. When you knelt in front of me on the ice—"

He wrapped his arms around me from the side, hugging me to his chest. "You don't owe—"

"I do, Colm. I need you to know everything. It was like I was back at the rink when he proposed, and all I could see was how he looked when I woke up upside down surrounded by glass and metal. Blood in his nose and the dashboard crumpled against his legs."

Colm dropped his cheek to the top of my head. "That had to be jarring for you. I know we were only talking about moving in. I'm sorry."

"Don't be sorry for showing me what was in your heart. I'm sorry I couldn't accept it." I pulled away from his chest and ran my hand over his cheek. "I was so scared and the thought of losing you like I lost him, it hurt so much, but Fern and Charlie sat me down and asked me what kind of life I wanted to live. And I found the answer.

"I'm ready now. That's why I did everything I did today. I needed you to know that I love you."

"I know you do. And I'm okay with things now. I've never loved anyone like I love you. I can't imagine what it would be like to lose—" He pinched his lips together. "I don't even want to say the words. But I can't imagine what it was like for you. And I know he was first in your heart, but I hope I can be the last." Tears welled in his eyes.

"How did I ever get so lucky to be so well-loved by two incredible men?" I brushed back a short lock of hair behind his ear and gazed into his eyes. "This isn't about places. There is no first or second. No winners and runners up. Preston was my love who knew me better than anyone. And you're my love who will be with me for the rest of our lives, and we'll learn everything we can about each other and make even more memories. There's room in my heart for the two of you and for this little one and any others we have in the future."

"You're up for more kids?"

"I've always wanted a big family. Growing up, I only had my stuffed animals and I know how close you and Liv are. I'd want at least that, if not more."

"Just when I think I can't love you any more." Colm kissed me in the way I'd come to learn was his way. Like he was afraid he'd forget the taste and feel of my lips if he didn't explore and devour every inch of them.

The taxi arrived curbside in front of the brownstone. Colm opened the door to his house. Our house. I was happy to be home. We had so many new memories to make and joy to embrace together.

Without a word, we went upstairs, not letting go of one another's hands, like we didn't want to break this connection between us until it was absolutely necessary.

Inside his bedroom, which hadn't become a hermit's cave in my absence, he unbuttoned my coat. I unbuttoned his and we kicked off our shoes. Undressing each other, I let my hands linger on his body. I'd missed the feel of his arms around me and the press of his chest against my back.

His fingers trailed over the curve of my shoulders, teasing the undersides of my breasts and resting on my stomach.

"Your stomach popped." He smiled his wide and infectious grin at me.

It seemed overnight I'd gone from 'hmm, did she have a massive lunch' to 'oh wow, she's totally pregnant'. "It did." I rested my hands on top of his.

"Let's get a shower."

He grabbed us a pair of fluffy towels and led me into the shower. We cleaned one another, like a ritual in new beginnings, washing away the fear and sadness of our past.

The sexual tension was there, but this was beyond sex—although I won't say I didn't moan when his fingers sunk into my hair as he worked the shampoo into a lather. Bracing my hands against the wall, I let him work his finger magic and added showering together to the list of things we'd be doing a hell of a lot more often, at least until Baby Frost arrived.

Even with the very present swell of his erection, Colm didn't make any moves. Not to say that there weren't a few lingering touches on my nipples or an extra thorough exploration of my pussy with a graze of my clit.

As turnabout is fair play, I soaked his cock extra well, giving his thick mushroom tip some extra attention that drew shudders from him. But he didn't take the bait. Reaching around me and placing a kiss on my wet shoulder, he turned off the water.

Stepping out of the shower, he grabbed one of the towels, holding it out for me. He dried me off and then himself before getting us both into bed. I hadn't thought I was tired after the intensity of the day, but as all the adrenaline wore off and the quietness of our lives settled in, I was beat. It had been an eventful day with the best end imaginable.

He'd known before I had exactly what I'd need.

Turning to face him, I dragged my fingers through his hair.

He dropped his hand to my stomach. "I can't wait to show you both how much I love you."

I draped my arms over his shoulders, locking them around the back of his neck. "You can start showing me right now."

Lifting my upper body, I peppered his neck and shoulders with kisses.

His insistence at not having sex only made me crave it—and him—more. He'd never seen me as spun glass or fragile and I wasn't going to let him pull that now.

His hardened cock rubbed against my ass. I shifted my hips, letting his erection massage my clit. I shuddered, dropping my head back to gaze into his eyes.

The burn of desire filled them and I couldn't stop my smile. I'd tease him until he gave in.

He groaned and jerked his hips forward.

Didn't he know how determined I could be?

43
─────

COLM

S he wrapped her legs around my waist. Her heels dug into my back.

My cock slipped lower, teasing her soaked opening. I bit back another moan. I was supposed to be letting her rest. It had been an eventful and emotional day. The last thing she needed was me releasing all that pent up tension that hadn't left me since she'd walked away our first night back together.

"But we just got cleaned up." Be a gentleman.

"I don't mind getting a little dirty as long as it's with you." She lifted her head and kissed me. Hungry and longing like we hadn't been inseparable since I slipped that ring on her finger.

"Aren't you tired?" *Don't overwhelm her.*

"Not in the slightest." She bit back a yawn.

"We can pick this up tomorrow."

Staring into my eyes, she shifted her hips and I dropped my head back, another moan shooting from me. "I want it all tonight. No kid gloves. No holding back. No more walls, Colm."

The cold metal brushed against the back of my neck, spurring me on. This was my soon-to-be wife. The woman who'd gotten through to me when no one else had, and who'd lost so much, but was still brave enough to be here with me. And I'd make sure she never regretted it a day in our lives together.

Shifting my hips, I sank into her velvet vise. Pure blissful heaven. How I had resisted this long was surely a marvel of the modern world.

"Yes!" she shouted, her hips spurring me on.

"I love the sound of that word from your lips. I can't wait until your voice is hoarse from saying it."

She looked at me with sex-glazed eyes. Her fingers tugged at my hair and I dropped even lower, pinning her hips to the bed, sinking in even deeper.

"You feel so damn good, Imo. Too sweet not to taste as often as you'll let me."

"Anytime. All the time." The words were on the razors edge of a keening cry. Her back arched, pressing her stomach against mine. Her moans were a symphony of pleasure and I was the conductor.

Lifting one hand, I cupped her breast, rolling her nipple between my fingers.

She hissed, low and hard, circling her hips and driving me wild.

We raced together, pushing each other higher and harder until the cascade of electric brilliance rocketed from my toes.

Changing my angle, I drove into her.

Fluttering spasms gripped my cock. Under me, she tensed, burying her face in the crook of my neck. The nip of her teeth against my sensitive skin set me off.

I thrust into her, burying myself as deep as I could with toe-curling rapture firing through my system.

Collapsing onto my side, I pulled her close, panting.

Her hair fluttered with each exhale. I wrapped my arm around her and settled my hand over her growing bump. A not-so-small kick whacked against my hand.

"Baby Frost is wondering what's going on out here."

Baby Frost. The first of many to come.

"Mom and Dad were just wrestling. Nothing to worry about."

Imogen laughed, her whole body shaking.

Rolling off the bed, I grabbed a cloth and cleaned her up before settling back into bed.

A contented sigh and she rolled over, facing me. "Look what you did, you got me all sweaty." She laughed, walking her fingers along my chest.

"I think you had a hand in this as well."

Tapping her finger against her lips, she looked up at the ceiling. "We seem to be remembering how this started in very different ways."

Her peals of laughter filled the room as I attacked her with my fingers.

"Okay, I'll admit it. I might have had a hand in it."

We settled into an easy silence, cocooned in body heat under the thick blankets.

"I love you, Colm. Thank you for not giving up on me."

I buried my face in the curve of her neck. "I love you too, Imogen. Thank you for caring enough to not let me give up on myself. You're stronger than you know, and I can't wait to be the man at your side for as long as you'll have me."

She held on to my arm wrapped around her. "It seems we both have a lot to be thankful for."

"I guess we do." Even with everything I'd lost, the pain of

that no longer overshadowed everything I did. It wasn't a reminder of how things could've been, but a reminder of how every moment going forward shouldn't be taken for granted and should be cherished. And that's what I'd do every day I drew breath: I'd cherish my wife, children, and family because in uncertain times, those memories and looking to brighter days were all I needed to make it through anything.

She was my strength, my heart, my love.

EPILOGUE

"**G**o. Just go! We'll catch up to you," Ford shouted, nearly tripping over his goalie pads as the locker room door closed behind me.

I'd set a land speed record in showering, and my button-down shirt clung to my chest in a mixture of water and newly sprung sweat.

I'd ducked out of the locker room before the press conference. Scoring a hat trick during a game should be cause for celebration, but right now I couldn't pretend to care. My heart had been in overdrive since the chorus of text messages had blared from our phones in our bags after the game.

I should've known something was up when our box had been empty. Imo and the rest of the Queens of Rittenhouse, as they'd dubbed themselves, had been at every home game.

The taxis I'd ordered idled outside the tunnel exit behind the stadium. Three sat ready to go behind the one I got in. I waved to security for doing me a solid and jumped in the back. Without a word, the taxi peeled out and I swore I could smell burned rubber.

We took a corner hard and I slammed against the back door. It seemed the driver had taken the bonus for getting me there as soon as safely possible to heart.

Sweat poured down my back. I hadn't trusted myself or any of the guys to drive. The glowing red sign of the Hospital peeked between the budding branches of the trees. My fingers tightened on the seat of the taxi driver.

As much as I loved the game, the past month had shown me how important the people around me were, and I wouldn't take them for granted. This would be my final season. On my own terms. I'd proven I could do it and that was all I needed. There was always enough new blood to continue the winning streak we'd forged this season.

One final run for the cup with the Kings and I'd spend the rest of my life spoiling my new wife and baby.

I flung the taxi door open before he'd even come to a complete stop. A quick pause—more like thundering up to the reception desk and gasping out a request for the labor and delivery floor was all I could get out.

Using my hands to propel me up the steps to the fifth floor, I burst through the door probably looking like a madman.

The nurses beside the reception desk's eyes widened when they spotted me. I'm sure I wasn't the only frazzled guy to burst onto this floor today.

"Colm." My name came from the other direction.

Imogen stood in a doorway doing the mom bounce she'd adopted over the past month. The little bundle strapped to her chest sent a flurry of warm and gooey feelings running through me.

I kissed Imo, keeping my chest from crushing our little girl. Imo tasted better every time I sampled her lips. From the day I slipped my ring on her finger to the day we stood in my backyard and exchanged vows to the day she labored for eighteen hours to bring our sweet baby into this world.

I smoothed back the hair on top of Abby's head and kissed her while I inhaled her new baby smell.

"How are my girls?"

"We're good." Liv leaned over in her chair in the waiting room behind Imo, setting down the magazine. "Oh, you were talking about them." She motioned to Imo and Abby.

"You think you're no longer in the club anymore?" I lifted my sister off her feet and squeezed her tight.

The door out in the hallway banged open and a stampede of footsteps hammered against the floor.

"We're in here." Imo waved the guys into the room.

They were out of breath and panting, like we hadn't given our all only thirty minutes ago out on the ice.

"Looks like someone needs a bit more conditioning." Liv wrapped her arms around Ford's neck and planted a kiss on him.

Imo slipped in close to me. "I never thought I'd see the day."

"What day?"

"The day you'd smile like that seeing them together." She continued her bounce and dropped a kiss onto Abby's head.

"What's not to be happy about? My grown up little sister and best friend have found love with one another. Someone would have to be an idiot not to see that."

She laughed. "Do you want to hold Abby?"

"Like you ever have to ask. I always want to hold her, but I know how you hate it when I steal her from you."

"Yeah, when she's in the middle of breastfeeding." She pinched my side.

"Ow, so mean."

"You love it when I am."

"You know I do." I kissed her again, never ready for it to end, and helped her unstrap the baby carrier and cradled my little girl in my arms.

She had bright blue eyes like her mom, and my curls. Her beauty and perfection made it hard to believe she was part me.

"It's only a matter of time before this little cutie has boys showing up on your doorstep with dug up flowers and worms." Heath ran his fingers over her toes.

"It's a good thing they'll have four uncles to deal with in addition to me." I rubbed my nose against Abby's and laughed as she latched onto my cheek.

I know everyone said that about their babies, but this time it was true. That she would one day grow up and have a life of her own made it hard to breathe. I needed to treasure every single moment I had with her. With everyone in this room, because we were family.

"Has anyone come in with any news yet?" Declan held onto Mak with his arm draped over her shoulder.

"Nothing—"

Emmett skidded into the doorway, bumping into the doorjamb and not even wincing. His massive smile melted away any of the tiny fear dancing in the back of my mind.

"It's a boy! Avery and Lucas are doing great."

He was buried under the pile-up of hugs. Tears, high fives and even more hugs filled the room.

"Our little family's getting bigger every day, big brother." Liv squeezed me in a side hug and kissed Abby's chubby cheek.

"It sure is, Olive." I kissed the top of her head, tearing up as she stepped away and held hands with Ford. The two of them peered down at Emmett's phone as he flicked through the pictures.

We sat in the waiting room for our turn to go in and meet the first Prince of Rittenhouse.

"So, can we start placing bets on the Abby-Lucas courtship in another eighteen years?" Heath clapped his hands together, rubbing his palms.

My glare didn't go unnoticed.

Heath held his hands up in surrender. "Just throwing that out there. So touchy."

Imo laced her fingers through mine and ran the backs of her fingers down Abby's cheek. "I love you, Mr. Frost." She stared into my eyes and I'd never felt like a luckier man.

"I love you more, Mrs. Frost."

Thank for you joining me for the final Kings of Rittenhouse novel! I know you've been waiting patiently—okay maybe not so patiently, but I'm so happy you're here with me and the rest of the gang to celebrate.

If you'd like one more day with them, you can grab Colm and Imo's bonus scene here.

Looking for another sweet and steamy sports romance read?

The Perfect First - A First Time Romance

Persephone has a list of firsts to tackle in her senior year of college and her biggest is lose her V-Card. Reece is a cocky football player who stumbles into her interview session for candidates can't help, but want to protect her and keep her from making a big mistake. He volunteers to help her with everything on her list--except her No. 1, but then everything changes.

A HEARTFELT THANK YOU

I can't lie, I cried writing this epilogue. It has been an emotional journey with the Kings and their Queens.

This was my first series centered around a tight group of friends and they became even more like family as I wrote their books. Saying goodbye is never easy, especially when these are friends you've come to love over so much time.

That doesn't mean I won't revisit them at some point in the future and that they won't pop up in what I have planned, but they've all got their happily ever afters and I can't be happier about that! So thank you for coming on that journey with me and them.

Thank you so so much again for all your support and I can't wait for you to see what I have coming up next!

Happy reading!

Maya xx

ACKNOWLEDGMENTS

Wow...I truly can't believe this series has come to an end. It's crazy to think a little under two years ago, the novella hit kindles all over the world and we're here at the end.

I want to thank my editing team, Tamara, Sarah, and Sarah. This series means so much to me and thank you for helping me bring it to life.

I wanted to thank every blogger, bookstagrammer, and reader for sharing all the news about these two as we lead up to the release. Your energy helped kick my butt when I needed it to get everything as perfect as possible.

It really means so much to me that you've taken the time to share and talk about how one of my books has brought all the feels, made you want to throw your kindle or needed a cold shower afterward.

Thank you and happy reading!

Maya xx

ALSO BY MAYA HUGHES

Fulton U

The Perfect First - First Time/Friends to Lovers Romance

Kings of Rittenhouse

Kings of Rittenhouse - FREE

Shameless King - Enemies to Lovers

Reckless King - Off Limits Lover

Ruthless King - Second Chance Romance

Manhattan Misters

All His Secrets - Single Dad Romance

All His Lies - Secret Romance

All His Regrets - Second Chance Romance

Under His Series

Under His Ink - Second Chance Romance

Breaking Free Series

Blinded - Second Chance Secret Baby Romance

Mixed - Enemies to Lovers Romance

Served - Enemies to Lovers Romance

Rocked - Rockstar Romance

Standalone

Passion on the Pitch - Sports Romance

CONNECT WITH MAYA

Sign up for my newsletter to get exclusive bonus content, ARC opportunities, sneak peeks, new release alerts and to find out just what I'm books are coming up next.

Join my reader group for teasers, giveaways and more!

Follow my Amazon author page for new release alerts!

Follow me on Instagram, where I try and fail to take pretty pictures!

Follow me on Twitter, just because :)

I'd love to hear from you! Drop me a line anytime :)
https://www.mayahughes.com/
maya@mayahughes.com

Made in the USA
Monee, IL
22 May 2020